A NOVEL BY

NISA SANTIAGO

Cartier Cartel. Copyright © 2009, 2010 by Melodrama Publishing. All rights reserved. Printed in the United States of America. No part of this book may be used or reproduced in any manner whatsoever without written permission except in the case of brief quotations embodied in critical articles or reviews. For information, address Melodrama Publishing, P.O. Box 522, Bellport, NY 11713.

www.melodramapublishing.com

Library of Congress Control Number: 2007943740

ISBN-13: 978-1934157343

ISBN-10: 1934157341

Mass Market Edition: September 2010

10 9 8 7 6 5 4 3 2

Cover and Interior Design and Layout by candace@candann.com

Cover Photo by Frank Antonio

CHAPTER ONE

1997 – The Declaration

The loud rumbling in Cartier's stomach kept her awake all night. Her mother, Trina, promised that she was stepping out with a male friend and would return shortly with an order from the Chinese restaurant. Cartier waited up, desperately, until she finally realized she would go to bed hungry, again. Cartier's mother often put her own needs before the needs of her child. But leaving Cartier hungry was going too far.

Cartier didn't wait for the alarm clock to ring before getting ready for school. She was already dressed and waiting on her best friend, Monya, to meet her so they could walk to school together.

Cartier sat on the windowsill of the quiet, messy apartment and looked at the street down below. Buses zoomed up and down the boulevard, while pedestrians made their way to work and school. Soon she spotted her mother walking down the block in a micro-mini skirt, waist-length leather jacket, and stilettos. It was deathly cold outside, but that didn't stop her mother from dressing so scantily. Trina's dyed blond hair against her dark chocolate skin grabbed everyone's attention. And her walk—more like a bop—was priceless. Cartier often joked that even Stevie Wonder would recognize Trina's walk.

At thirty-two, Trina still possessed the shape of her youth. She was petite up top with A-cup breasts, wide hips, a round ass, and thick thighs. Her stomach was washboard flat, showing no signs that she'd ever given birth. Trina was severely bowlegged, but instead of hobbling, she switched her hips hard, so hard it served her desired purpose—a distinctive strut that men loved and found sexy.

The closer Trina got to the apartment, the angrier Cartier became. She watched her mother casually stroll to the tenement building without a care in the world, although their refrigerator echoed from a lack of food and the cupboards were bare.

Where is she coming from? Cartier wondered.

When Trina realized she was being watched, her eyes instinctively looked up to the window. Her smile quickly faded when she saw the glare in Cartier's eyes. She knew she'd fucked up. She also knew she would have to hear her young daughter's mouth about not coming home last night. After she climbed the two flights of steps to the apartment, she wasn't in the mood to listen to Cartier's foul mouth.

"Where were you?" Cartier screamed. "I waited and waited all night for you."

Shaking her head, Trina began her explanation. "I told that motherfucker I needed to get home, but he wasn't tryna let me go."

"What do you mean he wouldn't let you go? You're grown!"

"You know how KP is." Trina paused for emphasis and then began taking off her jacket. "I told him it was over and the next thing I knew we were having breakup sex."

"Ma—"

"That motherfucker was like, 'Now take this . . . take my baby . . . now you're gonna be with me forever." Trina chuckled, reliving her night of sexual fun.

"You kept me in here starving so you could have sex? With a loser? If you get pregnant that's one more mouth to feed and you can't even feed the child you already got." Cartier was furious at Trina's immaturity and she also hated that her mother spoke to her as if they were friends.

"You know you're my only baby. I love only you, and I ain't having no more kids."

"You're not gonna keep rocking me to sleep every minute with your lies!" Cartier yelled. "I'm sick of living like this! I don't have any clothes and there's never any food! I'm sick of being poor!"

"See, now that's where you're wrong. You're not gonna put all the baggage on my shoulders. It took two to make you, so you can go and lay some of that blame on your dead father! I done got you through the years that matter the most. It's time you start doing for yourself around here. You're fifteen years old. At fifteen, I was already out of my mother's apartment, living with my man and keeping house—"

"I'm tired of hearing this same ole story," Cartier interrupted. "It's getting stale. And you weren't keeping house. You were playing house and look where that got you."

Trina was tired and her body was sore from an all-night fuck marathon. She was in no mood to argue a moot point with her daughter. In some ways, Trina was disappointed in Cartier. She felt her daughter lacked the independent nature that Trina had at her age. When Trina was young, if there wasn't any food in the house, she didn't wait around to be fed. She went out and got herself something to eat. Whether she walked into a grocery store and stole food or got some trick to buy her something, she made sure she ate.

All Cartier was good for was complaining.

Trina looked at her daughter intently. She was a combination of both her parents. Cartier had Trina's dark complexion and body, but sadly, she had her father's features. Cartier's broad nose and full lips, reminiscent of an African sculpture, were traits inherited from her father. Yet when she smiled, her face softened. Just like her mother, her thick wavy hair was a trait of the Timmonses', much like her fiery personality.

"If you don't like living here you can get the fuck out!" Trina yelled. "This is my house and I pay the motherfucking bills up in this crib."

"And you remind me every day!"

"You damn right I do. If you were smart you would have learned a thing or two from your momma."

"If school was ever in session with you, maybe I could

learn a thing or two from you. But it seems that you're always out to lunch."

Trina couldn't figure out if that was a jab, but she knew it was some slick shit. She could tell by the tone of Cartier's voice.

"Say something else smart and see if I don't shove my fist down your throat."

Cartier recoiled. She feared her mother's violent nature.

"I need five dollars to buy a ham and cheese hero from the bodega," Cartier demanded.

"Girl, don't work my nerves. I don't have five dollars ... I might have three. You can buy the sandwich and you'll have to drink tap water or bum something in school."

"Jeez, you're such a great teacher. I guess I'm supposed to learn how to go fuck a nigga all night and come back broke!"

"Cartier Timmons, I will slap you into next week! Keep it up!" Trina threatened. "Now fuck you! Eat your fucking fingers, bitch!"

Trina stormed into her bedroom, slamming her door. Cartier was so annoyed and frustrated by her mother's actions that she wanted to cry, but she refused. She walked over to the empty refrigerator once more and stared hopelessly into it until she heard Monya knocking on the door. It was time to leave for school.

Cartier flung open the door and peered at her best friend. They had been best friends since they were born. Monya was just as poor as Cartier, they had so much in common, and their mothers were best friends too. The two connected on those levels.

"I heard y'all arguing from down the street," Monya said as soon as Cartier opened the door.

"What else is new?"

"What happened now?"

"She left me in the house all night without anything to eat," Cartier said and then grabbed her book-bag.

"Well, in a few days she'll get her assistance check and then you'll have food for at least a couple weeks."

Cartier shook her head. "Nah, I'm gonna have food today!"

"You got money?"

"We won't need money."

That day was the first day either girl stole anything. And neither felt an ounce of guilt behind their actions. Stealing was a survival mechanism. No longer would Cartier look to her mother to feed her. From this day forward she was feeding herself daily. She reveled in her newfound independence.

CHAPTER TWO

Ballin'

"Listen," Cartier began as Monya, Lil Momma, Shanine, and Bam all gathered around. "I'm tired of walking around here looking all bummy while other girls our age are dressed fly."

The crew all looked down at their worn, outdated clothing.

"So, I've put in a call to Shorty Dip and she's agreed to take us out."

"Take us out where?" Shanine asked.

"To the department stores. She's going to take us to the expensive stores in the city and bag us up."

"I'm not walking out of nobody's store with stolen merchandise," Lil Momma exclaimed. "I'm not built for such things. Bottom line, if I got caught my mother would beat fire out of my ass."

"Will you stop being so negative?" Monya interjected. "Ain't nobody getting caught. Cartier and Shorty Dip already worked out the plan. All we gotta do is walk calmly out the door. Dip and her crew will do the rest. They'll remove all the sensors from the clothing, bag it up nicely in a large department store shopping bag, make sure none of the undercover detectives are on to us, and then we will do the easiest job, which is walk out the front door."

"If that's the easiest part then why don't they do it?" Lil Momma was relentless in her objection. Her pride wouldn't allow her to be what the streets called, a *vic*. Meaning, she would forever be looked upon as a slouch. A person who allowed herself to be used.

"Look, either you're down or you're not. It's that simple." Cartier had had enough of Lil Momma and her annoying ways.

"Well then, I'm not down."

Without hesitation, Cartier retorted, "Then bounce."

As the cold winter months came and went, Cartier, Monya, Bam, Shanine, and Lil Momma began dressing in the latest outfits. Though Lil Momma wasn't down with boosting, her girlfriends still treated her as an equal. When they boosted a store, they always added something extra to their bag for their friend.

Their popularity at school and around the neighborhood skyrocketed. Cartier was the ringleader of the crew, who planned their heists and provided guidance and advice. The crew, which she aptly named the Cartier Cartel, all looked up to her.

When spring rolled around, Cartier had a new outlook on their situation. Something Lil Momma had said months ago stuck in her head. Cartier realized she and her crew was doing the riskiest part of the heists. They were the ones walking out of Bloomingdales, Macy's, Sak's Fifth Avenue, Bergdorf Goodman, and Barney's with thousands of dollars worth of merchandise. A few of the Cartel crewmembers had open court cases for shoplifting and all of them had been caught in the act at least a half dozen times.

Yet Shorty Dip walked home with most of the merchandise. She took home seventy percent of the merchandise. She rationalized that it was only fair since she brought the young girls in. After all, she was twice the young girls' ages and young girls their age didn't need the best clothes or accessories.

They sat outside in Dip's 1998 Lincoln Navigator and took turns going in and out of those high-end stores like cattle. Dip loved taking Monya inside stores. She had a light-brown complexion, as if she were a foreigner, possibly of Indian descent. When she dressed properly, her looks were deceiving. By the time the store got wind that she was up to no good, she was already out the door and inside the safe haven of Dip's truck.

Each girl couldn't deny the adrenaline rush getting away with stealing gave them. Business was good and *interesting*. Popping off tags on $1,800-shirts was incomprehensible. They had clothing that they couldn't even pronounce and shoes they couldn't even walk in. Cartier finally understood what her mother had been trying to convey to her regarding independence. Boosting had afforded her and her crew a new lifestyle that consisted of getting their hair professionally done, manicures and pedicures, movies, and taxicabs. Additionally, the girls sold some of their merchandise at the local beauty parlors. The Cartel was making moves and handling their business. But business could always be better.

Cartier watched as Dip grabbed one item each of the new Gucci summer white line in Bergdorf Goodman's. Dip loved to take Cartier into the large, ornate store because Cartier had the most heart. She was fearless and would run, fight, and maneuver her way out of the store with the merchandise if need be. Bergdorf was the type of establishment that relied on their surveillance cameras. You had to be swift and stoic in order to evade the security system or guards. The security guards who worked the exits were diehard enthusiasts who loved busting thieves.

Inside the store, Cartier and Dip pretended to be strangers. Cartier's role was to peruse the aisles and not touch anything that would cause the sales associates to take notice of her. A skilled booster had to be unassuming and invisible while standing in front of a store employee. Your biggest job was to go undetected.

Cartier walked past a dress that she had seen the week prior. The price tag was $2,299. Then, Dip had promised to put it in the bag for Cartier. She didn't do it. And it appeared to Cartier that Dip wasn't going to steal the dress this week either. For some reason, Dip only wanted the girls to dress in jeans and sportswear, while she dressed in the high-end fashions. Cartier and her crew were inundated with Guess, BCBG, Juicy Couture, DKNY, and bebe, while

Dip gravitated toward Cavalli, von Furstenburg, Moschino, and Gucci.

Cartier observed Dip go to a table and pick up three pairs of Versace jeans. Cartier knew she and her crew would be given those as consolation for today's work. She was furious. The Cartel had more Versace jeans in all flavors than they could wear.

What the fuck was Dip thinking? Cartier gave Dip a signal and pointed toward the dress. Dip grimaced in disapproval. She frowned and her forehead creased. Cartier watched in horror as Dip stuffed a large shopping bag minus the dress Cartier so desperately wanted.

At first, when Dip placed the bag underneath a rack of clothes and gave Cartier the head nod to go and retrieve it, she hesitated. Cartier wanted to tell Dip to take the fucking bag and shove it up her ass, but she held her tongue. She watched as Dip headed down the escalator, making her way out the store.

Cartier looked around and all was quiet. Slowly, she walked over to the clothes rack and peered down at the neatly packed, large shopping bag. Her eyes darted around the area and all was quiet. Cartier gripped the heavy bag and made her way toward the elevators. When the doors flung open, there was an undercover detective inside and she clearly heard his conversation over the radio. The male's voice on the other end excitedly shot off a description of a black female known for stealing. Cartier knew the description was Dip's. The voice informed the undercover detective of Dip's location on the second floor, in the shoe department. The commanding voice also emphasized to his fellow detective to be on high alert. The detective never glanced at Cartier, whose heart was in her throat by now.

As Cartier was getting off the elevator, making her way toward the exit, she knew what she had to do. But the decision she'd make would solely depend on whether Dip was a team player or not.

Back at the car, she hipped the girls to her plan. At first, they resisted, but since Cartier was the leader of the Cartel, they knew they had to follow her lead. In the close quarters of the SUV, the girls waited patiently for Dip to come back so they could continue shopping.

When the undercover detectives spotted Shorty Dip, her hands were buried deeply in her coat pockets as she walked briskly down the block toward the car. Dip was on point, continually looking over her shoulder to see if she were being followed. It wasn't uncommon for store-employed detectives to follow known boosters from the store to their cars. Sometimes they would get lucky and catch the boosters with merchandise from numerous stores.

To be safe, Dip usually parked blocks from the store they would hit.

As Dip got closer to the SUV, her eyes searched the car to see if Cartier was safely inside. When she spotted Cartier, she exhaled.

"Girl, it was so hot in there," Dip began. "I didn't know if you got knocked."

"Nah, I was straight. But they were looking for you."

"Yeah, they found me, but there wasn't shit they could do but escort me out because I didn't have shit."

"They walked you to the door?"

"They sure did."

"That's embarrassing," Monya commented. "I hate when they do that stupid shit."

"I don't give a fuck," Dip replied. "They can walk me from here to Brooklyn as long as I got their shit. We G'd off in that motherfucker."

Unable to contain the excitement she felt about getting the new Gucci line, Dip grabbed the bag and began pulling out the garments. Although she didn't say anything, in fear the girls would start to finally wise up and realize she kept all the good quality clothes for herself, the expression on her face was priceless.

Cartier began, "Did you get me that dress I wanted?"

"What dress?" Dip was a bad actor Cartier surmised.

"The dress that I pointed to inside the store?"

Dip shrugged. "Oh my God, I didn't know you wanted that dress. Why didn't you say something? It would have taken two seconds to put it in the bag."

"What do you mean why didn't I say something? You knew I wanted that dress last week and I reminded you again today!"

"All I had on my mind was getting y'all these fly-ass jeans." Dip pulled out the three pairs of Versace jeans. It was beyond her that four girls were in the SUV. "I should have gotten myself a pair too. Y'all gonna be some fly bitches. Don't nobody have these."

"That's 'cause nobody wants them!" Cartier blurted out and then reminded herself that she needed to chill in order for the plan to go accordingly. She had recently made it a point to be a better leader, definitely a better leader than Dip.

"Look, calm down with all that fucking yelling!" Dip responded. "I always get y'all what the fuck you ask for. In that store it's different. You see how they be on my ass up in there. My time is limited and I don't have time to linger. If I sleep, then, we get nothing. I only have a matter of minutes in any department before they call the Ds on me, so I don't have time to decipher hand and head movements. Next we about to go to Macy's, and I won't get shit. I'll pick out a whole bag for just you girls."

Cartier couldn't believe how selfish and greedy Dip was. Macy's had the bullshit and she knew it. Cartier knew that in Macy's they'd be walking out with Guess and Mudd jeans. Instead of flipping out, she said, "Are you serious? You're gonna dedicate a whole bag just for us?"

"Yeah, I'm serious," Dip replied. "That's because I'm not a selfish bitch. This shit don't mean nothing to me. I'm the flyest bitch in Brooklyn. I don't have shit to prove to these hoes. They all know what time it is. I got so much shit in my closets I can't even close the doors. I'm not greedy at all."

"Well, who's going to go in with you?" Cartier asked.

Dip thought for a moment. "I think I'll take in Bam. She has the perfect look for Macy's." Dip always mentioned that Bam was really of no use other than a low end store like Macy's. No matter how you tried to clean her up, there was something deceptive looking about her. She was dusty looking and only good for crowded, affordable department stores.

"That's what's up," Bam acknowledged.

"You know what?" Cartier began. "I think you should go up first and let Bam wait around ten minutes, and then meet you up there. That way if the Ds are on to you, Bam won't get knocked. Macy's Ds are a lot smarter than Bergdorf's, and they are on to the whole decoy thing. What do you think?"

Dip hesitated for a moment. She was torn between cursing out Cartier for trying to dictate the next move and also thinking about the household goods she was going to steal for her new apartment. Dip didn't have any intentions of packing one bag of shit for them. She was going to have Bam's stupid ass walk out with two stuffed shopping bags, most of which would contain bed sheets, towels, and dishes. The latter prevailed and Dip realized she needed time to find everything and prepare the bags before Bam could leave with them.

"OK, you're right, Cartier. Bam meet me in exactly twenty minutes in the Cellar."

"The Cellar?" Bam asked in a confused state.

"Look, I got this. Just meet me in the Cellar." Macy's Cellar was the bottom level that held all the household goods.

Despite Dip thinking the girls were stupid, they weren't. She never thought the girls were smart enough to figure out her scheme, or strong enough to stand up against her.

"OK, sure. Twenty minutes and I'll be there," Bam replied.

The crew waited five minutes before they hopped out of Dip's truck. Cartier's plan consisted of them leaving the SUV in the no-parking zone, taking all the merchandise that was stolen that day, and hopping on the 3-train back to Brownsville, Brooklyn.

Their take for the day was over twenty-five thousand dollars of stolen merchandise. The only thing that stopped the crew from having a big celebration was the infamous reputation of the woman they'd just crossed. Shorty Dip wasn't going to take what they'd done to her lightly.

CHAPTER THREE

No Shook Hands in Brook Land

For two days, the girls didn't walk the blocks alone. They were all too familiar with the code of the streets and knew that their actions would beget an action from Dip. No one had to tell them that they now had beef with Dip. Not only did Dip's truck get ticketed and towed, but they heard that the tow-truck driver fucked up her rims as well.

It was only a matter of time before Dip and her crew from Flatbush, Brooklyn ran up on the Cartel. Dip couldn't be disrespected. She had a reputation to uphold, and if she didn't respond appropriately, then she would be opening up a can of worms for other motherfuckers to try and play her.

Shorty Dip didn't work a nine to five. Her job was boosting. Boosting paid her rent, paid her car note, put food in her refrigerator, sent her daughter to a private school, and paid for a host of other things. The common thread that afforded her lifestyle were *vics*—a steady stream of young girls with heart—willing, ready, and enthusiastic about walking out of department stores with stolen merchandise. And the so-called Cartier Cartel was the best. She had never run across girls as ruthless and full of heart as Cartier and her crew.

Bam was the first to notice the black Lincoln Navigator creep up the block, as the Cartier Cartel sat on the stoop. Lil Momma, Bam, Shanine, and Monya looked toward one another and then bolted down the block. Only Cartier hesitated, eventually deciding not to run. She thought back to when she was eight years old and had gotten jumped by two neighborhood girls. Cartier ran inside her house crying for her mother. Trina told her that she better go back outside and give those girls the fight of their lives.

"In the hood either you fight and earn respect or you run and lose respect," Trina's words resonated in her head. "You better go back out there and earn *your* respect!"

Shorty Dip exited the car first in her toughest gangster imitation.

"Oh, bitch, you think you tough?" Dip asked in a gruff voice, trying to antagonize the girl who was half her age.

"Ain't no shook hands in Brook-land," Cartier spat and prepared herself for battle.

"Bitch, I will beat the Brooklyn out of you if you don't give me back my shit," Dip threatened.

Cartier, still not bowing down, stood firm. "I'm not giving you shit and I'm not gonna be too many more bitches—"

"Yo, Dip, punch that little smart bitch in her fucking face!" Angie said from inside the SUV.

Cartier cut her eyes toward the SUV and said, "Why don't you come do it?"

The remaining three women inside the Navigator got out and surrounded Cartier. Each woman looked as if they'd been in a war. They had battle scars etched into their hard, leathery skin. Their beer bellies protruded from their jeans and not one of them tried to hide their muffin tops with the tight tank tops they wore. The variety of colorful weaves—orange, blond, and burgundy—accentuated their ugliness.

Yet Cartier refused to be intimidated. She hated Dip and really wanted to spit in her face for the way she treated her crew who had been loyal to her. All Cartier wanted was a measly dress and that was too fucking hard for Dip to comprehend. And what killed Cartier was that the dress was f-r-e-e. Dip acted as if Cartier wanted her to toss it on her credit card.

"This between me and Dip—one on one," Cartier declared. "But if y'all wanna get in it, then we can all toss it up. Whatever, however, is how I get down!"

Dip knew Cartier was tough and could bring the heat. She looked into Cartier's eyes and knew she was prepared to give her a fight. Several things raced through Dip's head in a matter of seconds. She wondered if she still had it in her to stomp out a girl half her age. Although an avid fighter all her life, Dip hadn't had to beat on a bitch in years. Her reputation preceded her and usually kept people at bay. Dip also knew if she backed down now, with Jacki, Karen, and Angie watching, she'd never live that down. Dip fingered the screwdriver she had stuck in her back pocket and decided to ask Cartier one last time to give up her shit, or else she was prepared to go all out.

The loud banging on her front door almost gave Trina a heart attack. Instinctively, she knew something had happened to her only child. She ran and flung open the door, only to see Monya, Bam, Lil Momma, and Shanine standing there.

"Where's my child?" Her words were laced with panic.

"They're gonna jump her!" Monya cried.

"What? Who? Where the fuck is she and why the fuck are y'all not with her?"

"It's Shorty Dip and her crew," Monya replied.

"Shorty Dip from Cypress projects?"

"Yeah, her," Lil Momma answered.

"Why the fuck is that grown-ass bitch fucking with my child?" Trina was asking questions as she dressed feverously. "Where's Cartier!"

"She's in front of my building. We all took off running and we thought she was behind us, but she stayed," Monya explained.

"You damn right she stayed 'cause a Timmons don't run from no damn bitch! They bleed like we bleed."

Trina couldn't wait to get her hands on Dip. She and Dip were a year apart and had beef back in the days when they were in high school. Of course, they argued over what women of all ages fight over: a nigga. But they never came to blows. Each woman knew the other could handle her own.

As they ran down the block, Trina called Monya's mother, Janet, who happened to be her best friend, to meet her in front of the building. Trina didn't hesitate to threaten the Cartel that if something happened to her daughter, she was going to personally whip each and every one of their asses and then make Cartier whip their asses, too.

As the crew came running down the block, Trina saw a crowd of women surrounding her daughter. She called out, "Dip!"

Hearing her name stopped Dip in her tracks.

"Who that?" Dip asked. She was confused when she saw an unrecognizable face racing toward the ruckus. As the crowd drew closer, the face came into focus. It was a face she didn't want to see.

Trina looked up and saw Janet only a few steps behind them.

"What the fuck is up with you in my daughter's face?" Trina demanded.

Dip was more than stressed at the newfound news that Cartier was Trina's daughter, yet she had to keep it gangster.

"Yo, tell your daughter to return the shit that doesn't belong to her."

Trina looked to Cartier. "You all right?"

Cartier nodded.

"Cartier ain't returning a motherfucking thing! Possession is nine-tenths of the game. Whatever my daughter got that's yours is now hers! Let's set it off in this bitch! Cartier, I got this one!"

As Dip went to reach inside her back pocket for the screwdriver, Trina smashed her in her face with a strong right hook. Dip stumbled backward and the crowd began thumping. Janet jumped on Jacki and then Cartier Cartel took care of Karen and Angie. Punches began flying, hair got pulled, and even a few bites caught flesh. These women were fighting for respect, which wasn't given freely or easily in the streets. Trina was trying to damn near kill Dip for fucking with her daughter and settling a score from back in the day. Trina had a lot of pent up anger and knew if she didn't end it today, then this would be an unsettled beef.

The two-block radius was a tight-knit community, and once word got out that they were fighting outsiders, it was a wrap. On that day, not only did Dip and her crew get the shit beat out of them, but the neighborhood made sure they totally destroyed her Navigator. They smashed all the windows out, kicked dents into her exterior, and slashed all tires. When they were through, the car looked totaled.

Dip and her crew were literally chased out of the neighborhood. When it was all said and done, Trina and Janet had a chat with Cartier's crew.

"I'm so disappointed that you girls would leave my baby out here alone," Trina began. "Anything could have happened. She could have been jumped or stabbed. Janet and I never got down like that—"

"You know that's right," Janet interjected. "If I had

a beef with somebody, then Trina had a beef with that same person. And Monya, I'm really surprised at you of all people. You lucky I don't whip your ass right here and now!"

"Nah, don't do that, Ms. Janet," Cartier defended her friend. "It's all good. I know Monya has my back. She just got spooked. Ain't that right, Monya?"

"Yeah, you right," Monya answered weakly. She was afraid of her mother, and although Janet stood strong, Monya knew she was embarrassed her daughter had run away.

Cartier took up for her best friend, because Ms. Janet gave Monya the worst beatings. And Cartier knew Monya wasn't really a fighter. Monya was interested in boys, money, and clothes. If she never had a fight in her life, Monya would be happy.

Trina concluded, "Well, from now on remember this, y'all crew. Don't let nothing—fear, an ass-kicking, a nigga, money, or bitches—come between the crew!"

That night when Cartier and Trina were alone, her mother told her how proud she was of her for standing up for herself when nobody else was there to have her back.

"Ma, I only did what you taught me to do."

"That don't minimize how I feel. You could have run like the rest of your crew and I wouldn't have known shit. So I know this wasn't about me. I know you did what you felt was right in your heart, and for that I'm really proud of you."

Trina walked over to Cartier and they both embraced.

Cartier couldn't explain how fighting on the streets of Brooklyn could bring her and her mother closer, but strangely that was exactly what it did.

CHAPTER FOUR

Wifey Material

A couple weeks after the brawl, Trina took Cartier down to Atlanta for the wedding of one of their relatives. While there, Cartier picked up on a scheme and couldn't wait to put it to use in New York. Cartier knew this could make her and the crew some money. Just thinking about it made Cartier antsy with anticipation. She figured with this newfound knowledge, they could take over Brooklyn first and then the entire city, one borough at a time.

In the confines of her bedroom, Cartier worked diligently making boobie bags. The scheme Cartier scoped in the ATL consisted of boobie bags dismantling the sensormatic alarm box, rendering the alarm system useless. Sensormatics were the alarm items placed on clothes in department stores that had to be removed by the cashier before customers left the store. If they were not removed, the alarm would go off soundly and immediately. With the sensormatic disarmed, they could fill the bag to capacity within seconds, and casually walk out of the store.

The boobie bag contraption was almost like magic. Cartier took two large shopping paper bags. The first one, she lined it with aluminum foil, taping the foil in place. Once the bag was wrapped, she then slid the wrapped bag into a perfectly crisp large shopping paper bag! It took her three days to manufacture twenty bags before she called her crew up to her bedroom to explain how the bags worked.

Monya was the first to ask a question. "So you saying that we can drop anything we want inside this here bag without taking off the alarms and when we walk out the front door of the store, the alarm box won't go off?"

"That's exactly what I'm saying."

"But how do you know this works?" Lil Momma, who wasn't down with boosting, asked. "This could be an urban legend or some shit."

"I know it works, because when I was in Atlanta, I saw it for myself, with my own eyes."

"Jeez, do you know how much money we gonna make?" Monya asked. "If this works out the way I think it will, in a couple years we'll be able to get our own apartments and won't have to live with our mothers."

"We should all save up our money to buy a five bedroom apartment in the city and go to all the hottest clubs each night and hopefully, meet all the rappers." Lil Momma was fully enthralled in the conversation.

"What do you mean *we*? You ain't down," Bam was quick to point out to Lil Momma.

"If I wanna get down, I can!" Lil Momma challenged.

"Right, Cartier? If I wanted to get down, I could?"

"Listen, we got better things to discuss right now than talk about whether Lil Momma is going to move with us from now on. We gotta make a pact that these bags will be our secret. No one must know how to make them or use them. Understood?" Cartier looked in each one of their faces to get a feel for each girl's thoughts.

"Understood," they all said in unison.

It only took a couple of days before the weekend came and the girls went out to test the bags. Lil Momma was a willing participant, but now roles had switched. Cartier and Monya were the ones who went into the stores and gathered the clothing and packed each bag, while Bam, Lil Momma, and Shanine took turns walking out of the stores. Each bag always had five of each item. If there was only four pieces of an item in the store, then that item, no matter how fly it was, had to be left. Every member of the crew got treated equally; that way no rifts or animosity would arise. Within a couple of weeks, each girl had more clothing than they could wear in a month's time. They had a steady stream of customers, and even had the local neighborhood and surrounding neighborhood boys interested in them.

The one who was most pleased with all the attention she was getting was Monya. Her long, silky hair was now cut into shiny layers, and her light brown, Indian-looking complexion made her look older than her crew.

That, coupled with the skintight jeans, high heels, and large, oversized purse she wore, gave her a mature look. Her dainty facial features were complemented by the theatrical hairstyle, and the look enhanced her already sensual personality.

It didn't take long for Monya to get scooped up by a dude who had his own ride. His name was Wise and he claimed to be the nephew of one of the members of the infamous Fat Cat crew located in Queens. At twenty, he was five years older than Monya. He cruised onto the block with music blaring, in a deep lean in his new peanut butter and chocolate Mercedes AMG with custom bucket leather seats. That car made everyone's mouth drop open with envy. As Monya came switching down the steps of her stoop, her friends were proud.

Cartier, Shanine, Lil Momma, and Bam couldn't believe Monya's luck. They all figured he had to be a millionaire. And they wanted to know what all girls wanted to know: Did he have friends?

The crew watched Monya slide into the luxurious ride as the car sat idling. Soon Monya rolled down the window and called, "Cartier, let me holla at you for a second."

Cartier hopped up and walked toward the car. She was looking equally cute in her skintight jeans and halter top, all dressed up with nowhere to go. That was their daily routine. She bent down and peered inside only to see one of the cutest guys she'd ever laid eyes on. Wise had a low-cut Caesar with deep, shiny waves. Long sideburns and a thin mustache complimented his smooth, light brown skin. He had small, sneaky eyes and a slim frame.

"What's up?" Cartier asked.

"I wanted to introduce you to Wise. Wise, this is my best friend, Cartier."

Wise did a head nod. "Nice to meet you."

"You, too," Cartier replied. This was followed by an uncomfortable silence. Cartier ended the awkward moment, "See you guys later."

"A'ight."

Cartier went back to the stoop and told the girls how cute Wise was.

"I wonder where he's going to take her tonight?" Shanine stated.

"Monya said they were going out to eat," Cartier said, still admiring his car.

"In Queens or Brooklyn?"

"How the fuck should I know?" Cartier snapped.

Just as a brutal debate was about to kick off, Monya exited the car and began walking toward them. She tried her best to conceal her embarrassment from her friends, while also trying to put on a sexy switch in her hips, just in case Wise stayed around long enough to watch her walk away. He didn't. No sooner had the passenger's door closed than he hit the gas pedal.

Cartier reacted first. "What happened?" She knew Monya didn't sit in a beauty parlor all morning and put on her tightest jeans and brand new Prada shoes to see this kid for five minutes.

Monya began shaking her head wildly. "He got a

phone call, said he had to bounce, and he'd call me later."

"Bounce?"

"That's what he said."

"He probably going to meet some bitch," Bam said.

"Why the fuck would he be going to meet some bitch when he's with a bitch?" Cartier snapped, in defense of Monya. "Look at Monya. Ain't too many females out here prettier than my homegirl."

"Exactly. Ain't no other bitch out here prettier than me!" Monya ran her hands through her hair. It was something she did when she was nervous or embarrassed. "He know he want this. Besides, we ain't even fuck yet. He probably had to go and take care of business."

"That sounds about right," Cartier agreed.

"Well, what about the money she spent on her hair? Is he gonna give that back?" Lil Momma couldn't believe that they were taking up for him. "And her nails? She spent all her money trying to look cute for him and he's talking about he had to bounce."

"Don't be stupid," Cartier snapped. "She would play herself asking for seventeen dollars back!" She paused and looked at Monya. She was steamed. "He gotta know he can't just disrespect you like that. Did you tell that motherfucker that your time isn't to be wasted?"

"Nah, I didn't say shit," Monya replied weakly. "I was so stunned that he was ushering me out of the car. What do you think I did?"

"You ain't do shit!" Cartier blasted. "That bitch-ass nigga think it's like that 'cause he got money. I can't wait until we get our own rides so we can stunt on people too."

Cartier looked off and began thinking. Although they were doing well with boosting, it was just enough money to get by. Plus, she was tired of boosting. She knew they had to do something to make more money, but she didn't have a clue what that could be. They could only go boosting on the weekends, and after they divided the clothes and sold what was left, they only made a couple hundred for themselves. After manicures, pedicures, doobie wraps, lunch money and taxicabs, none of the five could save any money.

They all decided to go to the Magic Johnson Cineplex on Linden Boulevard in the East New York area of Brooklyn. After the movie, they all walked to the Lindenwood Diner one block over and ordered seasoned crab legs and shrimp Caesar salad. It wasn't until a few guys from their neighborhood walked in that the real fun began.

Jason, Maurice, and Wonderful made their way over to the crew. Over the past year, Jason had come up in the drug game. For years, he had sold hand-to-hand, but now it seemed as if he was pushing weight on a small level. At nineteen, although he was considered ruthless, he had a soft spot in his heart for Cartier. Jason had a light complexion and loved dark-skinned girls with thick thighs. Not to mention, he loved girls with sassiness. He deemed Cartier his perfect match.

"What's up, ma?" Jason asked Cartier as he slid into the booth next to her.

"Jason, what you doing here?" a surprised Cartier asked.

"I came here to see you," he replied and licked his full, juicy lips.

Giggling, Cartier replied, "No, you didn't."

Jason didn't miss his opportunity. He moved closer and draped his arm around her neck. The other crew members had broad smiles on their faces. They all felt Cartier should hook up with Jason, but for some reason she wouldn't. She was more interested in his man, Wonderful. Cartier had no idea that Wonderful thought she was ugly. Although he would fuck her, that was as far as Wonderful would take it with her. In fact, he didn't find any of the Cartier Cartel attractive. Bottom line, he loved Spanish girls and had no interest in sistas.

Internally, Cartier was hoping Wonderful was getting jealous over the fact she and Jason were flirting. She stuck her fork in her shrimp and fed it to Jason.

"Damn, ma, this shit is good. Excuse me, waiter," Jason began. The waiter quickly came over and gave Jason his attention. "Let me get another order of the shrimp Caesar. What y'all niggas want?"

"I'm straight," Maurice said. He was the broke one out of the crew and sometimes, Jason could flip. Sometimes, Jason would pay for Maurice, other times he'd leave him hanging.

"Yeah, order me one, too," Wonderful replied. Jason and Wonderful were best friends like Cartier and Monya. Jason never screamed on Wonderful or tried to play him.

"Yo, give me three orders of the shrimp Caesar salad," he looked to Maurice, "Motherfucker I know you hungry . . . and let me get three double shots of Hennessy."

The waiter took the order and didn't bother to ask for identification. He didn't want any kind of altercation with the young gangster. He knew asking for a simple ID card could lead to a beat-down or the end of his life. It was that serious in the hood.

"Order me a shot of Henny too," Lil Momma asked Jason. When he didn't acknowledge her request, she barked, "Oh it's like that?"

"Stay in ya lane little girl," Jason replied and then playfully plucked a toothpick at her. Only Lil Momma didn't find anything funny.

As the night went on, Jason would allow Cartier to take sips of his Hennessy, and before anyone knew it, she was tipsy.

"Do you know that nigga named Wise?" Cartier asked Jason.

"Wise from Queens?"

"Cartier!" Monya wanted to keep her friend quiet, but Cartier wasn't having it.

"What? Jason peoples. Besides, we don't know shit about that kid."

"Oh, Monya, you frontin' on me?" Jason asked.

"Nah, it ain't even like that," Monya replied. "Wise and I are only friends."

Cartier turned her body toward Jason. As she spoke, he couldn't help but want to take her home and eat her pussy. Jason loved to eat pussy. It gave women the most pleasure and he had made a concerted effort at being the best. Additionally, he believed eating pussy could compensate for his small dick. The girls he was with didn't consider him to be packing, and Cartier looked like she could handle a big dick. He was almost sure she wasn't a virgin the way she and her crew ran around. Word on the street had them boosting and running around all the boroughs thinking they were cute.

"So that punk ass comes around supposedly to take Monya out to eat and five minutes later, he's out, talking about he had somewhere to go!"

"Damn, Monya. You running niggas out of town like that?" Wonderful asked.

"Whatever."

"You sure ya breath wasn't lightin' up the car?" Wonderful joked.

Everyone began making jokes at Monya's expense. She glared at Cartier, who then tried to redirect the conversation back to her original question.

"But what's up with him? He got a girl or something?"

"I ain't into snitching on a nigga," Jason began. "But that nigga be getting rep from his uncle. He run around here like he thorough like them real niggas in Fat Cat's crew. And who's to say he really blood to one of those niggas?"

"He got money?"

"I don't give a fuck what that nigga got and don't got!" Jason was suddenly upset at Cartier's interest. His jealousy took over and he forgot that the questions were in her friend's best interest. Not hers.

Cartier rolled her eyes, "Calm the fuck down."

"Calm me down—"

Cartier playfully slapped his face.

"You lucky I don't hit girls, 'cause I don't let nobody be touching my face."

"Please, you know I will fuck a nigga up."

"Word? I heard how you and your crew put in work on those old broads."

"Nah, that was her moms out there getting busy," Wonderful interjected.

"What? It wasn't only my moms . . . that was me too!" Cartier was insulted. "And my crew. We were all out there thumping."

"Yeah, give my girl her props," Jason said defensively.

Wonderful looked to Bam, Shanine and Lil Momma who had basically sat quiet throughout the whole meal.

"Y'all was out there thumping too?" he quizzed the three girls but only Bam nodded her head. "Why y'all so quiet?"

Lil Momma snapped, "I don't talk when my throat is dry," and the whole table erupted in laughter.

After they finished eating, Jason paid the check for everyone and they all squeezed into his green Nissan Pathfinder. When he pulled onto the block and dropped off the girls, he called out to Cartier.

"When you gonna give me the digits?" he asked.

"What? You know you're like a brother to me,"

Cartier replied coyly.

"Fuck that brother shit. You know how I feel about you. Let's make it official."

Cartier truly didn't want to hurt his feelings. He was always good to get a free meal, free ride, or sound advice and she didn't want to ruin that.

"I'm not looking for a man right now, but when I do, it will definitely be you."

"I like that answer, ma."

Cartier exhaled. "Goodnight."

"Goodnight, wifey."

CHAPTER FIVE

1998 - Charge it to the Game

With a silk scarf tied tightly around her head, Cartier headed out to the corner store to buy her mother a pack of Newports and a sour pickle. It was eleven o'clock in the morning and she had every intention of going back to sleep. Every Saturday morning, her mother woke her up early to help clean up the apartment. The routine was always the same. Her mother would wake up and put on all her favorite music from the late sixties and seventies: Aretha Franklin, Prince, Diana Ross, and Donna Summer. To make matters worse, her mother didn't have CDs. She had vinyl albums.

Cartier bought her mother's pack of Newports and bought herself a loose one. As she stood there puffing on her cigarette, she watched as a few neighborhood boys she knew do hand-to-hand transactions. They all stood huddled around talking smack, and when someone came through, one of the boys would step off to the side to serve them. When she thought about it, one of the boys, Kenny, had recently purchased a 1993 Honda Accord. As Cartier walked home, the light bulb went on in her head. She figured that there was a lot more money in selling drugs than in boosting. She also knew the risk would be less. She reasoned with herself that those who bought drugs wanted to get high. And everyone knew nothing could stop a fiend from getting high. Additionally, she and the crew would be able to spot an undercover cop a mile away. Hell, none of the boys on the block had ever been bum rushed by the cops. She knew what they could do, she and her crew could do ten times better. She still needed to think her plan through, but for now, she couldn't contain the excitement she felt in her stomach.

Diana Ross was belting out tunes from her *Boss* album, and Trina knew all the words. When Cartier walked in, her mother had a pile of her stolen clothes on her bed.

"Don't none of this shit fit me," Trina complained. Trina was pregnant and starting to show. Both she and Cartier chose to play dumb.

Cartier was really disgusted Trina was pregnant in her old age. If her mother chose to keep the child, Cartier would be sixteen years older than her baby sibling. She thought that was ghetto as hell.

"Then maybe you should lose some weight," Cartier replied, playing into her mother's deception.

"Maybe you should steal some shit that your momma could fit, perhaps some maternity clothes."

Cartier didn't miss a beat. "What I look like? Your baby daddy?"

Trina rolled her eyes and then went and embraced her daughter.

"Ma, stoooooppp," Cartier said, whining.

"Give your momma some sugar."

"No!" Cartier screamed and then giggled. "So, I guess that means you're keeping your baby?"

"How long did you know?"

"I'm not stupid. I know what pregnancy looks like."

"Well, you just better not come up in here pregnant."

"That will never happen."

"Well, let's not get carried away. I do want grandbabies. Just not until you're married."

"Ma, you really want to do this? Have a baby when you don't have a job? And what about the father? What's he saying?"

"You know he's all excited. This will be his first child."

"But what about you? Is that what you want?" Cartier wasn't crazy about the situation. Recently, she was the one acting like the grownup. She could only hope the father came through, but her experience in the hood told her that was a long shot.

"Girl, stop sounding like the mother. I know what I'm doing and I want my baby. You won't understand. I had you too young and I missed out on a lot of things. I took a lot for granted and let your grandmother raise you. I missed your first steps and that hurt. I've already forgotten the scent of a baby that I loved so much. This time I want things to be different. I want to enjoy motherhood and do better. You deserved better than I could give you, Cartier. Hopefully, I can give to your little brother or sister what I couldn't give you."

Cartier didn't know what to make out of her mother's admission about not really being there for her. She felt something, and it could have been a sting of jealousy, but she hoped it was mixed with the right amount of eagerness about the prospect of having a little brother or sister.

"How far along are you?"

"six weeks," Trina replied as she dusted off one of her end tables.

"Hmmm, you still got time to do the do," Cartier said jokingly referring to an abortion.

Trina tossed the dirty rag at her and they both chuckled at Cartier's dark humor.

After they cleaned up the house, Cartier took a look around and decided they needed towels and toiletries. She decided she would put that on her list of things to get when they went boosting this afternoon. But for now, she needed a nap.

As her mother's belly grew, so did Cartier. She grew up. She saved up enough money to purchase herself a new five-piece bedroom set, one that was made of real wood and sturdy. She also bought two gallons of paint and had the maintenance men paint her bedroom. Next came the new carpet for the apartment. She felt really good about herself. With the summer ending and school rolling back around, her days of going to bed hungry were long gone. She and her crew now had the reputation that Shorty Dip once carried. Her cell phone rang all day with the *flyest* chicks from each borough wanting to be friends, but mostly wanting to go boosting with her and her crew. But that was a no-go. There wasn't any way they would put another bitch on.

Each night from her window, Cartier watched Manny, Reggie, and Kenny sell weed from their stoop. From what Cartier was told, they had some good shit. She watched intently, studying them night and day, and paid close attention to the hours they kept. Everything she saw fed into her method to her madness. Their success became her hunger. She scoped the new clothes and sneakers, the cars, the money, and even the cute chicks on their arm. Besides the females, they had what she wanted—success.

For Cartier, selling drugs was the next logical step in the Cartel's progression. If done properly, then she and the crew could make more money than they'd ever dreamed of having. And yes, the money was appealing. She was the breadwinner in the family now, and taking care of Trina and her new sibling were her responsibility now.

Cartier shook her head as she thought about the baby's daddy bouncing before the baby was even born. It was the way of the hood. Like Trina, Cartier wanted the baby to have everything she never had. She and the Cartel had already stolen four garbage bags worth of baby clothes, from newborn to twenty-four months. The doctor said her mother was having a girl and her mother chose the name Prada. They also began to steal a few items from Babies "R" Us. Cartier didn't really care for the store. She had gotten knocked twice trying to roll out a high chair in a shopping cart. Each time she was fingerprinted, but let go because of her age. On her third try, she got it. She caught the guard slipping and eased out without detection. Within two months, the baby had enough shit to last two to three years. The only thing her mother would be responsible for was feeding the baby, which the government would assist with. Between food stamps and WIC, Cartier thought all should be fine.

By the time fall rolled around, each member of the crew had officially dropped out of school. At sixteen, they all functioned as if they were grown women. Cartier had men coming and going in and out of her small bedroom and Trina said nothing. History was repeating itself. Trina was able to have boys sleep over when she was Cartier's age, so it was perfectly natural for her to allow her daughter to do the same, although truly Trina didn't like it. It didn't feel right to her.

One part of Trina wanted to step up and be the parent Cartier never had and start laying down rules and regulations. But the other part—the stronger part—felt like Cartier was the sister she never had. By the time Cartier reached twelve years-old, everyone mistook her for Trina's baby sister, and when Trina would tell them that Cartier was in fact her daughter, they were always surprised. Trina did look good for her age. Each day Trina promised herself she would raise her new baby the right way. Her second child would not only go to school each day, she would graduate and go all the way to college. That was Trina's only wish.

Trina watched as her first born walked around the house cleaning up for her impending company and was somewhat proud of her accomplishments. Cartier had grown so much in the past year and a half, and although she wasn't heading to college, Trina was still proud of the newfound independence Cartier exuded.

"Who's coming over?"

Cartier stopped in her tracks to respond. "The Cartel. We have a few things to discuss and they should be here shortly. I just wanted to clean up a bit and get a few things out the way."

"OK, well y'all keep it down in here. I'm going to go in my room and get some rest."

Monya got a tip that there was a small boutique in midtown Manhattan that was sweet for mink coats and ripe for the picking. In their realm, you weren't considered fly until you owned a mink coat. It was a sign of opulence and status.

"You know doofy Claudia came off the other day with two mink coats," Monya explained. "And you know if that clumsy bitch could catch two, we all could finally get our coats."

"All right, bet," Cartier agreed. "We gotta dress the part and work in pairs. I'll work with Lil Momma; Monya, you work with Shanine; and Bam, you can go in solo. Everyone wear their most expensive conservative outfit and make sure your hair and nails are done. And we gotta wear lipstick and heels to appear older. We can't fuck this up, because I want my coat."

It was Cartier's idea to go on a weekday, since the stores were always on higher alert on the weekend. They dressed professionally as if they worked in an office building or at some high-end job. They looked the part and easily passed the businesswoman test. From across the street, the girls watched the movements in the store. It was virtually dead, which was what they had anticipated.

Each pair of girls and Bam filed into the small, quaint boutique and overwhelmed the two sales associates. They all inundated the two women with dozens of questions while making them go back and forth pulling various styles of mink coats.

Lil Momma, Bam, and Shanine each had two garment bags draped over their arms. The top garment bag was filled with a puffy coat and there was an empty garment bag inconspicuously hidden from sight underneath the top bag. With coats piled to the ceiling, working in teams, each girl began putting mink coats inside an empty garment bag. Bam was the first to put one inside her bag and then skillfully replace the already full bag on top.

"I'm oodgay," she said in pig Latin, meaning she was good. This got everyone excited. There wasn't any way they were going to let Bam be the only one to get a mink coat. Monya and Cartier looked at each other, eye-to-eye. As if reading each other's thoughts, they both grabbed two beautiful swing mink coats and zipped them up inside their garment bags. This was done quickly. Monya handed the full garment bag to Shanine and Cartier handed the other full bag to Lil Momma.

The unsuspecting saleswomen continued to assist the women, hoping to get a nice commission right before the holiday.

"Let's ogay," Monya stated, but Cartier had other plans. As Bam, Shanine, and Monya began to exit the store, Cartier felt the situation was sweet enough inside the store to get an additional coat for herself. She put her hand on Lil Momma's arm and stopped her from leaving.

She whispered, "Wait. We can get more."

Lil Momma's eyes looked down at the *one* coat in Cartier's hand and knew how it was about to go down. There wasn't any way she was walking out with three not four coats. Greed had now taken over her as well. Cartier tugged on the garment bag, but Lil Momma wouldn't release it.

"Get me another one, too," Lil Momma demanded in a hushed voice. Cartier knew that four coats couldn't possibly fit inside the bag. Additionally, as the leader of the crew, she felt she should be the only one afforded two coats.

"A'ight, just give me the bag and then I'll get yours."

Reluctantly, Lil Momma gave her the garment bag. Quickly, Cartier stuffed the third coat inside the bag and as she was about to zip up the bag, Lil Momma stopped her. Without observing her surroundings, Lil Momma snatched the garment bag from Cartier and began shoving another coat for herself inside the already tight space.

"What are you doing?" Cartier asked. She was furious

at her clumsy friend. Cartier stood there in shock as she watched Lil Momma try to frantically stuff the coat inside. Cartier took a few steps back and watched in horror as both sales associates noticed what was going on and rushed toward Lil Momma. Cartier began to make a speedy exit as one woman firmly grabbed Lil Momma's wrist and the other lady snatched the bag. A struggle ensued as Lil Momma tried desperately to overpower the petite white woman. In Lil Momma's head, she could upgrade from boosting to burglary. Surely, she could whip both of these women asses and take what she wanted.

"H-h-help!" the sales associate screamed. "Let go of the coats!"

Lil Momma began to punch the lady in the face and head, while trying desperately to get her to release the coats. In the chaos, Cartier thought about going to jail if she didn't get out of there quickly. As she got closer to the door, the other sales associate was locking them inside with keys.

"Let me out of here!" Cartier demanded.

"Not until I call the police!" the sales associate responded.

"You let me out of here. I don't have anything to do with this," Cartier protested. "Or I will sue this damn store, the owner and your ass."

The sales associate didn't know what to do. To her knowledge, the women were together. But what if they weren't? She'd only seen the other woman trying to steal and the woman standing before her looked angry and intimidating. The commotion got louder and when the female standing before her reached out for the keys, she relented and let her out. Once she locked up again, she ran to the telephone and called 911.

Outside, Cartier took off down the block. She ran until she reached the subway station. She thought about calling Monya to see where they were, but it was too hot. She needed to get to the safe haven of Brooklyn. Cartier took the 4 train to the 3 train.

Meanwhile, Monya, Bam, and Shanine were starting to get nervous about their other crew members. When they walked back on the block and saw a New York City police car parked outside the store, they knew something had gone down. They weren't sure, but chances were good that Cartier and Lil Momma were busted. Monya's heart stopped. She couldn't understand what happened.

Immediately, she stepped up and took charge. She didn't say anything. She just placed her hand in the air and flagged down a yellow cab. They had three stolen coats in their possession, probably worth an estimated thirty thousand dollars. If they were caught, they'd get in serious trouble.

"1475 Rockaway Boulevard, in Brooklyn," Monya rattled off.

The cab driver peered in the back seat through his mirror at the three young black ladies. They looked clean enough and he could see that they'd been shopping. Only he didn't like the Brooklyn address they were heading. Too much violence in that area, and he didn't want to take the chance that he would get stiffed for his cab fare.

"I don't go to Brooklyn," the driver said in his thick Albanian accent.

Monya wasn't in the mood to play musical cabs. She pulled out two twenty dollar bills and handed it to the driver. "You do now!"

Now she was speaking his language. As he drove toward the FDR Drive, Bam and Shanine began asking questions.

"What the fuck happened?" Bam asked. "It was so sweet in there."

"How should I know? I wasn't there," Monya snapped.

"I know they are stressed out right about now," Shanine stated. Although Cartier was the head member in the crew, Shanine was most concerned about Lil Momma.

"Wouldn't you be? I bet Lil Momma fucked up somehow." Monya ran her hands through her hair.

"I'm just glad that we got our coats," Shanine added.

"Damn, like how you sound? Two members of our crew just got busted and all you can think about is yourself." Monya wanted to slap the black off Shanine. She couldn't wait to speak to Cartier and tell her what Shanine had said.

The rest of the ride home was in silence. When the cab was approximately five minutes away from their destination, Monya's cell phone began ringing. She looked down and was delighted to see that it was Cartier.

"Bitch, where you at?" Monya said.

"Yo, Lil Momma got knocked. It was crazy. I'm home. Where are you? Is everyone safe?"

"Yeah, we straight. We're in a cab and should be on the block in five minutes."

"Come straight to the compound."

When the girls arrived at Cartier's apartment, they were hyped to know what happened. Trina showed them in and they walked back to Cartier's room. She'd already taken off her conservative clothing and put on a pair of sweatpants and T-shirt. Cartier and Monya warmly embraced, lingering in each other's arms longer than Shanine or Bam cared to witness.

"Yo, shit was crazy today," Cartier began. "They got Lil Momma."

"How did they get on to you?" Monya asked.

"That stupid bitch, Lil Momma—"

"See. What the fuck did I tell y'all?" Monya interrupted. "I knew Cartier was too good to get knocked on a humble when it was so sweet. What did she do?"

Shanine was saddened Lil Momma was knocked. Lil Momma was her best friend and she didn't like the way Cartier and Monya were talking shit about her. Since Lil Momma was always taking up for Shanine, she decided to do the same.

"Well, what did she do, because the last time I looked we all had our bags packed and the only thing Lil Momma had to do was walk out. You telling me she didn't know how to walk?"

Her sarcasm didn't go unnoticed.

"Her walking the fuck out wasn't the problem," Cartier said with attitude. "The problem was that when I told her ass to walk, she refused."

"What sense does that make? Why would she want to hang around in a store with stolen merchandise in her bag? Was she afraid to leave?" Shanine was giving Cartier the third degree.

"She wasn't afraid of shit. She was stupid. I went to add a third coat to the bag—"

"A third coat? Why? That wasn't the plan. And who was the coat for, Cartier? There's only five members, not six."

"I can count, bitch!" Cartier had had enough of Shanine. "I safely put a third coat in the bag, so we could sell the sixth and make money for the crew. Once I successfully put the coat in the bag, Lil Momma went berserk and got selfish. She wanted two coats for herself, while we all got one. When I refused and told her to bounce, she began trying to stuff a fourth coat inside that tiny little bag without paying attention. They peeped her and she got knocked. I mean, it was crazy. They were fighting and shit. At first, they was gonna take me down, too. But I wasn't having it."

"So you just left her?"

"What's the point in both of us getting knocked?"

"I can't believe that Lil Momma would want two coats for herself. That's so unlike her," Shanine still refused to believe Cartier's version.

"Let me see the coats," Cartier began as she looked at the two garment bags. Excitedly, the girls began pulling out beautiful mink coats with shiny skins. There wasn't any way Cartier wasn't keeping a coat. She'd already decided that on the train. As they lay on her bed, she began trying on each coat until she found the one she wanted. With the coat still adorning her shapely body, she tossed the next best one to Monya. "Monya, try this one on."

As both girls modeled coats, Shanine and Bam began to get nervous. Bam reached out and grabbed the last coat, which was the coat she'd picked out. Shanine was left coatless.

"Cartier, let me try on my coat," Shanine began.

With a straight face, Cartier began to put a spin on things. "Your coat got knocked with Lil Momma."

"What?" Shanine raised her voice. "How my coat got knocked? That was all you."

"You must be crazy. From jump I told Monya to pick out my coat and put it in your bag. Lil Momma was picking out y'all coats and your bag got knocked."

"That's a damn lie!" Shanine yelled.

"Monya, am I lying?"

"Cartier told me in the beginning to make sure I got her coat. And even if she didn't, there's no way that the head of the Cartel is gonna walk around without a mink coat. She and I set this whole operation up. If it weren't for us, y'all wouldn't have half the shit y'all do."

Shanine looked to Bam for support, but Bam was just happy they didn't try that bullshit with her. She had a coat and couldn't wait to walk home with it.

Instantly, Shanine burst out into tears. "Y'all both

know that shit is fucked up."

"What are you crying for? We can go back and get you and Lil Momma coats." As Cartier spoke the words, she ran her fingers up and down the soft hair of her coat.

"Yeah, right! You know it will be hotter than hell in there," Shanine exclaimed and ran out of the room and headed home. It was an awkward moment. Bam decided to pack up her coat and leave as well, leaving Monya and Cartier alone.

"We shoulda took Bam's coat too and sold it for some dough," Monya said. "We should be the only ones in the crew to have minks. We shoulda never took them with us."

Cartier contemplated Monya's thoughts. "Nah, we could let Bam keep her coat and make money some other way. I don't want them to think this is a dictatorship. As boss lady, I gotta keep the crew happy or else it will draw dissention."

"Well, you ain't keeping Shanine happy."

"She'll get over it. Besides, her and Lil Momma are close. If Lil Momma don't have a coat, neither should Shanine."

Monya tried to understand Cartier's logic and realized it wasn't logical. Cartier said all those words trying to make a point, but the point was she wanted a coat and took Shanine's. That's all, folks.

CHAPTER SIX

❖

1999 - The Compound

It was the first week of January when Lil Momma was released. She'd spent thirty days in Spodford, an inmate facility for juveniles, only she was seventeen. She lied about her date of birth in order to avoid being treated as an adult. Sixteen and up is when they can send you to Riker's Island, depending on the crime. Lil Momma and the Cartel had been lying about their ages since the first day they started boosting. The judge remanded her into custody because of her horrible record for shoplifting. When she looked over her shoulder and saw the Cartel, she glared at Cartier. She was angry with Cartier for not helping her fight the sales associates. She was the one who got busted. And why? Because her illustrious leader got greedy. They both could have had mink coats to keep them warm this cold winter. Lil Momma had a lot of regrets, but when the judge said thirty days, she regretted being a member of the Cartel.

Now that she was home, she was ready to make up for lost time. While in lockdown, she met a few girls who had actually heard and looked up to the Cartel. Lil Momma felt famous that the streets were telling her story. She had second thoughts about her regrets. The Cartel had given her what she never had before—a name and notoriety. She wasn't ready to give up the game. It was a part of her. The itching inside her was desire.

Her issue with Cartier was past news. Yes, she was disappointed Cartier had lied to the crew, but it was a dead issue. In her heart of hearts, she knew Cartier wasn't stuffing a third coat to sell. But she also knew she couldn't prove otherwise. Cartier didn't actually say that the coat was for her to keep. Lil Momma deduced that from the look in Cartier's eyes. Nevertheless, it was the past. It was time to move on.

"So you not going to say something about Cartier taking my coat?" Shanine drilled Lil Momma.

"What I look like getting on her bad side right now when I'm fucked up and starving? My cousins took all my shit while I was locked down. I practically gotta start from scratch. If I start beefing about a damn coat, they could kick me out of the Cartel. At this point, I got the worst record and most of the Ds know my face. I'm hot as chicken grease and I need the Cartel. You know that you, me, and Bam are the weakest links with this boosting shit. You know that Cartier and Monya are far more skilled than all of us put together. They got the most heart. Without them, we're going to be looking bummy or being some old school bitch's vic like Shorty Dip. I don't know about you, but that's not cool with me."

Shanine wasn't trying to hear this bullshit. She'd waited four weeks for Lil Momma to come home and start beefing with Cartier over her coat. Lil Momma was the most outspoken of the crew. She spoke her mind and wasn't afraid of disagreeing with Cartier and Monya. Shanine didn't have the guts Lil Momma possessed. But Shanine realized Lil Momma wasn't going to go to bat over her coat, especially when she didn't have one.

Shanine sucked her teeth. "Whatever."

"Don't get mad with me," Lil Momma began. "You shouldn't have let her take your shit. Be mad with yourself."

Cartier called a meeting in the compound, the name she called her bedroom. It was time to disclose her plan. She had been putting together this plan for over six months, and after the incident in the city and Lil Momma getting locked up, she figured it was now or never. She had marinated this plan over and over in her mind. She admired that about herself—how she was capable of formulating a plan and thinking it through before she brought it to the Cartel.

Cartier waited until all members were present and then she closed her bedroom door for complete privacy.

"After the little situation last month," Cartier began. "And one of our members going down for thirty days, I've come up with a plan that will increase our profits and lessen our risks."

"Wow . . . that's what I'm talking 'bout," Bam screamed.

"Quiet, please!" Cartier snapped. "Let me tell you the

plan before y'all interrupt me. As I was saying, our profits will increase and our risk will lessen. We're going to leave this boosting shit alone altogether and begin hugging the block."

Cartier watched as everyone shifted in their seats. She knew they had questions, but no way were they going to interrupt her again.

"I've already spoken to Jason and he's agreed to supply us with the weight at one hundred dollars above wholesale value. So what that means is if we start with an ounce, he'll only make one hundred dollars on us—"

"Why would he do that?" Lil Momma asked. "What's in it for him?"

"He thinks pussy," Cartier deduced. "Anyway, as I was saying, he's going to give up the product for dirt cheap. Once we get it, we're going to start hugging the block and make this paper. And as I said, we'll be making money hand over fist and we won't be in any danger, because we'll all be lookouts for each other."

Finally, the Cartel got to speak. Monya went first.

"I'm hearing everything you saying, but this shit sounds too risky. What do we know about hugging the block? Niggas get shot over the drug game all the time."

"Ain't nobody getting shot." Cartier couldn't take Monya and her scary ways.

"But she does have a point. We could get shot or stuck up or worse, murdered," Bam added.

"Look, if y'all wanna keep boosting and eventually do serious jail time for a bunch of labels, then go right ahead. But I'ma get out here and get this paper. And while I'm driving in hot whips, y'all be hopping in and out of cabs. While I'm blinged out, y'all be wearing Canal Street jewels. While I'm shopping on Fifth Avenue, y'all be getting chased from Fifth Avenue. A'ight, meeting over."

Cartier terminated the meeting and dismissed the crew, only they didn't leave. They needed Cartier. Their lives revolved around their leader. They sat around, thinking about going against the grain. She was their backbone. Cartier was the one who got them in the game. She was the driver of the ultimate ride they had taken the past few years. Boosting had been their livelihood, an addictive habit, but now it was stale and played out. It was no longer fun and now, because of their success, it was more dangerous. Store-employed detectives and security guards were hot to catch them in the act. And they knew the day they got caught, hard time in Riker's Island or Nassau County was mandatory. A slap on the wrist wasn't even an option. The only deal anyone could possibly cut for them included selling out the other members of the Cartel. Jail time for shoplifting was stupid, yet they could all see that that was where they were headed. They were now cavalier and reckless in their antics. They knew Lil Momma was lucky getting only thirty days, but like everything else, luck ran out.

Again Monya was the first to speak. "Well, if you got our backs, then I'm down with you. You know you're my girl."

Cartier knew she could always depend on Monya to

have her back.

"Yeah, I'm in too," Lil Momma added. "I need all the money I can get."

"Just tell me what to do and I'm in," Bam stated.

"Me too," Shanine said, completing the group.

"OK, good. Well, we're gonna start small. I need everyone to put in two hundred dollars from their stash. Lil Momma, if you're tapped out, then I'll cover you. But I'll need that paper today."

"No, I have it. I can go get my share now," Lil Momma volunteered. She wanted to please Cartier and show her bygones were bygones.

"Good. A'ight, then everybody go and get your paper and meet back here in an hour."

CHAPTER SEVEN

Money Over Niggas

Cartier leaned against the side of the cold concrete building as the frigid air attempted to freeze her toes and fingertips. In the beginning, she entertained herself by blowing smoke rings out of her mouth; now she stood stone as her mind raced. In a few hours, she and the crew would call it a night from hustling. She had contemplated alternating shifts, but for now, having everyone on the street cut down the stress. Cartier reasoned that with all five playing a significant role, it would play out better for the Cartel.

Bam held the product while Lil Momma took the money. Shanine then walked the money to Bam and the process reversed. Bam gave the product to Shanine, who walked it to Lil Momma, who completed the transaction with the customer. Monya was the lookout while Cartier provided the muscle.

Cartier relished her role as the muscle. She knew they were susceptible to all types of violence. Some of the boys in the hood didn't appreciate their entrepreneurial spirit. She felt she was prepared to do damage with the knife she kept tucked in her back pocket and the baseball bat she hid on the side of the building. Since she started boosting, she had been playing with knives. She now considered herself a self-taught expert with any blade.

In the first three weeks of selling hand-to-hand, the Cartel brought home five hundred dollars each after buying their reup. Shanine, Bam, and Lil Momma were ecstatic, but Monya and Cartier weren't so pleased. Monya already had plans for her money. She was saving up to buy diamond earrings, and Cartier had her eyes on a ride.

Cartier wanted to stack paper like her male counterparts did. For her, five hundred large wasn't stacking paper. That was chump change, little boys' money. She wanted to move up the ladder and didn't have the patience to go slow. By the third week, she figured she needed to call a meeting.

Everyone gathered in the compound, her newly furnished bedroom, as she closed and locked the door behind them. With business first on her mind, she didn't have time for Shanine and Bam's arguing over petty shit.

"Why don't you knock it off?" Cartier blasted as she took command of the meeting.

"Then tell her to leave me alone," Shanine suggested.

Cartier disregarded Shanine's childishness. It was getting harder and harder for her to tolerate Shanine and her petty ways. "OK, look, I got to say something that I'm sure y'all aren't going to like, but just hear me out and see my logic."

"But before you say what you gotta say, let me say this," Lil Momma interrupted. "Everything is going great and I don't think we should switch up our game plan, because that could be bad luck."

"Why the fuck you gotta go and jinx us?" Cartier snapped. "You know I hate it when you start bringing up that voodoo shit."

"How's that voodoo?" Lil Momma snapped back. "If I'm saying we're on the right path? We're all making money. We don't got Ds breathing down our necks and we're all on our way to sitting on top of big money."

"That's exactly what I want to get at. Our paper. Yes, we're at a really good start, but in order for us to come off and really get paid we'll need to do two things. One, we need to stop selling weed and move up to dope—"

"Cartier! That's way too dangerous!" Lil Momma replied.

"Will you keep it down before you wake up my moms and then I gotta hear her mouth all night about how hungry she is?"

"My bad, but you can't be serious."

"As a heart attack," Cartier continued. "Like I said, we need to flip the switch and start selling dope. And not only that, our profit for this week needs to be reinvested to buy our package."

"What? Now you done said the wrong thing fucking with my money," Monya stood up from the bed and placed her hands on her hips. "I was riding with you for a moment, but now you're talking crazy."

"Sit your bony ass down!" Cartier barked. She wasn't in the mood for Monya's act of defiance. Best friend or not, she regarded Monya as bitchy and hoped she didn't have to bring her down a peg or two. "This week we're going to reinvest every dime of our profit into our reup. And though I'm not crazy about this, we're going to start working in shifts. And here's my reasoning. Fiends walk the streets all day and night, twenty-four seven, 365. Not just during a particular hour. Now, if we have more product and divide our shifts by four, then we got the whole neighborhood locked down. We will work in six-hour shifts, with two of us covering the graveyard shift. I will take the graveyard shift, while all of y'all can alternate. The graveyard shift is from midnight to six in the morning. The other shifts will be put inside this hat and y'all stick your hand inside and choose. Please don't make this a difficult process. It's not brain surgery."

The whole crew was getting tired of Cartier's sarcastic remarks and bossy attitude. But they weren't tired of the money, so no one tried to check Cartier.

Each girl took turns pulling for a shift. Shanine drew the first shift, from six in the morning until noon. Lil Momma pulled the second shift, from noon until six, and Bam drew six until midnight. Monya was tasked to team with Cartier from midnight until six.

The first week was tough. Each member wasn't used to the strict hours, and it was especially rough on Cartier. But she thugged it out; the success or failure of the Cartel rested solely on her shoulders.

By week two, the Cartel was subject to idle threats by the neighborhood boys they knew and had once called friends. They felt that the Cartel was taking their clientele. Initially, they all were accosted by slick remarks from their childhood acquaintances. But when the boys' boss, Donnie, stepped to the Cartel, things got more intense.

One morning, shortly after three, Donnie rolled up on Cartier and Shanine. Donnie stepped out of his luxury SUV with an ice grill plastered to his face which transformed into a smile, a smile of deception. The past week, his money had dropped drastically. The Cartel was selling dope on his corners and they were doing what no one else could do—affect his profit margin. He heard they were running a twenty-four hour operation, thus monopolizing the drug game. He had to admit it was a smart move. However, it would have been smarter to do it elsewhere; anywhere except his corners. Out of respect and deference to their gender, he'd decided to give them one warning and only one. Had they been men, he would have gotten out of his ride, bucking shots.

"What do we have here?" Donnie said, standing two feet from Cartier. Her sidekick, Shanine, was servicing a customer.

"Whaddup, D?" Cartier returned the half-hearted greeting.

Donnie cleared his throat by sending a wad of spit only inches from Cartier's new Air Force Ones. "You tell me."

Cartier's pressure rose. She didn't appreciate being spit at in the middle of the night by some lame-ass dude. She was tired. Her feet hurt. Instead of buying her proper size seven, she bought her sneakers a half size too small to make her feet look smaller. Now all she wanted to do was get in her new comfortable bed.

"I don't know what you want to hear," she stated.

"Why y'all on my corners, that's what."

"Oh, Harpo, dis here yo corners?" Cartier said mockingly in her best impersonation from *The Color Purple*.

"You think that shit is cute, bitch?" Donnie retorted excitedly as he stepped closer to Cartier. "I'm not playing with your silly ass—"

"Who you calling silly?" Cartier cut him off.

"You, bitch!" Donnie shot back.

Cartier turned to walk away from him and he reached out and grabbed her. She wiggled out of his grip. "Get the fuck off of me!"

"Cartier, I know you think you all tough, but you ain't no nigga. I will fucking break you in two if you keep slinging rock on my blocks."

Cartier walked away, tossing her middle finger over her shoulder, and kept it moving. There wasn't any way she was going to allow Donnie or anyone else to prevent her from establishing her drug empire. *Fuck Donnie. He's a loser,* she thought.

"If I have to come out here again and see any one of your crew on my corner pushing work, I'ma push your wig back. Take me for a joke if you want to." Donnie jumped back in his ride and pulled off, screeching his tires as he sped away.

Cartier was hardly moved by his antics. He was acting as if he was the major of Brownsville, saying shit like, *his block, his product, his customers,* when that motherfucker didn't even own his car. Cartier heard he was leasing his shit from the dealership. *What kind of kingpin drives a damn leased vehicle?*

Donnie hardly made her hands tremble. If he got out of line again and confronted her, then the Cartel was going to jump his ass and give him a severe beat-down. If she had to, she was prepared to get Ms. Janet involved since Trina was eight months pregnant. Ms. Janet had already proved that she still had what it took to get busy as if she was still twenty years old.

"What was that all about?" Shanine asked after the commotion had died down.

"That punk motherfucker out here trying to push his weight around."

"What he say?"

"That we gotta stop hugging the block or else."

"Or else what?"

"He didn't say."

"Please, he better go on with that bullshit. He been watching too many mob movies. This ain't the mafia, where he owning blocks and extorting motherfuckers. This the fucking hood and any and everything goes. I hope you told him to kiss your ass!"

Cartier loved that four out of five members of her crew had heart. Had she been out there with Monya, the conversation would have gone differently. Yes, Monya loved money, but she was scared of her own shadow and always predicted gloom and doom. She decided not to tell Monya about what had happened tonight.

"Hell, yeah, I told him to bounce," Cartier stated. "Let's just keep this conversation between us. I don't want the rest of the crew to get antsy and not be able to concentrate."

"Do you think that's wise? I mean, shouldn't they be on point?"

Cartier could hear the concern in Shanine's voice. But she was the leader and she had to make the tough decisions. "They'll be more alert if they're not worrying. Besides, I always work the graveyard shift and if he wants to start beefing, he's going to come for me, and I can handle me and mines."

Shanine didn't think it was a good idea not informing the Cartel about Donnie's threat, and although she didn't want to go against Cartier, she knew that keeping the Cartel in the dark about a possible threat wasn't just a bad decision; it was just plain stupid. She couldn't wait for morning to give the crew the 411.

They both finished their shift and headed home to get some rest without another mention of Donnie.

CHAPTER EIGHT

Caught Up

Cartier and Monya both had hot dates tonight. They were at Cartier's, getting dressed so they could examine what the other was wearing. It was the mandatory pre-date inspection; the critique among friends.

Monya didn't like the body hugging cat-suit Cartier wore. Although she agreed it was sexy, she thought it was too much for her age. The revealing outfit showed every mountain, hill, and plateau on Cartier's shapely body.

"I don't like that outfit," Monya said. "It looks a little dated."

"Are you crazy?" Cartier asked as she looked at her firm, round butt protruding in the flimsy material. You couldn't tell her that she wasn't hot shit. Cartier thought either Monya was bugging or blind. "That nigga gonna be all over me."

"But who wears a cat-suit to the movies and dinner?"

Cartier could hear the envy in Monya's voice. "Since when do we follow tradition? I will wear a cat-suit to the movies and dinner, and I'm sure Ryan won't complain."

Cartier had met Ryan while attending a Bad Boy concert at Madison Square Garden. He was from Harlem and sported a perm blowout afro. He was half black and half Puerto Rican, drove a BMW 525, and had a street name for himself.

Monya didn't like their relationship, but she kept that to herself. She had spotted Ryan first and told Cartier to walk to the area where he was standing with his boys. Monya knew exactly who Ryan was. But once Ryan got a look at Cartier's fat ass, Monya wasn't even a consideration. Monya was burnt as she watched them exchange numbers. She could hardly believe Cartier had stolen her man. Monya was seething. She saw how Cartier took off her jacket to show her big ass and pranced all up in his face. As far as looks, Monya knew hands down she was prettier than Cartier. She even had a cute shape to be so thin; a shape that sported her small waist, nice size hips, and flat stomach. The only thing missing was an ass like Cartier's. It wasn't flat, it was just small and Monya hated that. As fine and nicely proportionate as she was, she felt the big-ass girls ruled the land.

Monya was relentless. She walked to Cartier's closet and ruffled through a few dresses. "I think this would be more better, don't you?"

Cartier stopped dead in her tracks. "Bitch, what you trying to pull?"

Monya turned to face Cartier and swallowed hard. She ran her hands through her hair and began to wring her hands. She realized she might have overplayed her hand.

Deep down, she didn't want Cartier to use what Monya thought was her strength, which was her body. She hadn't ever lost a guy to anyone, and although Ryan wasn't her man, she'd been plotting on him for months. She'd even had dreams about being his girl, sitting shotgun up in his ride and going on shopping sprees. Monya had studied him and learned his brief history. But she focused on the material, her true interest and love in life. She knew Ryan had made his name slinging drugs and making paper. She was intrigued that he bought his last two girlfriends brand new cars. He bought the first a new Honda Accord. When they broke up, he took it back, traded it in, and bought the next girl a brand new Infiniti jeep. When that relationship didn't work out, girlfriend number two wasn't as gullible. She didn't give back shit. She kept the ride and was still riding that jeep up and down the streets of Harlem.

"I was only trying to help," Monya explained weakly. "You know you're my girl, and since that nigga is into buying cars, I want you to look your best. You know the Cartel needs a whip."

Cartier wasn't born yesterday. She rolled her eyes at Monya's bullshit excuse. She knew jealousy when she saw it. Cartier wanted to play it cool, but she was prepared to slap Monya senseless if she didn't get over herself. Cartier knew how to get Monya's pressure up and she knew the more she piled on, the more pissed off Monya would get. When she put on her Christian Louboutin stiletto pumps and mink coat and paraded around the room, she could see envy and jealousy on Monya's face.

"Oh my gosh, damn, I look fly," Cartier bragged. She didn't need Monya to kiss her ass. She had enough confidence for the both of them. "I can't wait to see his face when I pull off my coat."

"It ain't even that serious," Monya sourly replied. She'd just put on her dress. "How I look?"

Cartier stopped prancing around long enough to look at her friend. Her eyes scanned Monya up and down and she didn't get it. She knew guys loved Monya's cute face, but Cartier thought Monya was a lost cause. At one point, her body matured faster than the rest of the Cartel's bodies. But as fast as it grew, it seemed to stop just as fast. Regardless of how many guys pushed up on her, Cartier thought Monya's body was that of a ten-year-old.

"You look stupid," Cartier said matter-of-factly. "Why are you always wearing those baby doll dresses?"

"How I look stupid and you don't?" Monya countered.

"I'm just saying that you're going on a date, not to the mall with friends. You're supposed to look sexy. Why don't you throw on a pair of tight jeans and halter shirt and your mink coat?"

"Because he already saw me in jeans. I gotta switch it up and give him a little variety. That's why I put my hair in curls and not let it fall straight."

Cartier knew she had gotten under Monya's skin, just as Monya had tried to get underneath hers. And she loved it. Payback could be a bitch just as payback could be rewarding. Monya was insecure and that insecurity was woven in every fiber of her body. It was easy for Cartier to pull back the layers and find her buttons. She knew Monya needed validation, validation she would never receive from Cartier.

"Look, just as you were trying to help me, you need to help yourself and take a good look in the mirror. That's all I'm saying."

Monya wanted to curse her out, but she didn't. She did look hard in the mirror and at the last minute settled on a pair of jeans and tight sweater. Internally, Cartier was laughing. Monya looked twenty times better before, but it was the price she would pay for trying to sabotage Cartier first. It was about having a strong will, and Cartier knew she possessed the will and confidence to bring down mountains. Her best friend didn't.

"I hope I have fun with this kid tonight. He seems a little boring on the phone," Monya began. "But if I have a boring time, hopefully Karon will make up for it tomorrow night."

"You going out with Karon tomorrow?"

"Hell yeah, why not?"

"What about Wise?"

"What about him? If a dude wants me to be exclusive, then he better make me exclusive," Monya explained. "There're too many men out here to put all my eggs in one basket, especially considering how men play. They have a stable of bitches and they want you to be faithful." Monya sucked her teeth as she admired her pretty face in the mirror. "Besides, Karon is all sweating me. Did I tell you last night he was crying for me?"

Here we go again, Cartier thought. *Monya on this fairest-of-them-all shit again. She's always telling tales about how some dude is crying over her bony ass, begging her to be his chick, or dissing some chick for her. Please, bitch, can the Cartel see this shit just once?*

Cartier didn't feed into Monya's ego. She excused herself and went in the room with her mother. She knew if she stayed, her thoughts would become verbal, and she didn't want to crush Monya's spirit or her own spirit before their dates.

Wise came to pick up Monya ten minutes prior to Ryan picking up Cartier. Cartier watched as Monya and Wise drove off. One part of her wanted Monya to lock it down with Wise, while the other part wanted Wise to shit on her and crush her huge ego. Although Cartier loved Monya like a sister, there was still a competitive streak for both of them and it seemed their interest in men was bringing that to the forefront.

Monya relaxed as the car glided over the pavement. She felt more like she was riding on a magic carpet than in a vehicle.

"Where we going?" she asked as they headed down Atlantic Avenue toward the FDR.

"I was thinking that we go to eat at Benihana's. Would you like that?"

Monya looked into his dreamy eyes and got lost. She really wanted to be his girl.

"Yeah, that's cool."

"You ever been there?"

"Of course," she lied. She really didn't know why she lied, but Wise was her first adult boyfriend. She didn't want him thinking she wasn't used to shit. Truth be told, all her other boyfriends didn't have money to take her to a nice restaurant, didn't have a vehicle, or didn't have any style. She'd gone out to dinner before, but Red Lobster was the closest she'd gotten to upscale.

"I love their food," she lied again.

"I mean, it's a'ight," Wise commented. "I would have taken you to Mr. Chow's, but I couldn't get a reservation." Now it was his turn to lie. In the matter of women, Wise was a practical guy. He wasn't about to drop $300 for a good time that didn't include him getting pussy later. *She's lucky I brought her ass to Benihana's.* He knew her full resume and knew she had an ulterior motive, just like he did.

"Well, we can go there next time?" Monya asked joyfully.

"No doubt," he paused. *Shit better be tight and tasty to get that kinda money out of me.* He knew it was best to change the subject. "You looking really sexy tonight. What's the name of those shoes you got on?"

"Thank you." She smiled. "These are Jimmy Choos."

"Word? How much those joints cost?"

Monya got excited. Was he going to take her shopping? Perhaps she didn't miss out on anything with Cartier bagging Ryan. She possibly had the moneymaker sitting next to her.

"I paid four hundred for these."

"You bought those?" Wise asked with surprise in his voice.

"What do you mean did I buy these?" Monya questioned with shock on her face. "They ain't free."

"You paid cash out of your wallet for those shoes?" Wise still had doubt in his voice.

Monya didn't know what he was trying to say. She wondered if he thought that some other dude bought her shoes and he was getting jealous. She didn't know how to handle the situation and wished Cartier was there to help her. She decided to calm the situation and show him her independence.

"Of course I bought them myself. Ain't no nigga give me the money for these."

Wise hated the way she spoke. She had such a pretty face, but her speech told a different story. The women he usually dated were well-spoken and educated. Monya was the typical Brooklyn broad—ghetto as hell.

"Get the fuck outta here," Wise said laughingly. "You trying to rock a nigga to sleep with that bullshit."

Now Monya was truly confused. If Wise had a point, she wished that he would get to it.

"So how did I get them?" she asked.

"Don't you be boosting?" he retorted.

That mere word, *boosting*, sent waves of embarrassment down her spine. Then she remembered she and the Cartel had a reputation that preceded them. She wasn't down for games and saw no point in lying.

"I mean, hell yeah, we be getting that paper, but your question was about my shoes and I bought these."

"So it ain't that easy boosting shoes?"

"It depends on the store and the salesperson. Sometimes, they get caught slipping. Other times, they're not having it."

"So when you gonna get me some shit?"

Monya sunk even lower in her seat. She couldn't believe that this nigga just tried to play her. Disappointment immediately set in, but she wanted to rise above the feeling.

"Well, if you were my man and if I was still boosting, then maybe I would."

"Oh, now all of a sudden you stopped boosting?" Wise's voice was laced with sarcasm and Monya wasn't feeling him at all. She resented that he put her on the spot and didn't like the interrogation.

"It's none of your business when I stopped or if I stopped," Monya snapped back. She was too cute to be under such pressure. *This nigga can bounce for all I care. There'll be another one rolling through soon.* "I don't know what the fuck you thought, but you got me mixed up."

"Do I?"

Monya hated the sarcasm in his every comment. "Truly you do," she said with equal sarcasm.

For the rest of the ride, they sat in uncomfortable silence. When they pulled up to park on the side block, Monya decided to make small talk.

"I'm so hungry right now. What about you?"

"That's the reason we're going to eat, right? Because we're hungry?" the sarcasm continued to drip in his every comment. Not waiting for a reply he stated, "Watch my car door when you open it."

Monya could sense his mood had shifted and she didn't want it to be a dull night. Not one to stay in a funk, she hoped she could put a smile on his face before the night ended.

Cartier and Ryan hit it off from the start. When he pulled up to her apartment building, he actually got out of the car and opened her car door. Cartier was impressed. She'd never experienced such chivalry. Most of the boys she grew up with couldn't spell or ever heard the word chivalry. That one act had already placed Ryan above the guys she had dated before.

"When I saw you I was mesmerized," Ryan stated on the ride to the restaurant. "I was like, 'I gotta get to know shorty.'"

"I didn't even know you were checking for me. I thought you were checking for my homegirl."

"Which one? The skinny, Indian-looking chick?"

"Yeah, her. But she's not Indian, she's black."

"Yeah, yeah, I know who you talking about. But nah, I didn't even see shorty. All I saw was you. You were wearing the hell out of those jeans."

Cartier giggled and was totally consumed by Ryan's compliments. She couldn't remember the last time she'd blushed. "When you stepped to me I was thinking how sexy you were. I knew you weren't from Brooklyn."

"What gave me away?"

"Your blowout," Cartier said with a smile.

Ryan looked at himself in his rearview mirror and then profiled to see each angle. He knew he was eye candy and few women, if any, could resist his charms. "Yeah, most girls think this is a good look."

"Most girls? How many do you got?" Cartier asked, with a half-hearted smile.

"I don't got none at the moment, but I see one that I definitely want."

"Oh really?" Cartier said coyly.

"Umm hummm. And she's sexy as hell. And she has the perfect lips . . . can you kiss?"

Cartier waited until they stopped at a red light, then leaned over and kissed his soft lips. His tongue game was perfect. He was a man who knew how to kiss. The kiss wasn't too wet, and he teased her with just enough tongue. He wasn't one of those brothas who forced his tongue down your throat. Cartier felt all tingly inside as she pulled back and relaxed into her seat.

Ryan's dick immediately got hard as he put his hand over it and adjusted his boxers. "Damn, ma, you see that shit?"

How can I miss it? Was what she wanted to say. His dick was bulging through his loose-fitting jeans and she was impressed. Instead of speaking, she just giggled.

"You got a nigga all hard just from your kiss. I see you dangerous and I gotta watch out for you."

She wanted to say something about that too, but once again, she just played it off.

Cartier liked the chemistry between her and Ryan. Both had expressed in the car how nice it would be to get fucked up on wine or hard liquor at the restaurant.

"Cartier," a voice called. Cartier searched the crowded tables and her face lit up when she saw Monya. She was waving her hands wildly in the air and gesturing for them to come over.

Cartier looked to Ryan. "That's my best friend, Monya. Can we sit with them?"

"It's all good," Ryan said as he addressed the waiter. "Can we sit at that table?" pointing to the table next to Wise and Monya.

Wise and Ryan gave each other a head nod, while simultaneously closely examining each other's bling. They were both iced out with platinum watches and rings, and dressed neatly.

"I can't believe we both ended up at the same restaurant," Cartier exclaimed. She took off her mink jacket and both men's eyes quickly darted toward her big ass.

This moment didn't go unnoticed by Monya. A shot of jealousy surged through her body. She was tired of Cartier showing off her body. *Why don't the bitch just sign up for a strip club and jump on a pole?*

Cartier enjoyed the moment. She stood for several seconds, letting Ryan, Wise, and others in the restaurant get an eyeful before finally retiring to her seat. She knew how to play the game.

"I know . . . what a shock to see you," Cartier began. "Hi Wise." Wise gave her a head nod in return. Cartier could clearly see he was in a sour mood. "Wise, this is Ryan. Ryan, Wise."

Both men exchanged nods again.

Ryan leaned over and whispered in Cartier's ear, "Damn, you're trying to give a nigga a heart attack tonight in that outfit." He then put his hand on Cartier's thigh and squeezed.

Monya watched with envy as the two lovebirds cuddled throughout dinner. It was noticeable to Wise. They didn't talk to each other throughout dinner. When it was time to pay the check, Wise got his revenge. He dropped fifty dollars for his half of the check and left Monya hanging.

"Oh, it's like that?" Monya asked in disbelief.

Wise pulled up, adjusted his sagging jeans, and replied, "You already know what it is," and walked off. Monya eyes popped open like saucers, with a look of surprise plastered on her face.

"What the fuck is going on?" Cartier asked.

"That motherfucker is bugging," Monya replied, getting hyped.

Ryan quelled the situation by paying for the check in full. He had his own bad ways, but he wasn't petty over nickel and dime shit. It was boyish and childish to disrespect a female, especially in public. He wasn't a chump like that. Regardless of the situation, he would have manned up and paid the check. There were other ways to get payback, if payback was truly needed. If not, he would have just left the bitch alone. Wise was a petty brotha and petty brothas didn't get or deserve respect.

On the ride home the two women wouldn't stop clowning Wise.

"I can't wait to get on the horn and tell everybody what the fuck he did." Monya glared.

"He's a crab-ass nigga!" Cartier added.

"He gonna get his. Don't let me see him when I'm with One-Eighty or those other niggas from the Stuy. They will seriously beat his Queens ass down!"

"I know that's right. In fact, we don't need to get no one to beat his ass, we can do that shit ourselves," Cartier retorted and Monya knew she was dead serious.

When Ryan pulled up in front of Monya's building, he wasn't ready for Cartier to leave. He squeezed her hand and gave her a look. Cartier knew exactly what that look meant.

"Monya, I'll see you tomorrow," Cartier said.

"What? You not coming with me?" Monya asked weakly.

"I said I'll see you tomorrow. That means don't wait up, bitch."

Monya smiled and got out of the car, but inside she was steaming. She knew Cartier was about to get some dick, the dick that was supposed to be hers. The dick she had dreamed about and wanted for months on end.

Slutty bitch, was her lasting thought.

CHAPTER NINE

American Gangsta

Over the next couple of days, Cartier and Ryan were inseparable. When she wasn't overseeing drug deals, or hanging out with the Cartel, she and Ryan were developing a serious relationship.

Their relationship didn't sit well with Monya and Jason. As a distraction, Monya had fucked through the borough. Some joked she was the neighborhood ho now.

Jason, on the other hand, was stunned. Cartier was the love of his life and it hurt him to see Cartier with Ryan.

"Yo, I should just knock that nigga off," Jason said.

"You can't kill him," Monya replied, thinking that this wasn't a part of the plan.

"And why not? I can post up out here and wait on that silly motherfucker to pull up for Cartier and push his wig back." Jason was so angry his nose flared as he spoke about murdering a man he didn't even know.

"Because that's stupid, that's why. She ain't worth taking a life over."

"She's worth that to me," Jason replied stubbornly.

Jason was in love with the only girl he ever had eyes for—Cartier. Since grade school, she had been his future. She was the girl, and now the woman he always wanted. Watching Cartier with another man hurt. He couldn't take seeing Ryan and his luxurious ride while he still drove a used Pathfinder, or watching him spoil Cartier with gifts and money while she wouldn't give Jason the time of day. Jason didn't think of himself as a jealous guy, but he had never dealt with someone having something or someone he wanted. He was jealous of this mysterious uptown dude who had stolen the love of his life, the woman who had his heart.

He and Monya sat in his jeep, sipping on a small bottle of Hennessy, commiserating. It was a pity party for two. Monya didn't like seeing Cartier happy, but she couldn't explain why. She wanted Jason to step up his game and pull Cartier. She didn't want Cartier and Ryan falling more in love, and Ryan buying a car for Cartier. As bad as the Cartel needed a whip, she didn't want it to be Cartier who provided it by way of Ryan.

"Why don't you ever tell her how you feel?" Monya asked.

"What the fuck you think I've been doing? Cartier knows exactly how I feel."

"Well, obviously, what you've been doing ain't enough. There's no way this outsider should have been able to swoop down and bag her." Monya knew what she was doing. She knew what buttons to push. And she needed Jason to be pushed.

Jason's anger was increasing. He felt like a chump, a loser who couldn't even pull the girl he dreamed about. But what he couldn't understand was why Monya cared so much.

"Monya, you and I ain't never been cool. Why the fuck you care if I get with Cartier? What's in it for you?"

Monya didn't expect the question, but she had confidence on her side. She thought she was smarter than Jason and could easily manipulate him. "This really ain't even about you—"

"That's exactly what I mean. If this ain't about me, then what's it about?" Jason snapped back.

"It's about my best friend," Monya tried explaining. "This guy is no good for her and I hate to see her making a big mistake."

"Then why don't you tell her?"

"I did," Monya lied. "She just won't listen to me."

"Then let's go back to plan A and let me push back this nigga's wig!"

Monya thought about it for a second before coming to her senses. She couldn't believe she'd actually entertained the thought of having an innocent man murdered. Quickly, she snapped back to reality. There wasn't any way she could have blood on her hands. That was just bad karma. Plus, she still had feelings for Ryan, and the last thing she wanted was for him to die. And worse, she didn't want to be a part of such a death.

Monya was aggravated. She looked at the pitiful look in Jason's eyes and listened to the yearning in his voice, and for the life of her, she couldn't understand why he liked Cartier so much. What in the hell did these men see that she didn't see? On a scale of one to ten, Cartier was a struggling four. And three out of those four points were for her body. *Why can't anyone else see this?*

"Calm the fuck down," Monya snapped. "You ready to do a bid over Cartier? I don't know what the fuck is so special that motherfuckers are losing their minds over her."

"Let's keep this gangsta. Ain't nobody losing their mind," Jason said. "I'm just saying that I have more to offer than that lame, permed-hair faggot."

"Whatever."

Monya was disgusted and felt that they weren't getting anywhere. She decided to carry her ass back upstairs. Tomorrow was another day.

CHAPTER TEN

What's Beef?

The anger brewing inside the young black male was palpable. He told those hard-headed little bitches not to sell shit on his corner, and they defied him. He couldn't fucking believe it. He sat inside the front seat of his black Yukon watching as Bam did a hand-to-hand transaction to Shirelle, one of the local fiends.

Each time she served a customer, Donnie rationalized that they were taking food out of his daughter's mouth and money out of his pocket. As the car sat idling, a million thoughts flowed through his mind. But one thought remained constant: to bust a cap in the young bitch's ass.

Donnie took another long, steady pull from his blunt, ignoring the repeated calls his phone kept registering. He was in his world, contemplating doing the deed of a dealer and protecting his turf. As the purple haze permeated the confined space in the car, he began coughing, trying desperately to control his breathing. He was beyond fucked up. He reached inside his glove compartment and pulled out a small bottle of Hennessy to lubricate his dry, pasty mouth. The strong cognac burned his throat as he took a large swig of the dark liquid. His body felt warm as the alcohol traveled through his body. He loved this feeling.

Normally this would have been a job for one of his boys, one of the peons who worked for him. But tonight was about a statement, a statement he wanted the hood to hear loud and clear—that these young bitches and anyone like them would never punk him in front of his peoples. This was man business, and he was the man delivering the message tonight.

When the incessant ringing of his telephone blared again, he decided to pick up. It was his baby's momma, Pebbles. There was no reason for him to ignore her call when he wasn't out fucking some other chick.

"Yo!"

"Where you at?" she asked.

"Don't you know how to address a nigga?" he responded with attitude. "Damn. You can't say hello? How was your day? The first fucking thing out your mouth is where you at."

"Hello, motherfucker! Now, where the fuck you at?" she returned the attitude.

Donnie chuckled. He had the streets of New York on lock, people feared him, and no matter what he said or did, he couldn't get his baby momma to walk with trepidation. She was the realest chick he ever fucked with and she was nice with her hands. If she wasn't pregnant with their second child, she would be the one throwing down on the Cartel tonight. One-on-one, he was sure she would have whipped their asses—all by herself.

"I'm over here on Rockaway, scheming on this bitch, Bam. You know that bitch, right?"

"Yeah, that little nappy-headed bitch who thinks she cute. She hangs with those other chicks who call themselves the Cartier Cartel, right?"

"Yeah, that's her."

"Now that we got that out of the way, why you scheming on her? What that mean?"

"It means I'm about to give her a severe beat-down."

"For real? What she do to you?"

Donnie took another drag from his blunt and finally replied. "Those silly bitches out here taking away my customers."

"They selling product? I thought they hustled the stores?"

"They do all that good shit. But today is gonna be a bad day. I promise you that!"

"Whatcha gonna do?"

"Didn't I just say that I was gonna beat that bitch down!" Donnie barked, suddenly irritated.

Ignoring his outburst, Pebbles replied, "You want me to come and whip her ass 'cause you know I will snatch that bitch bald. I will rip her fucking weave out of her head—"

"Yo, calm down! You carrying my seed and you getting all hyped for no reason. I got this."

After Donnie ended his call, it was time to handle business. With his gun tucked snugly in the back of his jeans, he crept up on Bam, who was oblivious to her surroundings. He wondered how she managed to not get knocked by Ds. She was totally unaware of her surroundings, and that was the first thing you learn when slinging drugs. If you didn't learn, you died.

He was finally close enough that she couldn't ignore his presence. At first, she was hardly fazed by Donnie. That was until she took a deep look into his menacing eyes. She could smell his breath from a distance. Fear gripped Bam, but she was determined to put on a game face. There was no way she was letting down the Cartel. She was concerned about what Cartier would do if she backed down from Donnie, especially after Cartier had blatantly disrespected him. Bam decided not to go against the grain. She was Cartel, and Cartel didn't back down from shit.

"Why you standing there looking all stupid—"

Before she could complete her sentence, Donnie smashed her in the mouth with a solid left hook. Before she could fully process what happened, her left jaw was assaulted with a right punch. As Bam stumbled backward, Donnie grabbed her weave and held on tightly to keep her from falling. He wanted her face to sustain as many blows as possible and give her a beat-down she and her girls would remember. He put her in a headlock and began to pound the top of her head and face repeatedly while squeezing her neck tightly.

Bam tried to scream and wiggle out of his embrace, but Donnie was too strong. In desperation, she tried to flail her arms and kick him, but to no avail. Soon her eyes were swollen shut, and her whole body felt numb. She was unaware of her surroundings. Donnie ripped her weave from her head, and it lay on the ground.

When he was tired of using Bam as a punching bag, he reached around his back and pulled out his burner.

Bam lay on the concrete sidewalk, knowing her life was over. She knew she wasn't ready to die. What had she lived for? What had she done with her life? She reasoned that everything she'd done up until that night wasn't worth her life. She was dying over a corner. How fair was that? The money, cars, clothes, and respect were all meaningless now. She thought about all the warnings her foster mother had given her and wished she could go back in time and heed her words.

Donnie lifted Bam by what little hair she had left.

"Please . . . no!" Bam managed to scream before being silenced with the butt of Donnie's gun.

With each hit, Bam's blood splattered everywhere. Once again, her battered body collapsed on the sidewalk, and her voice whimpered for Donnie to stop. Donnie wrapped his hand around her neck and picked her back up. The last blow to the middle of her face knocked out her once pearly white teeth and broke her nose, rendering Bam unconscious.

Donnie looked down at his handiwork. The young girl lay in a pool of her own blood. Donnie stared at his blood-covered hands. *If only they listened to me,* he thought.

Donnie turned to walk away and saw that he had an audience from the neighborhood standing around, gawking at the drug kingpin and his victim. They didn't see a drug hustler when they looked at Bam, only a young female beaten nearly to death by a drug dealer.

"What the fuck y'all looking at?" Donnie screamed, challenging anyone to say something. "Anybody got a problem?"

"That shit ain't right," one young lady mumbled under her breath.

"What? What the fuck you say? Huh? I can't hear you!" Donnie pressed her, still hyped from the beating.

The young lady walked away and once she was out of sight of the drug dealer, she called 911. She didn't know if the young girl was dead, but she knew she needed immediate attention. When the operator asked for her name, she hung up, satisfied that she had hopefully saved a life.

CHAPTER ELEVEN

It Was All a Dream

It was almost midnight when Cartier was violently shaken awake by her mother.

"Get dressed!" Trina cried out. "They done killed Bam, Cartier. They done killed Bam."

"What? Who?" Cartier's heart began to thump. Her fingers trembled as she grabbed a pair of jeans and sweatshirt.

"I don't know all that, just get dressed!" Trina snapped.

"Where are we going?" Cartier asked.

"Brookdale Hospital," Trina answered. "I already called a cab. We're gonna swing down the block and grab Monya and Janet."

There was a million questions going through Cartier's head, but she knew better than to irritate her mother. The loud honking of the gypsy cab made Cartier more fearful. Visions of someone trying to rob Bam kept infiltrating her mind. Cartier knew something must have gone wrong while Bam was hugging the block. Guilt loomed over her head for coming up with the bright idea of each member handling a shift alone. It now seemed irresponsible and juvenile. If she had listened to Monya when she said it was a bad idea, maybe Bam would be alive.

Janet, Monya, Lil Momma, and Shanine were downstairs and squeezed into the back seat of the cab, while Cartier and Trina tried to squeeze in the front seat.

"Listen, y'all gotta pay extra for the additional passengers," the cabdriver announced.

Everyone went berserk and began screaming at once. Stupid motherfuckers, faggots, bitches, and crabs flew throughout the cab, words the average New York cabbie heard once each week, if not once each day.

"Get the fuck out!" he roared to the ladies.

"We ain't going a motherfucking place," Trina roared back. "We got a murdered niece and you better take us to our damn destination!"

"Y'all better get out or I'm taking y'all to the precinct!" the cabdriver replied, matching Trina's intensity.

"I wish you would do some stupid shit like that," Janet threatened.

The cabdriver huffed, and put the car in motion. The car erupted once again with a barrage of insults. Tuning out the ghetto-fabulous women, the cabdriver almost wished one of them was his lady. He would have given her a swift backhand in her smartass mouth.

"I should come up in that front seat and punch you dead in your face!" Janet screamed.

The cabdriver deduced this loudmouth was the alpha bitch in the crew. But the comment was the last one he was going to tolerate. He went ballistic. He didn't tolerate being spoken down to by anyone, and definitely not by a female.

"Bitch, I wish you would try it!" he challenged and hit the brakes, stopping the car abruptly.

Again, the car erupted with insults. Trina fingered her blade that was tucked snugly in her back pocket, but decided against it. There was too much at stake. She motioned for Cartier to get out of the cab and everyone followed. As he pulled off, Cartier picked up a bottle and launched it at the cab, just missing the back window.

"I'm so fucking heated right now," Cartier stated to no one in particular as they forged on. "Ma, what happened to Bam? Is she really dead?"

"Cartier, I done told you I don't know any answers," Trina responded. "Black Gena from the building said the ambulance took her away and they said she was dead on the scene. That's why we're going to Brookdale to see what's up."

They called another cab to take them to the hospital. This time each person sat quietly, wallowing in their own thoughts about Bam.

Trina's mind was on Cartier. It could have been Cartier she was getting a call about. Cartier was her daughter, the one she tried to make hard as nails, the one she refused to raise properly, the daughter she let the streets raise for her.

When they finally reached the hospital, Trina once again took charge.

"Hi, my name is Trina Timmons and I'm here about my niece, Bam . . . I mean, Bernice Jones. Her name is

Bernice Jones. Was she admitted?"

The young, exhausted receptionist hardly looked up to acknowledge Trina as she punched Bam's name into the computer. You could hear the tapping of each key as her extremely long fingernails hit the keyboard.

"She's in the OR," the receptionist stated.

"She's alive?" Trina asked, relieved.

"Obviously," replied the unenthused receptionist.

Trina couldn't resist a rebuttal. "What the fuck you say?"

"Excuse me?" the receptionist asked with attitude.

"Bitch, you heard me!" Trina screamed. "That's my niece you're talking about?"

"And I told you what you wanted to know!"

Trina's eyes grew small from anger. Her patience was consistently being tested tonight. "Where's your supervisor? I want to speak to your supervisor!" she demanded.

"I am the supervisor," she replied, trying to minimize the situation. This would be her third complaint within the week.

"Well, I want to speak to whoever's over you." Trina wasn't going to take the receptionist's word.

"Ma, come on," Cartier begged. Trina was seven months pregnant and Cartier didn't want her to upset the baby. "Let it go. She ain't even worth it."

Trina glared at her new enemy. "Bitch I'ma see you when this is all over!" Cartier pulled Trina's arm toward Bam's foster mother, Marianne. "Slap that smile off your face, stupid bitch," was Trina's last jab to the receptionist.

It didn't take long for them to realize Marianne didn't have any answers. She knew Bam was admitted and rushed into the operating room with severe head trauma, but that was it.

Marianne felt as if she had aged ten years as she paced up and down the waiting room. Bam was one of four foster children and the biggest headache of the four.

Six years ago, Marianne had the brilliant idea to become a foster parent in order to save up enough money to buy a house. It was her get-out-of-the-hood fast plan. The state paid $552 per child each month, and coupled with her own modest income, Marianne rationalized she'd be out the hood in no time. She thought she had devised a brilliant plan to save twenty-five hundred a month for two years. Since she had all girls, they could sleep in one bedroom with two bunk beds. Additionally, the rent, utilities, food, and clothing allowance were a drop in the bucket. That was six years ago and Marianne wasn't any closer to purchasing a house. Those girls had managed to drive her stress and blood pressure up, give her an ulcer and thinning hair, and push away each boyfriend she managed to snag.

At that moment, she decided to send the girls back to foster care. Let them be the system's problem and not her problem. The foster care agency kept putting pressure on her to adopt the girls for good. All she had to do was sign her name on the dotted line. But Marianne just couldn't do it. She couldn't allow herself to be attached permanently to those juvenile delinquents. At thirty-seven, she had plans of getting married and having her own children. And none of the girls would be a role model to any of her children. She had tried to be a good foster mother and it didn't work. She could do bad all by herself. This was worse than having a worthless-ass man by her side.

It was eight in the morning and Marianne had to call in and take a day off, a day she couldn't afford to take off. She could never go on vacation, because she'd used all her vacation days for crazy shit concerning her four delinquents. Whether it was talking to school principals, store managers and detectives, truant officers, or visiting hospitals in the middle of the damn night, she was always taking days. She could be sleeping in her warm bed right now, but instead she was standing inside a cold, dank hospital with a bunch of hooligans.

A weary-eyed doctor in a white lab coat and clutching a surgical hat approached Marianne. "Ms. Jones?"

Trina nudged Cartier, who had fallen asleep in the hard waiting-room chair. Everyone stood in anticipation of the news.

"Yes," Marianne responded.

"Your daughter's going to be fine," the doctor replied. "She's sustained severe head trauma, but once the swelling goes down, she should be somewhat all right. The parts of the brain that sustained the most injury were the cerebellum and brain stem that control motor skills and speech. With physical and speech therapy she should improve over time. She's stable and sedated. If all of you are family, you can go in to see her for five minutes. But realize she won't know you all are there.

"Also, there are a couple of detectives who'd like to ask you a few questions."

"But I don't know anything!" Marianne replied excitedly.

"They still need to talk to you, ma'am. Goodnight."

Everyone glanced at the two detectives. Out of respect, the detectives decided to wait until after the family saw Bam.

The group filed into the room and was immediately aghast at the sight of Bam. She was hooked up to a couple of machines with tubes running in and out of her nose, mouth, and arms. Her head was bandaged and her left hand was in a cast. Her entire face was swollen to an unrecognizable state.

Cartier, Monya, and Shanine burst into tears, while Lil Momma miraculously held it together. Trina and Janet embraced their daughters as Marianne held Bam's hand.

An overwhelming force of emotions came flooding out as Marianne realized one of her girls was lying in that hospital bed. Bam had been her child for six years and she couldn't give up on her, no matter what her mind told her. Her heart couldn't listen, wouldn't listen. She wasn't raised that way. Family stuck with family.

"Bernice, this is Mama." Marianne choked up. "You gotta be strong so I can get you out of this hospital, baby." Marianne was giving it her all to keep it together. "When you come home, I'm going to cook you your favorite dinner. You love my baked macaroni and cheese, don't you?"

Tears streamed down Cartier's face. "Of course she does. And when you get better you can borrow my Xbox for as long as you want and I won't pester you to give it back."

They hoped their words of encouragement somehow reached Bam. It was hard to see how she could hear them in her condition. And it was even harder to walk out of Bam's room and face two detectives who wanted answers.

"Who did this to my baby?" Marianne asked them.

"Well, ma'am, that's exactly what we wanted to ask you," the smaller of the two detectives replied. He was around five feet eight with a medium build, blond hair, and a thick mustache.

"Ask me?" Marianne replied. "How should I know? Aren't you the cops?"

"Yes, and we're doing our job," the second detective stated. He was the taller of the two detectives by several inches. His portly belly had seen its share of Budweiser and Miller, and nothing light. "We've already been on the block and tried questioning a few leads, but everyone claims they didn't see anything. We were hoping you could tell us who had a vendetta against Bernice."

Marianne looked toward her friends. "You know parents are the last to know if their child has trouble. You need to ask her friends."

Each girl had only one name in their minds: *Donnie.* He was their trouble with a capital *T.* He had warned them. He was the only one who would benefit from hurting Bam.

Neither girl spoke a word about their rival, because of the code of the streets: Don't Snitch.

"Do any of you girls know who would do this to your friend?" the lead detective asked.

Each girl either shook her head or shrugged her shoulders.

"If you're protecting someone, then sooner or later we're going to find out," the detective said.

"There's no one to protect, because we don't know nothing," Cartier answered.

"And your name is?"

"Cartier."

"Cartier what?" the second detective asked.

"That's enough, Officer," Trina intervened. "My daughter hasn't done anything, and I'm not going to allow you to interrogate her as if she's the bad guy. You need to go out and find out who hurt Bernice."

"And why don't you let us do our job?" The lead detective stepped toward Trina. He was short on patience and had an obvious disdain for the present company.

Trina looked to Cartier and her friends, while Janet grabbed Monya.

"Marianne, we'll wait for you over here," Trina said. "You know these girls don't know nothing."

The detectives asked Marianne a few more questions, handed her a business card and left. As everyone began to leave the floor, a registered nurse named Kathleen came from around the corner and approached Marianne. The nurse had been watching the events unfold from afar and she was certain that the coast was clear. She didn't want to get Bam in trouble after the ordeal she had gone through.

"Ms. Jones?" the nurse stepped forward.

"Yes," Marianne replied.

"These are your daughter's clothes," the nurse said as she passed a plastic bag of bloody clothes to Marianne. "We had to cut them off her, but I think you'll know what to do with what's inside."

Marianne opened the bag and peered down at the bloody, ripped clothing. "Thank you for giving me this, but you could have just thrown these in the trash," Marianne said. "They aren't any good anymore."

Marianne tried to give the bag back to the RN, who refused to take them.

"Don't throw that bag away if you know what I mean," the nurse stated. The nurse had a little sister, Regina, who knew Bam well. After Bam was assaulted, Regina called her sister at the hospital and told her to be on the lookout for Bernice. Regina wanted a play-by-play account of Bernice's injuries and if she was dead or alive. Kathleen wasn't any stranger to the drug game being born and raised in Brownsville. Her current boyfriend was a drug hustler who paid all her bills. Even though Kathleen had always been a good girl, she was only attracted to bad boys.

Cartier had intentionally overheard the conversation and knew exactly what the nurse was saying. Without hesitation, she took the bag from Marianne and said, "I'll take it. That's Bam's favorite shirt. I'll sew it back together and fix it for when she comes home."

Marianne was tired and making a beeline for home and getting some much needed rest was all on her mind. She would get some sleep, get on the other three girls, and return to the hospital to stay by Bam's side.

CHAPTER TWELVE

The Breakdown

Everyone was tired when they reached Trina's apartment. Trina headed straight to her bedroom to get some sleep while Cartier and her crew went to her room. "Y'all know what's in this bag, don't you?" Cartier asked.

"Bloody clothes?" Shanine answered.

"You're as dumb as the day is long!" Lil Momma snapped. "What do you think Bam was almost killed over?"

"Oh . . ." Shanine said.

Carefully, Cartier rummaged through the bloody, torn clothing until she reached inside Bam's inside ski jacket pocket and retrieved $2,200 in cash and another $300 worth of heroin. The crew thought Donnie had someone rob Bam and beat her down. But with the money and product still on her person, they didn't know what to think.

"Maybe she wouldn't give it up and that's why they did her dirty like that," Shanine commented. "All she had to do was give up the shit. Now look at her."

Shanine's comments instantly pissed off everyone.

"How you sound?" Cartier spoke up, rising up on Shanine. "You blaming Bam for getting a beat-down, instead of praising her for *taking* a beat-down. We crew. She stood out there and held her own for the crew and you talking down about her?" Cartier was disgusted with Shanine's accusation. As she glared into Shanine's eyes, she wondered what Shanine or the rest of the crew, including herself, would have done if placed in the same predicament.

"I didn't mean it like that," Shanine replied in her defense.

"Yes, the fuck you did!" Monya jumped in.

"How you gonna tell me what I meant, Monya? You don't even think for yourself. Whatever Cartier says, goes."

At this point everyone was shocked. Shanine was obviously speaking her true feelings, and no one appreciated her being candid.

Cartier was furious. She was the leader and what she said was supposed to go. And that included Shanine.

"First of all," Cartier began, "when I formed this crew it was understood by everyone that I was the leader. It if wasn't for me we'd still be out here starving and begging people for shit. My thinking is what got us—"

"Is what got Bam nearly killed!" Lil Momma spat.

Cartier got even more furious. She couldn't believe two members of her crew were turning their backs on her, or had the gumption to stand up against her. She was the leader. She ruled. She made the decisions, and whatever decisions she made, the crew suffered the consequences as one, as a team.

"How you sound, Lil Momma?" Cartier asked, looking back and forth between Lil Momma and Shanine. "You siding with Shanine and all of this is my fault?"

"Cartier, if you gonna take all the glory, then you gotta take the fucking guilt." Lil Momma stood her ground. "We all told you that it wasn't a good idea hugging the block alone, but you wouldn't hear it. Now look."

Cartier's first instinct was to bust Shanine's and Lil Momma's asses. She felt they disrespected her on two fronts: first, disrespecting her in her own house and challenging her authority. As her chest heaved up and down, internally, she calmed herself. She read only a fool reacts out of anger. She wanted to be diplomatic about this. She knew she had to choose her words wisely and hopefully come to some sort of resolution, while still maintaining her crew's respect.

"Look, we're all upset behind what happened to Bam, but at this point we don't know what happened until she's able to tell us," Cartier explained in her most rational voice. "We can sit around pointing fingers all day, but what's that going to get us? Not when there's still money to be made." She held up Bam's stash of cash and heroin to make her point.

"We didn't lose our reup money," Cartier continued. "And we can't allow Bam's tragedy to be in vain. Whoever did this to Bam, did it to drive us apart. Now, more than ever, we need to stick together and go back on the block and prove that the Cartier Cartel don't fold under pressure."

Lil Momma didn't like what she was hearing. She loved her life and from the moment she heard about Bam's beat-down, she had been reflecting on her life.

"Go back on the block and sling drugs?" she voiced loudly. "Are you crazy? Do you want what happened to Bam to happen to me, or Shanine, or Monya, or hell, even you? What's wrong with you, Cartier? You're not thinking straight."

"See, this is exactly what happened in the movie—"

"This isn't a movie and we're not actors, Cartier," Shanine said, cutting her off. "This is some real shit. Bam got her brain smashed in! What's it gonna take to get through your thick head that we can't hang with the big boys? We all need to stay in our lanes and go back to boosting."

Cartier had had enough arguing with her scary friends. She was disappointed and shocked that they wanted to throw in the towel so quickly.

"Look, whoever don't want to be a member of the Cartier Cartel, can get the fuck out," she offered. "But remember, if you walk out that front door there's no coming back. We will no longer be crew and I will walk past you on the street like we never met."

Shanine, Lil Momma, and Monya heeded her warning and thought about the consequences. For each member it was a tough call. Lil Momma and Shanine were the two who had to make a decision. They knew Monya's loyalty was to Cartier, although both Cartier and Monya were more jealous friends than true friends.

Lil Momma was the first to speak up. "I'm out."

"Me too," Shanine replied. Both girls looked at Monya, who shook her head. There wasn't any way she was going against the grain. She had big dreams now and boosting couldn't fulfill those dreams. Hugging the block for a couple years would get her closer to realizing her dreams. Plus, she did the math in her head and with Bam, Shanine, and Lil Momma out, the shares would be split into half. Her dreams would be realized faster now.

"OK, it's done. Shanine and Lil Momma, bounce," Cartier commanded. "We're no longer sisters!"

Both girls hesitated. They were hurt by Cartier's words and tone. But the one thing they had learned explicitly from the Cartel was business was business. They wanted their cut of the money.

"No problem, Cartier, we out," Lil Momma said. "But give us our share of the money."

"Nah, Bee, you knew what it was from day one," Cartier replied. "I specifically said that if anyone abandons the crew, they walk away from all stakes in the game. That rule applies to you and Shanine. I wasn't talking back then just for my health."

Lil Momma's rebuttal was stopped by Shanine.

"Cartier, it's all good, but God don't like ugly. Keep our money and I promise you, you won't get to spend it."

"Oh, you threatening me, bitch?" Cartier jumped in Shanine's face.

Shanine stood her ground and shook her head. "It's not a threat, it's a promise. The laws of the universe."

"Don't worry about them silly bitches," Monya interjected. "They just scared. They'll be back."

"Didn't you just hear what I said? They can't come back," Cartier replied, rolling her eyes. She opened her closet and pulled out the shoebox that contained the crew's savings. She dumped all the money on her bed, adding the money from Bam's earnings, and she and Monya counted the money together.

The crew had managed to save $31,800, not including the $12,500 of reup money. Cartier and Monya figured at this rate, they'd be millionaires in two years.

CHAPTER THIRTEEN

Set It Off

Attorneys hated crimes in the hood, because witnesses were scarce. A crime could happen and a hundred people saw it, but not one would step forward. However, that didn't stop information on the crime from spreading. What the justice system didn't know, the hood knew twelve hours after the crime occurred.

By ten o'clock that morning, Cartier's phone began blowing up. She was informed that Donnie had beat down Bam, and unfortunately not one witness had put an end to his savageness.

"Yo, he gotta get it!" Cartier spat at Monya. "That punk motherfucker gonna bleed just like Bam. It ain't over."

"That crab-ass faggot gonna get his one day!" Monya shouted.

"One day?" Cartier replied in a surprised tone. "Today is his doomsday!"

"Who you gonna get to fuck him up?" Monya weakly asked.

"Who? You gotta be kidding me. We gonna do it."

"What?" Monya knew Cartier was upset. She was hoping Cartier was just talking, but she knew her friend. She saw the seriousness on her face and the venom in her voice.

"Donnie is a little punk. He ain't thorough. I know I gets busy with my hands, and if we catch him slipping, it's a wrap. Just have my back," Cartier beefed.

"I don't know about this, Cartier. You know he carries a gun at all times."

"He ain't gonna use it. If he was, why didn't he use it on Bam? 'Cause he's more pussy than my vagina, that's why. I'm tired of motherfuckers thinking they can play us. If we fuck up Donnie, do you know how much rep we'll get off that? Way more than we got off Shorty Dip. You see how no one wanted to give us our props off Dip 'cause our moms helped us fight. If we do this, then we'll get the props. No one else!"

"Are you crazy?" Monya yelled, questioning Cartier's sanity. Her voice quivered with each word. "That motherfucker carries a gun and pistol-whips bitches. What part of that don't you understand? Do you want to end up like Bam, 'cause I sure don't!"

Cartier sucked her teeth. "Listen to how the fuck you sound. You saying we should just let this shit slide? I don't know about you, but my moms didn't raise me to back down to anyone!"

Monya cut her eyes at Cartier's implication, and then ran her hands through her hair. She knew trying to talk Cartier out of confronting Donnie was like talking to a brick wall. Hopeless. Cartier was ready to set it off for her peoples and she needed Monya to have her back.

"Cartier, I got a bad feeling about this," Monya pressed the issue, "but if you want to do this, then you know I got you."

Monya knew it was useless trying to talk Cartier out of this. She was obsessed with fucking up Donnie. She had to go along to get along in this matter and hope it ended for the best.

That night Cartier got Jason to help lure Donnie back on the block. Donnie pulled up and immediately his eyes widened at the sight before him. Monya was hugging his block, slinging. Donnie jumped out of the car and started running toward Monya.

When Monya spotted him, she ran. And just as they planned, Donnie gave chase. Monya bent the corner and ran into the narrow alleyway, before she eventually slowed down.

"I'ma whip your bony ass, bitch!" Donnie managed to get out. He was winded. Although still young, his days of smoking had caught up with him, and those two blocks of running were gruesome. He leaned over, braced his hands on his thighs, and began to take deep breaths.

Cartier witnessed everything. She was waiting for an opportunity to get Donnie when he was vulnerable, and this was the perfect moment. Cartier crept up behind him with a steel pipe in her hands and swung wildly. The first hit caught him by surprise, thrust him forward, and he landed on one knee. The second blow knocked him off balance and he collapsed face-forward.

Before Cartier could swing the pipe a third time, Donnie swung around and caught the pipe with his hand and pulled Cartier to the ground.

Monya stood frozen with fear as Donnie and Cartier struggled. She heard Cartier call her name, but fear gripped her. She could see Donnie's hands wrapped tightly around Cartier's throat and Cartier fighting frantically for her life. She had never known fear like this, a fear that controlled her whole body. Although she tried to will her feet to move, she stayed in the same spot, as if she was lifeless.

As Cartier and Donnie continued to fight, Cartier was finally able to bite down on Donnie's thumb. She held on like a pitbull, until she tasted blood. The pain that shot through his body was enough to get him off Cartier. Donnie hopped up quickly and kicked Cartier in the abdomen with his size twelve Timberland boots.

Cartier folded into the fetal position and clutched her stomach. She could hardly catch her breath. She gasped for air as she watched in horror while Donnie reached into his waistband for his burner.

"Monya, help!" Cartier managed to scream before the loud blast of his cannon reverberated through the air.

Cartier didn't move. She didn't know if it was seconds or minutes that passed. Time stood still for her. When she opened her eyes, she felt the heavy weight of a collapsed body lying on top of her. Her eyes popped opened in shock as Donnie's lifeless body covered hers like a sack of heavy rocks.

Monya stood over both bodies, hysterical. Once again she was frozen with fear. She was terrified still. She saw Cartier's lips moving, but couldn't make out the words.

Cartier knew Monya was catatonic for now. She saw the large, fourteen-inch butcher knife protruding from Donnie's back. As he lay on top of her, she could feel his heartbeat slow down until it permanently stopped. Although she was mortified, she knew she couldn't panic. She pushed the heavy man off of her and got to her feet. It took all of her strength to dig the knife from his back. Next, as her hands trembled, she reached into his pockets and retrieved two wads of bills held together with rubber bands, his makeshift money clip. She then slid the Rolex watch off his wrist, and took his diamond chain and pinky ring.

"Here, Monya, stuff this in your jacket!" She reached out to Monya.

"Huh?" Monya was still in another world, grasping with what she had done.

"Hurry up and listen to me or we're both going to jail," Cartier hurried, trying to stay on point. She didn't have time for Monya's feeling. She wanted to do what had to be done and worry about the rest later when they were safe and sound. "Stuff this in your jacket and put your hood over your head."

Cartier wiped the knife on the back of Donnie's shirt, stuffed it in the sleeve of her jacket, put her hood over her head, and both girls calmly walked out of the alleyway.

They knew someone probably heard the shot and would be calling the police soon, but they were in Brooklyn and Cartier knew the cops wouldn't be rushing to respond fast. Still, she decided to stay on the side of caution by exiting quickly.

Her mind was reeling. Once again, she had underestimated the streets and put her and her friend in danger. She had no idea Monya had snuck a knife out of the house and she certainly didn't think Monya had the guts to use it. But the more she thought about it, the more it made sense to her. Monya was the scariest one in the crew, and she hated fighting and altercations. If anyone would make sure she had a weapon, it was Monya. Cartier realized what she asked Monya to do was way over her head.

Once they were safe inside the confines of the apartment, Cartier sprang into action. She ensured they both washed their hands thoroughly. Then she grabbed several garbage bags from underneath the kitchen sink. She led Monya to her bedroom.

"Stand exactly where you are and strip off all your clothes," Cartier told Monya. "Put everything inside this bag." She laid a bag on her bed for Monya.

Monya remained quiet. She refused to say a word. She began stripping as Cartier had told her to do.

Cartier began doing the same. The front of her jacket was soiled with Donnie's blood. All the evidence of the crime was going inside the plastic bags.

"What are you doing with that jewelry?" Monya asked as Cartier began to dump it inside of the bag.

Cartier looked at her, glad she was snapping out of her temporary coma-like condition. "We gotta get rid of it," Cartier explained. "If the police comes around asking questions, or get a search warrant and find it, then we're going to jail for the rest of our lives."

"Cartier, ain't nobody see us do nothing," Monya reasoned. "We could sell his jewelry and add that to our stash."

"No Monya," Cartier began shaking her head. "I don't think it's wise. We can't afford to be greedy, that's how you get caught."

"Then why did you take it?"

"So the police will think he got robbed and murdered," Cartier continue to explain. "If this were a movie, this move is what would get us caught."

"But this ain't the movies!" Monya's voice raised an octave. "And there ain't no CSI team coming up in the hood looking for trace evidence and hair samples to solve no murder in Brooklyn. This is the hood and people get murdered. That's the price we pay. They don't give a fuck about no dead drug dealer. A million motherfuckers could have wanted him dead and our names are at the bottom of the totem pole."

Cartier exhaled. And against her better judgment, she thought about the events of the past few years. Monya was right. She personally had heard of at least nine murders in her hood and not one had been solved. And out of those nine murders, six of them weren't a whodunit. The whole hood knew who committed most of those murders, and yet nothing. No arrest.

"OK, we'll keep the jewelry and get rid of our clothes," Cartier agreed. "But we gotta sell it off as soon as possible."

Cartier couldn't believe she actually saw a smile form on Monya's face. She didn't know what to think. The last thing she thought she would see tonight was a smile from Monya after she had just murdered a man.

Cartier tied up both bags and they took turns getting in the shower. Monya thought this was stupid too, but didn't want to hear Cartier's mouth. Once they got dressed, Cartier washed off the front doorknob with bleach, poured bleach down the bathtub's drain to wash away any trace evidence, in case any of Donnie's blood or hair was on her, and wiped off the bathroom and kitchen's faucets. After she was satisfied she'd done all she could, she and Monya left with the bags in tow.

As the girls walked down the building's staircase, one of Cartier's neighbors stopped them. "What y'all selling?" the heavyset brown female asked.

"Ummm, we taking this stuff to Bedstuy," Cartier replied.

"I thought you girls stopped boosting," the woman stated.

"We did, but this is some leftover shit we had lingering around."

"Well, why go all the way over to Bedstuy, when you could get a sell right here? Come inside my apartment, I got a few dollars."

They both hesitated. "We cool," Cartier said. "We

already have the money for this stuff, so we gotta go. But if we go back out, we'll stop by."

Cartier and Monya took a cab to East New York and dumped the bags in an alleyway dumpster in the Cypress projects. The cold night air put an eerie feeling inside the pit of Cartier's stomach. She knew it was a new day, a new beginning. She just hoped they survived it.

When they returned to the block, they had the crowd standing at the entranceway of the alley, the same alley they had been in several hours prior. The police had the alleyway and the sidewalk taped off with crime scene tape. The yellow tape was a solemn reminder of what had transpired. Neither one of them realized it, but their eyes were stretched open wide like saucers.

Cartier and Monya inched closer to the crowd. From where they stood, they could see Donnie lying stiffly on the ground with a white sheet on top of him. Cartier looked at Monya when she saw the forensics team snapping pictures and the meat wagon waiting to haul him away.

Shanine and Lil Momma were among the spectators. The girls all looked at each other. Lil Momma gave Cartier a knowing nod as if to say, *I know what happened here.*

Cartier was paranoid. Many thoughts raced through her head.

Will Lil Momma and Shanine be a problem in the future? Will the forensics team find something that leads back to me and Monya? Did anyone see Monya run into the alley, or see her enter the alley, or see both of us leave the alley?

It was the age of technology and she knew someone could have recorded the fight between her and Donnie on a camcorder, or Monya ultimately stabbing Donnie to death. Cartier was so deep into her thought, she was completely caught off guard when someone yanked her out of the crowd.

"Let's walk," Jason demanded as a startled look displayed across Cartier's face.

"Chill!" she retorted and wiggled free. "I'm coming."

They both walked down the block and he motioned for Cartier to get inside of his Pathfinder.

"What the fuck happened to Donnie?" Jason demanded to know.

"You tell me."

Jason wasn't down for any bullshit. He loved Cartier, but even love had its limits. "Cartier, don't play stupid with me, dammit," Jason calmly stated. "You ask me to get the nigga over here and when I come through, someone's done smashed him off? Who the fuck you get to take him out and why the fuck you got me involved in this bullshit?"

"I'm telling you I ain't have shit to do with this," she lied. "Come on, you know me better than that. I would never put you in the middle of no bullshit. And besides, what niggas I got that will body somebody for me? The only nigga I know that would be down for me is you, and you didn't do it."

Jason thought for a minute. He was a reasonable man and figured that Cartier wouldn't play him dirty. But no matter how you slice it, he was probably one of the last, if not the last call on Donnie's cell. The last thing Jason wanted or needed was po-po rolling up on him talking about let's talk. That thought alone made his stomach churn.

"Yo, where you coming from anyway?" he asked casually. "Did you even meet Donnie?"

"We were supposed to meet Donnie, then things got fucked up. Monya and I had it out with Shanine and Lil Momma—"

"I thought they were y'all homegirls" Jason interrupted. "What y'all beefin' about?"

"They both got issues with me, talking about I'm bossy and shit like that."

"Oh, that girly shit. They just jealous of you, ma. Don't let that shit get to you."

Cartier shrugged her shoulders. "It's all good though 'cause I'ma show them that they fucked up not being in the Cartel. They can't get any money without me."

"That's right. That's how you do it. Show those bitches who's boss," Jason couldn't help himself. Cartier could do no wrong in his eyes. He just wished she could see that he was the man for him. As they sat there, they watched the meat wagon pull away with Donnie's body. They both sat in silence for different reasons.

"You don't want to go get something to eat?" Jason asked.

"Nah, I'm good. I gotta go and check on my moms. You know she's pregnant and by now, I'm sure her nosey ass done heard what happened. I'll have to go and fill her in."

Cartier was glad to escape the minor interrogation inside Jason's ride. She walked briskly to Monya and gave her a look. As they both walked toward Cartier's apartment, she whispered, "Yo, you know we can't tell anyone what happened, right?"

"You don't have to tell me that . . . I'm the one who killed him. Do you think I'm stupid?"

"Of course not, just act normal and we should be fine. Didn't anybody see nothing so I'm sure we straight," Cartier tried reassuring Monya. In actuality, she was also trying to reassure herself. "Monya, I'm trying to be strong and I don't know how you're holding up, but I can't get my hands to stop shaking."

Cartier pulled her hands from deep inside her ski jacket. They were cold and clammy, and trembling from nerves.

For the first time in their lives, Monya saw something she had never seen in her friend's face—fear.

"Cartier, get a hold of yourself," Monya said. "By this time next week, we'll be fine. OK? I promise. I love you."

"I love you, too."

That night, Cartier went home and gave her mother the biggest hug she could muster.

CHAPTER FOURTEEN

———◦———

USUAL SUSPECTS

I t took one week before Bam was well enough to receive
visitors. All four girls decided to visit Bam as a cohesive
group. Although they still weren't speaking, they deemed
it important to behave in front of Bam. They all agreed she
had been through enough.

As the girls walked in, the two detectives they had
met before were walking out. They nodded their heads to
the Cartel, who refused to return the acknowledgment.

Bam was still fucked up. Her right eye was scarred
permanently and was only half opened. She had several
missing teeth, bald spots on her head, and as soon as she
opened her mouth, Cartier knew she had brain damage.

"H-h-h-hi f-f-f-friends," she stuttered and smiled a
toothless grin. She looked terrible, squeamish to the sight.
Cartier and Lil Momma, although no longer friends,
exchanged fearful glances. "S-s-s-so happy t-t-t-to s-s-s-
see."

Bam was embarrassed. She couldn't finish her
sentence and felt ashamed.

Her friends knew what she was trying to say. One by

one they embraced their friend.

Lil Momma led with the questions. "Did you tell the police who did this to you?"

Bam nodded her head in the affirmative, but said nothing.

Bam's answer raked Lil Momma's nerve. "Well? Who did it," she asked Bam in a less than friendly tone. Everyone glared at Lil Momma, who decided to soften her tone. "We're worried about you, Bam, that's all."

Bam shook her head again and finally replied, "H-h-h-he d-d-d-dead."

"Donnie? Was it Donnie who did this to you?" Lil Momma was relentless in her line of questioning. And it didn't sit well with Cartier.

Once again, Bam nodded her head in the affirmative.

Cartier and Monya exchanged glances. Both wondered how long it would take before the detectives realized Donnie's death was a revenge killing. This information made them antsy; so much so, they decided to cut their visit short.

Outside, Cartier said, "I think we should give Lil Momma and Shanine their cut of the money and make up."

"Nah, we'd be stupid to do that," Monya replied. "What for? They wanted out . . . hell, they knew the rules."

"I'm telling you I got a bad feeling about Lil Momma," Cartier retorted. "She keeps staring at us as if she knows we had something to do with Donnie's murder."

"You're being paranoid," Monya responded. "How the fuck could she know? Don't let that bitch play you.

You gotta be strong."

The roles had been turned. Monya was the strong, determined one since she'd killed Donnie. Cartier wasn't sure if she was coming or going.

"She knows because she knows us," Cartier reasoned. "She grew up around us all her life and she knows I wasn't gonna let Donnie get away with beating on Bam, especially after the guilt trip she put on me."

"You're going mental," Monya countered. "Besides, why you taking credit for shit I did? You talking like you murdered him, when it was me who handled my business!"

Monya's outburst startled Cartier. She couldn't believe they were in the middle of the street arguing about who was going to take blame for a murder. Since that day, Cartier didn't recognize this new Monya. This Monya didn't have any remorse for taking a life. This wasn't the scary Monya she'd known since birth.

"What the fuck are you talking about?" Cartier asked with attitude. "No one's taking credit for your shit. I'm just saying that Lil Momma ain't stupid. In fact, she's one of the smartest members in my crew!"

Cartier knew this would cut Monya's pride down to size. She got the expected result.

"And what the fuck is that supposed to mean?" Monya asked as she stepped toward Cartier in a confrontational manner. "You saying I'm stupid?" Donnie's murder had given Monya the confidence she lacked all her years.

Cartier recognized where Monya's strength was coming from. But she was stuck between a rock and a hard place. She could beat Monya to a pulp, but that was something she didn't want to do. The Cartel had fallen apart and she couldn't afford to lose Monya as well.

Cartier exhaled and took a step back. She needed to breathe and put space between them. "That's not what I'm saying," Cartier began. "All I'm trying to say is that we gotta watch Lil Momma. She's out for revenge, because she wants her eight large and I'm telling you that each day she doesn't get it is going to put our whole operation at risk. I don't even feel comfortable hugging the block, because she might call 5-0 on us. You feel me?"

Monya tossed her eyes in the air, and said, "I wish that bitch would call po-po on me. She better chill if she knows what's good for her!"

Cartier wanted so badly to tell Monya that Lil Momma would break her bony ass into several pieces, but she knew there was no point. Monya was riding high off her accidental murder.

Pebbles was a sight to the two detectives' weary eyes. Her brightly dyed red hair, against her pale, almost pasty white skin, brought immediate attention to the grieving woman. Although she was half-white and half Puerto Rican, she carried herself and spoke as if she were black. Her mother was white, born and raised in a trailer park off Eight Mile, in the heart of the Detroit ghetto. Her father was Puerto Rican and was only passing through long enough to get her mother knocked up. Life in

Detroit was too slow for the pregnant girl, so she followed another boyfriend to the hoods of Flatbush, Brooklyn, where Pebbles would be born and raised.

When Pebbles was twelve years old, she began dying her naturally brunette hair, red. By the time she turned fourteen, her boyfriend at the time stopped calling her by her God-given name, Belen, and began calling her Pebbles, after Fred and Wilma Flintstones's daughter. The name stuck ever since.

The strikingly beautiful girl with the dirty mouth wanted justice for her slain man.

"Those bitches gotta pay or so help me God, when I drop my fucking seed I'ma kill all of them."

"Ms. Gomez, take a seat," the lead detective began. "Calm down . . . before you hurt your baby. We're here to see that justice gets served, but you gotta help us out and tell us what you know."

"I'm too fucking heated to calm down!" Pebbles exclaimed. "Those bum-ass boosting bitches took my world away from me. I got two kids by Donnie. Now what the fuck I'm gonna do? His fucking mother done came through and looted all his shit before he was even buried in the ground. I came home from work and all our shit was gone and she talking about that was her son's shit? She done found the stash and everything! She gonna get hers too!"

"Ms. Gomez—" the detective tried intervening.

"Call me Pebbles."

"Pebbles, why don't you start from the beginning?" the detective said.

"When I'm done can I press charges on his moms for stealing our shit?"

Both detectives looked to one another and decided to appease their only witness. "Sure . . . sure . . . anything you want," the second detective chimed in. "Now start from the beginning."

"OK, check it. Donnie calls me and tells me that he's about to check this bitch named Bam for selling product on his block . . ." Pebbles paused. "Am I gonna get into trouble?"

Then she answered her own question. "What could I get into trouble for? I don't sell drugs. So anyway, Donnie was heated. When he got home that night he told me he thought he'd killed Bam, because he left her ass knocked out cold on her block and didn't nobody do shit. You see they all feared my baby daddy. Now, I told him that I would handle those bitches after I dropped my baby, but he wouldn't have it. He beat her down himself and now he's dead."

Pebbles looked to the detectives to put the pieces together.

"That's it?" the second detective asked.

Pebbles exhaled. She felt as if she was dealing with the Keystone Cops. "Bam was a part of the Cartier Cartel. There are five members, Cartier, the ringleader; Monya, the lieutenant; and Bam, Shanine, and Lil Momma—the flunkies. They formed this all-girl organization and began slinging dope on my man's block. They had been beefing for weeks. Donnie said that alpha bitch, Cartier, was stepping to him like she was a dude. And the night he got killed, he got a call from this kid named Jason, who's fucking Cartier."

"How do you know that?" the lead detective asked.

"Because I got all his numbers from Donnie's cell phone bill and called the last number. It was Jason."

Suddenly, a smile appeared on both detectives faces. "Tell us everything you know about Jason. Last name, address, telephone number, anything you can think of."

"What about the Cartel?" Pebbles asked.

"We think we got our killer, and it's Jason."

CHAPTER FIFTEEN

Hold Ya Head

Less than two weeks later after Donnie's murder, the police thought they had put the pieces of the puzzle together. Pebbles had steered them in the right direction. It was only a matter of days before they started building a case against Jason and received a search warrant for his crib.

Jason didn't sweat it. He knew the police wouldn't find anything. He made it a point to keep his crib clean, not even a burner. When they hauled him down to the precinct on suspicion of murder charges, he wasn't worried. He knew in his gut he'd get pulled into the mix. But he was confident shit wouldn't stick.

On the night in question he was around mad niggas at a dice game, so he knew it would be hard for them to pin shit on him.

Word traveled fast in the hood. Cartier had just walked into her building when she heard the news. Her heart plummeted as she remembered Jason's words. He told her this was going to happen. That she dragged him into this situation. She just hoped Jason didn't tell the police she had had him call Donnie to meet her. Since they already knew Donnie had assaulted Bam, they would come looking for her and her crew. Cartier ran up her stairs, two at a time. She was shaking, severely, too much to pull out her door keys. She began banging on the door.

"Ma! Open up!" Cartier demanded.

Trina waddled to the door at a snail's pace. She was already two days overdue and if the baby didn't naturally come soon, then her doctor said he was going to have to take the baby. When she flung open the door, she was frantic. She thought Cartier was hurt.

"Are you all right?" she asked.

"I'm fine," Cartier replied and dashed into her room. She went to the shoebox that held their stash: money, drugs, and Donnie's jewelry. Her first instinct was to flush it down the toilet as they do in the movies. As she was contemplating her next move, she didn't realize Trina was standing there looking over her shoulder.

"Where the fuck you get all that money from?" Trina asked. "I mean, I know y'all out there tossing it up, but never did I imagine you were holding it down like this."

Cartier was a nervous wreck. She didn't know what to say. Large tears began to fall down her dark chocolate skin. She knew she was in deep trouble and didn't have anywhere to turn.

"Mommy, I don't know what to do," she blurted out as tears streamed down her cheeks. "I'm in big trouble. I really think I've seriously fucked up."

"Fucked up how? What's going on?"

The loud banging on the front door was unmistakable. "Police! Open up before we kick in the door!"

Trina didn't hesitate. She took the contents of the shoebox and shoved it the front of her spandex pants, positioned the contents by her crotch and closed her housecoat. Her huge stomach hid everything nicely.

"Hold on! No need to break my fucking door," Trina said as she swung open the door. As the police trampled in, Trina was nearly tossed to the ground. "What's this all about?"

Two cops in blue, one black and one Hispanic, walked directly to Cartier. "Cartier Timmons," the Hispanic cop said, "we have a warrant for your arrest!"

"What? For what?" Trina asked.

"On suspicion of first degree murder!" the black cop stated.

"Ma!" Cartier cried out. "Help me!"

Forcefully, Carter was handcuffed by the Hispanic cop, while his partner thrust a search warrant into Trina's face.

"We also have a warrant to search your apartment," the black cop said with a smirk on his face.

"You can search all you like, but I'm going with my daughter to the precinct!"

The police allowed Trina to put on an overcoat. A ride in a separate squad car was provided to her. Trina prayed to God that Cartier didn't have any other drugs or money hidden in her room. As she walked outside, she saw two squad cars down the block, in front of Janet's apartment building. Trina realized whatever trouble Cartier was in,

Monya was involved as well. But murder? Who? There had to be a huge mistake.

At the precinct, almost relieved, Janet and Trina embraced. When they heard the commotion at the sergeant's desk, they realized Shanine and Lil Momma had also been arrested. Janet and Trina didn't wait to join the ruckus. Four mothers were raising hell inside the precinct, all demanding answers.

It took the precinct captain five hours before he told them why the girls were being held. They had been arrested for murdering Donald Williams, who went by the street name Donnie, and was one of the biggest drug dealers in Brooklyn. The women knew the name. Who in Brooklyn didn't know Donnie? Or heard about his death?

Trina was uncomfortable while in the precinct. She sat fiddling with the money, jewelry, and drugs in her twat. When she realized there wasn't anything she could do for Cartier tonight, she decided to take a cab to her mother's house. There, she could hide Cartier's stash and think about what she could do to get Cartier out of this mess she was in.

Trina needed to talk to her daughter. She didn't understand what Cartier had gotten herself into. She counted the money and was surprised at the amount. Did she steal it from Donnie's dead body? Did she really have anything to do with Donnie's death?

Trina couldn't handle the stress. First Bam, now her own daughter. She heard Bam had received a serious beat-down by Donnie and the only thing she could think of was Cartier and her friends had put a hit out on Donnie. *At least Cartier isn't in the shape that Bam is,* was Trina's only resolve.

The more the thoughts flooded her brain, the more stress she felt. Then the one thing she didn't dream of happened. Her water broke. In her mind, she facetiously thanked Cartier.

"Driver . . . please . . . I'm having my baby . . . please take me to the nearest hospital," Trina pleaded.

"OK, lady, hold on," the driver said in his heavy Middle Eastern dialect. "Do you want to go to Kings County or Downstate? I think I take you to Downstate. I hear they good for delivering babies."

"Make it quick, I don't have much time!" Trina pleaded.

The labor pains were more intense in her thirties, than when she was in her teens. When she went into labor with Cartier, it was a walk in the park. Trina realized she was too old to be playing mommy again. As she did her routine breathing in and out, the thought of Cartier in a dirty jail cell added more stress. She was worried about Cartier. She conceded she was tough, but Trina knew Cartier couldn't handle being locked away. None of the Cartel could. Trina was sure of that fact.

As she continued her breathing, she wondered where and if she had failed Cartier. How did her daughter end up in such a bad situation? Trina was sure she should have seen it coming. She knew she was the one who put the added pressure on Cartier to be independent and get her own money. And when Cartier did what mommy told her to do, Trina turned a blind eye to her dealings, her comings and goings. Trina knew it, but she couldn't accept it. She never thought that advice would land her daughter in such a shitty situation.

It was hard for Trina to accept. Of course she knew what Cartier was doing out in those streets. She wasn't stupid. But she told herself it was petty shit. *Weed.* Nothing too heavy. If Cartier would have gotten knocked it would have been a slap on the wrist. And when she was boosting, what could the police do? She was a minor. Again, a slap on the wrist. Never in her wildest dreams did she think she would be going to a precinct, hearing her daughter was involved in a murder.

Trina was afraid. She was in labor and had so much weighing on her mind. When they arrived at the hospital, she was rushed to the emergency room to prep her for surgery. She gave the nurse Janet's information and asked her to relay the news of the impending delivery. She never thought she and Janet would ever be in this situation with their daughters.

Eleven hours later, Trina welcomed her second daughter into the world. Prada Quinn Timmons came into the world weighing six pounds, eight ounces. Trina tried to celebrate the birth of her child, but the moment was tempered. She was a nervous wreck.

At the arraignment, Janet passed word to Cartier that Trina had the baby. When Janet came back to the hospital, she didn't have any new information.

"As it turns out," she began, "Donald Williams is Donnie, the drug dealer. The same shit we already know."

"The one they found dead in the alley?" Trina asked confusingly. She was still on medication after the delivery of her child.

"Yeah."

"Why would they say the Cartel killed him?" Trina asked.

"Same shit. You know everyone on the block know Donnie's the one who hurt Bam."

Both Trina and Janet were in denial. In some ways they knew the truth, but didn't want to accept it. The arraignment was only a preliminary procedure in the judicial system, but both women knew the prosecutor had a valid point: all four girls did have a motive to see Donnie dead. He had maimed their friend for life.

"Damn, Janet, do you think they did it?" Trina asked the question they both didn't want to know.

Janet shook her head from side to side. "I don't know, Trina. You know if it were you and me, we'd go to bat like that back in the day. But I never saw either one of our girls as murderers. And although Cartier has a little fire in her as we have, she's no killer. And you know Monya—my scary child—ain't no killer. It pains me to see her locked up." Janet was trying her best to keep it together. But the heart is a delicate organ and its worst enemy is emotions. She began to choke up and cry. "That's my little baby, Trina. She won't survive in jail."

"Don't cry, Janet. Listen, they ain't doing no time. We

gonna get them good lawyers and get them out, even if I have to sell my pussy on the corner!"

"That old shit? All that will get them is a public defender," Janet joked and they both chuckled through their tears.

"When they were remanded back into custody all you heard was Monya screaming and crying for me," Janet said. "It liked to break my heart into pieces."

"What about Cartier?" Trina asked.

"You know she had on her game face. She was strong and held her head up. You would have been proud. Just keep your cell phone on. I'm sure she's going to call you."

Cartier was the first to call her mother. Trina had nodded off from the medication they'd given her for her cesarean.

"Hello?" Trina's voice was groggy.

"Ma, this Cartier."

Trina sat up in bed as best as she could. "You know I would have been there if I could."

"You know I know that. Besides, you held me down when I needed you most when you—"

"Don't talk over those phones," Trina cut her off.

"Oh yeah, my bad."

"Now, when's the next time you get to see the judge, and who's the lawyer they appointed you?"

"All of us go back to court in two weeks and I got this bullshit lawyer who's already telling me I'm going to do life, even though I'm telling him I didn't do shit. I swear I wanted to punch him right in his cracker-ass face!"

"Don't go getting yourself into any more trouble," Trina tried to calm her down. "Look, Cartier, try to look out for Monya. Janet was here and she said Monya won't be able to handle the pressure. If they put you girls together, always make sure you got her back as me and Janet always got down. You know how we do."

"I hear you, Ma," Cartier said and exhaled. She didn't want to admit it but in a million years she never would have thought the Cartel would end up in jail for a murder. "I'll look out for Monya, but I need you to do me a favor."

"What?"

"Call Ryan and tell him what's up. He needs to hear from you what's happened to me before the streets tell him my story. And when you get him on the phone tell him to come and see me as soon as possible. OK?"

"Yeah, I'll call him later—"

"Ma, why can't you call him now?" Cartier whined. "As soon as we hang up the phone just give him a quick call."

"Calm the fuck down!" Trina yelled. Although she was in pain and weak, she felt her daughter should be more worried about getting out of prison rather than running behind some nigga. "I said I'll call him. I've been through a lot too."

Cartier realized how selfish she was being. "I'm sorry. Get some rest and when you're better make sure you come and see me too."

"I'll be up there to see you as soon as I get out of

here," Trina assured her.

"Oh, yeah, my bad. Congratulations. What we have?"

"A baby girl. I named her Prada Quinn Timmons."

"Ma, now you know that's some ghetto shit, right?" Cartier said, laughingly.

"Look who's talking?"

"You're the one who named me Cartier. Now it's Cartier and Prada, and yet we don't have a pot to piss in." In unison, they both said, "Or a window to throw it out."

Cartier felt good talking to her mother. Ever since Cartier stepped up to the plate and began relying on herself to get money, her and her mother began to grow closer. Seemingly overnight. Trina was now one of the coolest mothers around in Cartier's eyes. And if her mother told her it was going to be all right, then it was. Cartier tried to assure herself that the police only had circumstantial evidence. She was sure no one saw them do shit. Plus, she couldn't believe Jason would snitch. But if he did, she would turn it back around and say he lied. Anyway, the only thing he could testify to was he asked her to call Donnie, and the last time she checked, that wasn't a crime.

But the saving grace for Cartier was Monya keeping quiet. If Monya talked or bragged about being a killer, that was it. The worst thing that could happen would be Lil Momma or Shanine getting that information and using it against them. This was truly a game now and the players were plentiful: Cartier and Monya against Lil Momma and Shanine, the whole Cartel against the cops, and possibly, Donnie's people against the Cartel.

What Cartier didn't know was that the police didn't know anything. They were playing the system, and the judicial system was letting them do it. Technically, the cops didn't have any evidence, circumstantial or otherwise. The search of all four girls' homes came back empty, and they didn't have a murder weapon, eyewitness, or even a reliable snitch to rely on. They used the theory, let's arrest them all and let the pieces of the puzzle fall where they may. And they knew the weakest link always spilled the beans. It was a gamble, but they had a murder to wrap up. And they didn't want it to end up in the cold case files.

Jason was the first to post bail. The detectives had visited him often but he said nothing. He didn't own up to anything and never mentioned Cartier's name. He was a soldier, and true soldiers didn't break. He was innocent of any murder beef. They couldn't charge him for making a phone call nor could they prove that phone call led to Donnie's death.

"Picture that," he spat when Cartier's mother approached him. Trina was back on the block after visiting Cartier in jail.

"Yo, that girl is my heart and I would never do anything to hurt her," Jason continued. "Tell her to hold her head. They bluffing. Those cops ain't got shit! Besides, she told me she's clean. She ain't got shit to worry about. Matter-fact, I'ma go see her."

Jason was worried about the Cartier Cartel breaking. Jail was a different animal for those experiencing it for the first time. Those basic civil liberties people take for granted were no longer free. You paid with time. That's why they called it pulling time. And for young girls like the Cartel, it could be brutal. He was worried one may break and confess to all kinds of shit. And he couldn't live with Cartier being locked up for a dime or quarter.

Jason had heard all the horror stories from niggas who folded under pressure and copped out to crimes they didn't commit. He knew most suspects looked guilty and was afraid to go to trial for that reason. Hell, every detective and defense attorney who worked for the man knew that same fact. Add the pressure and stress from being locked up in the joint, it was a no-win situation. But once you copped out, it was a wrap. You couldn't come back later saying you were railroaded, because no one cared. He had to get at Cartier before she folded.

Tuesday was visiting hours and Jason made his way to see his sweetheart, Cartier.

When she walked through the visiting room door, her eyes lit up. She was outfitted in standard jailhouse garb: an orange jumpsuit. But the baggy clothes couldn't prevent her thick thighs and round ass from standing out. Her hair was pulled back tightly into a ponytail. Her face was void of makeup and her nails of polish. She also looked worn and dusty from her stay in jail, but Jason could see past her current living environment.

He greeted her with a smile. "What's up, gorgeous?"

Cartier blushed and felt self-conscious. She took her hands and ran them across her hair and looked down. Although Jason wasn't her man, she knew how he felt about her. He had her back and regardless of how many times she dissed him, he always came back, always stood strong for her. She couldn't say the same thing about Ryan.

"I'm surprised you really came," she stated.

"And why is that? You my peoples, right?" His everlasting smile made her feel good.

"But you know how guys feel about going to see women in jail." Cartier was really referring to Ryan. She had Trina contact him to tell him what happened and he gave her a song and a dance about not being able to take seeing Cartier locked in a cage. He promised to give Trina the money to post bail for Cartier, but to date, he hadn't came through.

"I don't give a fuck how guys feel, all I care about is how I feel about you."

Again, Cartier blushed.

"So look, peep this," Jason began his schooling. "You know I ain't tell them cats nothing about calling duke for you. Your moms came talking sideways."

"Yeah, she told me. Thank you for holding me down."

"No doubt. But I want you to stand strong. Those niggas are bluffing. They trying to rattle y'all to flip on each other and one false confession and it's a wrap."

Cartier shook her head.

"I'm serious," Jason tensed up. "When you get a chance, go back and tell those knuckleheads not to fold . . . to wait this thing out and all y'all will be going home soon."

"Ain't nobody to go back and tell. Lil Momma and Shanine aren't speaking to me and Monya." Cartier paused. She looked at Jason. He didn't press her. "And Monya is a zombie. She hasn't eaten anything since she got here. They got her on suicide watch. So it feels like I'm in here by myself."

"Well, hold your head. You the strongest one out of the crew. I always saw something in you that I didn't see in those other broads. I don't know why you even used to hang out with them. When you get out, you better do things differently. Put up boundaries and don't let motherfuckers in your circle. You feel me?"

"No doubt," Cartier pepped up. "I just can't wait to get out of here. You know I even miss going to school?"

"They done scared you straight in this motherfucker if you miss school. Hell, remember, you dropped out for a reason. Don't tell me you somebody's bitch and giving my pussy away!" he joked.

"Since when this your pussy?" she retorted.

"Well, not yet, but hopefully one day. You know I'm still waiting on you to recognize I'm a good dude."

Cartier looked at Jason and saw his sincerity for the first time. She was still young and really didn't know what she wanted in a man. It was about the status, but when she needed someone to come strong, it was always Jason. He would drop everything for her. She knew she could count on him, but thought he was only shooting shit her way, not sincerity. She was wrong.

"I know you are," she replied.

The visit ended with Jason promising to put money on her books and to check up on her mother and little sister, Prada.

"Jason?"

"Yes?"

"Can you put a few dollars in Monya's commissary too?"

He shook his head in the affirmative.

"And Jason?"

"Yes."

"One more thing . . . maybe two."

"What? I got shit to do."

"Can you put money in Lil Momma's and Shanine's?"

He thought for a moment and her request made him only love her more. "Oh, when you get out you're definitely hooking up with me!" He gave her one more big smile.

Cartier walked back to her cell and thought about her visit. She never thought he would be the one who came to her rescue. How could she have overlooked him all these years?

CHAPTER SIXTEEN

No Honor Amongst Thieves

I t didn't take long for Jason's prophecy to come true. That next day, the detectives began interviewing each girl, and the game plan was simple, *divide and conquer.*

Shanine was the first to be interviewed and play "let's make a deal." She was summoned into an interview room with the arresting detectives and her public defender, which she already wasn't crazy about. She was nervous and didn't know what to expect, but she composed herself for the worst.

"What did I do now?" Shanine asked.

"Shanine, please have a seat," her public defender said. He was a young white guy who looked as if he had just completed high school, let alone law school. "These detectives are going to ask you questions and you don't have to answer if you don't want to. If you decide to answer them, only answer what you know."

Shanine nodded in agreement.

"Shanine, we need you to talk," the lead detective stated as soon as her butt touched the chair. "You might be able to talk your way out of trouble."

"What do you mean?" she asked.

"Look, we know you didn't kill Donnie—" the detective iterated.

"Oh really?" she cut him off quickly. "Then why am I in here?"

"Because you need to tell us which one of the Cartier Cartel did him in," the second detective chimed in. "If you were there and didn't stab him, then we can get you a reduced sentence if you tell us which one of you did it."

Her voice raised an octave. "I told you that we didn't do it! We might do a lot of things, but we ain't no murderers."

After twenty minutes of trying to get Shanine to turn against her friends, the detectives gave up. She didn't give them anything. She didn't volunteer any information nor did she slip up and say the wrong thing. They wouldn't admit it openly, but the detectives were impressed by her willpower. They just hoped all the girls were not that strong.

Lil Momma was the next to be interviewed. She had a different public defender, a young white lady, who looked equally as young as Shanine's attorney. The difference between the two attorneys was Lil Momma's attorney didn't say a word.

When the lead detective repeated his opening line for Lil Momma, she started talking before he could get the words out of his mouth.

"If you asking me, it was Cartier," Lil Momma volunteered. "And if she did it, then Monya was her right-hand man,'cause those two don't do shit alone."

"Why Cartier and not Monya?" the second detective asked.

"Monya is scared of her own shadow," Lil Momma went on. "Cartier has the heart and the strength to overpower Donnie. And the night he was murdered I could just tell that Cartier knew something."

"What you mean you could tell?" the lead detective asked. "Did you ask her?"

"Nah, I didn't ask her 'cause me and that trifling bitch ain't speaking."

"So you're not down with her crew no more?" the second detective asked.

"That's what I just said," Lil Momma said with attitude.

"Do you think you could get her to admit she killed Donnie?" the lead detective jumped in.

"Didn't I just say that we ain't speaking?"

"I'm sure you're a clever girl ... you do realize Cartier is your get out of jail free card. If you roll on her and give us the evidence we need, then you get to go home."

"How come y'all coming to us?" she surprisingly asked. "If you had enough evidence to charge all of us with murder, then where the fuck is it at? I don't want to be just sitting in jail while y'all deciding my future. That shit is fucked up, especially when y'all know me and Shanine ain't have shit to do with no murder."

"Well, our snitch tells us differently," the lead detective explained. "And it's up to you to prove that wrong. So if I were you, I'd be thinking of ways to be back cozy with my former boss—"

"That bitch was never my boss!" Lil Momma exclaimed.

Monya rolled into the interrogation room in a wheelchair. She was lethargic and weak. She was on a hunger strike and scared out of her wits. Most days she didn't know if she was coming or going. It didn't take much to realize she was the weakest link.

The detectives decided to play the odds and see if they could break Monya to turn on her best friend, Cartier. Unfortunately for Monya, she had the same good for nothing attorney that Lil Momma had. The detectives knew any other attorney would have prevented Monya from even being in the room with them. Luck was on their side. Better yet, manipulation was on their side. They had convinced someone they knew in the PD's office to assign the young, dumb attorney Monya's case.

"We know you did it!" the lead detective yelled in Monya's face.

"I didn't do anything," she pleaded.

"You took a kitchen knife and plunged it into his back to take revenge for your friend, Bam." The detective was relentless. "Just tell us and we'll reduce the charges from first degree murder to manslaughter. You'll do seven to fifteen and be out in five years with good behavior."

"I can't do five years in jail!" Monya shouted.

"Then tell us what happened," the second detective said in a low tone. He was playing good cop to his partner's bad cop.

"Look, Monya, if you work with them they will help you," the young attorney volunteered.

"You're my lawyer, bitch! You're supposed to be helping me!" Monya looked at the young attorney with fire in her eyes.

"Tell us who fucking killed Donnie!" the lead detective yelled again. "Save yourself, because Cartier is already saving herself."

"Cartier?" Monya said in a low tone. She was confused and on the edge. *What's going on?* was her only thought.

"Yes, she's the smart one," the good cop chimed in.

"What did she tell you?" Monya asked. Just that quickly her demeanor had changed from fighter to weakling.

"Way more than you're telling us," the good cop stated.

Monya looked down at her hands and realized they were shaking. She wondered if Cartier could have betrayed her trust and told them who really killed Donnie. Monya was so confused. Could Cartier really fold under pressure and snitch Monya out after she had saved Cartier's life? Monya figured if Cartier did snitch her out, then she would tell them that Cartier helped. She wasn't going to take the rap by herself. Her head was pounding and she felt faint. She hadn't eaten in days and was living off a couple cups of water every day. She barely had the strength to think properly. She weighed her options on snitching out Cartier and giving herself up. Her better judgment told her to wait until she spoke to Cartier to see what the real deal was. *What if these motherfuckers are playing mind games with me?*

"I want to go back to the infirmary," was the next thing out of her mouth.

The two detectives tried their best to break Monya and it didn't work. She wanted to talk to Cartier first. Her attorney even tried to weigh in and Monya told her to go to hell on a fast plane. After another thirty minutes, the detectives gave up for now, but promised Monya they would be back and be back soon.

The next morning, Monya was transferred back to her cell. She was dying to speak to Cartier. When she was told Cartier had been released, she passed out on the spot.

Cartier was happy to be released. She didn't know why and didn't give a damn, as long as she was free. She ran to Monya's house, expecting Monya to be home waiting on her. When Janet told her Monya hadn't called saying she was being released, Cartier didn't understand what was happening. Had Monya confessed to the crime? Had the police got into her psyche? Jason warned her, but she couldn't get to Monya in the infirmary to brief her.

Panic sunk in. Cartier didn't know what to do. She called looking for Shanine and Lil Momma, but they weren't home either. She definitely didn't get it now.

As the days passed by, the neighborhood began to call Cartier a snitch. She heard the whispers, but chose to ignore them. She had to wait until visiting hours to see what was up. Even Trina and Janet had words over what was going on. It wasn't long before their thirty-something years of friendship ended.

At the first opportunity, Cartier went to visit Monya. She needed to speak to her friend face-to-face to see what was going on. She got there early and when Monya came walking out, her naturally slim frame was almost skeletal. Cartier was mortified. The glare, coupled with the hurt in Monya's eyes, spoke volumes.

"Well, well, look who's here," Monya began. "How does freedom feel?"

"Monya, I don't know what's going on or why they turned me loose," Cartier leaned forward in her seat to explain. "That's why I'm here . . . people are calling me a snitch."

"And I'm one of them," Monya said with venom in her voice.

"What?"

"You heard me, bitch," Monya stated. "I'm sitting in this jail rotting away! Why did they let you go unless you told them what they wanted to hear?"

"I swear on my father's grave that I didn't tell them anything!" Cartier's voice sounded desperate. She really didn't know what was going on and was surprised her best friend thought she would sell her out.

"Liar!" Monya shouted.

"Why would I lie to you? You're my best friend and I've done nothing but try to protect you all my life. I wouldn't abandon you when you needed me most."

"What do you call leaving me in jail on a murder case then? Donnie wouldn't be dead if it weren't for you," Monya spat. "I took his life to save yours!"

Cartier had to agree with her friend. Had Monya not took that butcher's knife and plunged it deep into Donnie's back, there isn't a doubt in her mind that he would have killed her that night in the alley.

"Monya I know you did but I didn't ask you to."

Monya was furious at Cartier's cavalier response. At this point she no longer trusted her friend.

"I better not find out that you've crossed me!" Monya threatened. "There isn't a reason good enough to explain why I'm in here and you're out there."

"They're playing us . . . I can't understand their logic, but they're playing us."

Monya shook her head from side to side and then collapsed her face in her hands on the table. She began sobbing hysterically. "I'm gonna kill myself! I can't live like this . . . I won't make it!"

The more Cartier had to comfort her, the more Monya screamed, repeating the same line, "I'm gonna kill myself!"

Their visit was cut short and tears fell from Cartier's eyes as Monya was dragged away kicking and screaming. She watched helplessly as her best friend was carted off back to the infirmary.

Cartier went home in a fit of nerves. The morning's event kept replaying in her head. When a week went by and Shanine and Lil Momma were released, Cartier heard Monya tried to commit suicide. The jailhouse nurse pumped her stomach after she took a handful of antibiotics.

Janet was a nervous wreck. After that incident, she and Trina began speaking again. Trina convinced her that the cops were playing the girls against each other and Cartier hadn't snitched on Monya.

As each day passed, Cartier got the report that Monya was withering away in jail. She reflected on recent events and how the Cartel ended up in such bad shape. She was the leader, the most vocal one. She remembered Lil Momma getting knocked, because she, as the leader, was the first one to get greedy for an extra mink. Thoughts and past events beat Cartier up throughout the day and night. She felt that she had failed badly as the leader of the Cartel. But the thought that kept beating her up was, *How can I lead anyone into battle, when I should be standing on the front line?*

Sleep was hard. She tossed and turned every night. She slept better in jail. *I abandoned the Cartel when they needed me most. Each fucked up decision, from boosting to selling drugs, was my call. And what do we have to show for it? Not a damn thing. The Cartel has dismantled and my best friend is locked up on a murder beef.*

Cartier had heard similar stories of guys that got themselves in a fix like this. But she thought they were smarter, younger and would always fly under the radar. But how can you fly under the radar when you like the limelight? And she did. She entered a world she was unfamiliar with, on a mission to prove she and her girls could hang with the big boys. Just like Queen Latifah, Jada Pinkett, and Vivica Fox did in the movie, *Set It Off. But this isn't a movie, is it?* She realized that the only thing the Cartel and the girls in that movie had in common was maybe an unhappy and empty ending.

When morning rolled around, Cartier got up early, kissed Prada on her cheek, took a long look at her mother, and left.

She realized she was going to grow up overnight.

CHAPTER SEVENTEEN

Taking One for the Team

Cartier and her lawyer, Nicholas Aponte, walked into the 83rd Precinct ready to make a deal if one was still on the table. She wanted to plead guilty in exchange for Monya's freedom. Cartier reasoned she would be a better candidate to do the jail time than her best friend.

"Are you sure you want to do this?" Nicholas Aponte asked for the last time before going into the Brooklyn assistant district attorney's office to negotiate for his client. He looked at the young, fearless girl and felt empathy for her. He knew she felt she was strong enough to handle what was coming her way. But the fact still remained that a man lost his life and someone had to pay for the senseless murder.

"If my client has information about the Donald Williams murder, what's on the table?" Aponte asked Michael Washington, the ADA for the Brooklyn Borough.

"What information does she have?" the chocolate skinned attorney asked.

"She has information that it was self-defense."

"We're not buying that," ADA Washington said as he

sat back in his chair. "A man was stabbed in the back and in anyone's mind that's murder."

"But he was trying to—" Cartier tried to say.

"Cartier, let me handle this," her lawyer, Nicholas Aponte, cut her off.

"If my client cops to this, we want man three. She's out in five years."

"No way!" the ADA leaned forward. "The evidence is saying *first degree murder*. If she pleads, then we won't seek the death penalty."

"Come on, Michael," Aponte began. "Let's be serious and stop the dramatics. It's only us three in here. Regardless of what you say or how much you try to scare my client, the facts are the facts. You and I both know no jury will ever convict her on the flimsy evidence you have. Plus, you are talking about one of the biggest drug dealers in Brooklyn. Hell, the right jury may actually let her go and you know that. And remember, there are three other girls who could be suspects as well as rival drug dealers and don't forget, your murdered drug dealer almost beat another young lady to death, and for all you know, one of her family members got revenge. So let's talk real, Michael, and stop showcasing when the cameras are not rolling."

ADA Michael Washington didn't like the way the white attorney, Nicholas Aponte, was talking to him in front of the young black girl. He wanted respect. He didn't live in the world of sympathy for his people. He thought the way he worked his way out of Queens to

become a successful attorney, they could do the same.
Instead, many of his people turned to drugs and stealing.

After a couple of minutes of silence, Nicholas Aponte signaled to Cartier to rise. "We'll take our chances with a jury of our peers. I'll petition the court for a speedy trial, I'll have my connections at the papers run story after story of the lives Donnie Williams ruined, and make sure they mention how a beautiful young lady nicknamed Bam had a promising future and instead, she will never be able to walk upright or speak clearly again. Plus, look into case law, *Aiello versus New York State*. She'll walk, Michael. I guarantee you that."

Aponte and Cartier headed toward the door before ADA Washington relented.

"The best we could do is *second degree murder*, Nick," Washington stated. "Take it or leave it."

"We'll leave it, Michael," Aponte replied. "Come on, Cartier."

As Aponte reached for the door, the ADA stopped him. "Hold on a moment, let me speak to the district attorney."

Cartier was dressed nicely as she sat next to Nicholas Aponte. She appreciated his efforts in getting her a deal. She wished she could have done things his way. He had assured her he could get them all off, without spending any time in jail or prison. But it meant Monya would have spent two to six more months in jail and Cartier couldn't take that. She knew it was only a matter of time before Monya confessed and then Monya probably would have received a life sentence, or worst, a death sentence. It wasn't a chance Cartier was willing to take.

As Cartier sat in the courtroom, she kept telling herself that she was doing the right thing. That she was taking one for the team. She knew she was fortunate; Nicholas Aponte had gotten her a sweet deal: five to fifteen years and she would be out in three and a half with good behavior. The only stipulation was she had to stand up in open court and give an allocution, admit her guilt, and tell what actually happened in open court.

"I was standing outside alone on my stoop when Donnie pulled up to the curb," Cartier began nervously explaining. She felt as if her insides were about to explode. "He sat in his car for a long time, before jumping out and running toward me. I was nervous so I ran. I ran into the alley and Donnie gave chase. In the alley, he and I began fighting, and he was getting the best of me. I tried to get away and tripped over a rock, and he fell on top of me. At that moment, I played as if I was knocked unconscious. Donnie pulled out his gun to shoot me, but something must have spooked him, because he spun around to see if someone was coming. That's when I pulled a large kitchen knife from out of my jacket that I carried for protection and stabbed him in his back. I didn't want to kill him. I only wanted to get away. I wanted to live. If I didn't stab him, he would have shot me."

As Cartier told her story, low sobbing was heard throughout the courtroom, coming from Pebbles, Donnie's mother, and other family members. For some of his family members, it was a bittersweet moment. They knew he was out there terrorizing the streets, and was possibly either heading to jail or the grave. The grave won. Donnie's mother prayed for him each night and hoped he would get out of the game before the game snatched him out. She also felt sorry for Cartier. The young girl had ruined her life all because her bully-of-a-son wanted the corner. She glanced over at the young girl's mother and realized they both were losing their children, only in different forms.

As the bailiff handcuffed Cartier and began to lead her into the back, Cartier took one last look over her shoulder and mouthed the words to her mother, "I love you."

"Keep your head up!" her mother replied.

"We gonna hold it down," Monya yelled, as others yelled and shouted, before the judge called for order in the courtroom.

Cartier looked at Monya—the weak link. She knew she had done the right thing. Monya had saved her life.

In her mind, this was day one. She just hoped she could do the next three and a half years standing on her head.

CHAPTER EIGHTEEN

Hold You Down

Cartier knew the key to doing her time was staying focused on her future. She enrolled in the GED program and scored 265 on her test, which made her feel as though she'd accomplished something. She felt bad for dropping out of high school now. When she received her diploma, with her name written in large script letters, she felt an overwhelming sense of responsibility. She made a promise to herself that when she got out, there was no way she would allow her sister, Prada, to travel the same paths in life she'd taken. She wanted to be a good role model to her younger sister.

By the next September, Cartier had enrolled in the prison's two-year college associate's degree program. She was disappointed the state had gotten rid of the bachelor's degree program due to budget cuts. She didn't understand why people had a problem with inmates getting a free education while incarcerated. As she rose out of bed, Cartier was eager to see her mother, Prada, and Monya. The first Saturday of each month, which was when Trina received her check, was the Timmonses visiting day. Trina would leave money on Cartier's commissary account before she left and often brought recent pictures of the family for Cartier to see. Trina had changed. This whole experience had turned her into a better, more responsible parent to both Cartier and Prada. At least twice per week, Trina would write Cartier, and send her books and cards with inspirational messages enclosed.

Cartier's hair had grown out of her perm and it was all natural. In the beginning, during her transition, she would let one of the girls straighten it with a hot comb to keep it straight. Now that it was in its natural state, Cartier would just wash and condition it, grease her scalp, and braid it into two neat plaits. Her naturally tight, wavy hair looked healthy. In her spare time, when she wasn't in her bunk or the library reading, she polished her fingernails and toenails to keep in touch with her feminine side. When she looked down at her nails, it was a message to not give up, that one day soon prison would be something in her past and she would be resuming a normal life.

As much as it pained her, this was Cartier's favorite moment in prison—being led from the back, past the heavy cement doors, to the visiting room. It always brought instant joy to her heart. And as always, the first thing she would do when those doors to the visiting room opened was look for the familiar faces that put a smile on her face.

"Cartier!" the small voice shouted. Cartier followed the voice and saw Prada in her mother's arms. She walked toward the table with the same huge smile on her face.

"Girl, I know you didn't just be-bop to this table?" Trina asked.

"Ma, whatcha talking about?" Cartier said, definitely not in the mood for Trina's tripping.

"I hope you're not letting these girls turn you out in here," Trina commented.

Cartier nodded her head toward Prada and said, "Ma, watch your mouth."

"She don't know what we talking about," Trina assured Cartier. "Now answer my question, you in here playing house with these other girls?"

Cartier's face turned red from embarrassment and insult. The last thing on her mind was allowing some dyke chick to eat her pussy. The thought was repulsive. People had it so mixed up about what goes on behind bars. There were enough gay and lesbian chicks in here for you not to get jumped and raped.

"Ma, since when you know me to want to go the other way?" Cartier asked.

"Not no child of mine . . . but you need to keep your femininity in here. Put a little switch in your hips when you walking. Don't let this place steal that from you."

Cartier held up her hands to show her mother her painted fingers. "You and I are on the same page."

"Good," Trina said and smiled.

Cartier looked around again searching for Monya. When she initially came out, she figured Monya was in the bathroom. Trina noticed what she was doing.

"Monya ain't come with us," Trina added.

Cartier didn't sweat it. Sure she was disappointed, but she was used to it now. This was the third month in a row Monya hadn't come to see her. "Really? What reason did she give this time?"

"She stopped giving reasons," Trina said. "She just said she didn't feel like coming."

"Well, what is Janet saying?" Cartier asked.

"Janet ain't saying too much. She said she tried talking to Monya, but her daughter don't listen to her no more. Monya think she grown and can't nobody tell her shit—"

"Ma, watch your mouth!" Cartier interrupted.

Trina rolled her eyes. She always cursed around Cartier and didn't have anyone tell her she couldn't. Now all Cartier did was repeatedly scold her on how she was raising Prada. Trina wanted to tell Cartier that Prada was her child and she could raise her any way she wanted. If that meant cursing like a sailor, then so be it. But she didn't want to upset Cartier since she was locked down.

"You right, my bad," Trina apologized. "But if it weren't for Janet, I would catch Monya and beat her little bony ass down." Trina paused for a second, having used profanity yet again and then she continued. "She walking around the neighborhood like she some big time dealer."

Cartier moved closer to her mother to fully hear what she was saying. Suddenly, her interest was piqued.

"Monya is hugging the block?" Cartier asked inquisitively. "After all we've been through? I mean, after all *I'm* going through?"

"I know. And it ain't just her. She got the members

of the Cartel back together again and from what I hear, they're doing pretty well for themselves. I hear that Monya is now the head of the Cartel. They're all riding dirty up and down I-95 from what I'm told. They've upgraded from selling hand-to-hand. I hear they're moving keys."

Cartier shook her head. She was disappointed with the news.

Trina continued. "Well, all them are back slinging except Bam. She's the only one who's doing the right thing. I guess that boy knocked some sense into her head, because she's working a part-time job at the public library and also went back to high school to get her diploma. She said she's going to walk down the aisle this June."

Cartier was happy about the news regarding Bam, but she and Bam weren't best friends. They weren't as close as she and Monya. Cartier figured she should have heard the news about Monya from Monya. Although it wasn't Monya's idea for her to cop out to the crime, the fact of the matter was she did. And if it wasn't for Cartier, Monya wouldn't have a life to throw away. She'd be sitting in jail counting down the days until her release instead of vice-versa.

"That's all good about Bam," Cartier half-heartedly replied.

"I ran into her two weeks ago and she gave me her information to put on your visiting list. I told her you would like that very much."

"Yeah, you did right," Cartier faintly replied. "It would be nice to see her again. . . ."

Cartier returned to her cell feeling down. So many things went through her mind. She was fearful for her scary friend and wondered how Monya would handle being head of the Cartel. What if someone like a Donnie threatened the Cartel again? What would Monya do? Would she be able to handle those type of situations? Cartier knew she had to do something. She picked up a pen and paper and began to write in hopes of getting answers.

> *Whaddup Monya,*
> *Long time no talk. I would be lying if I said I didn't miss you. I do. I hear you got a lot going on out there and I'm concerned. Come holler at ya girl.*
>
> *Friends forever,*
> *Cartier*

Cartier dropped her letter into the prison's mailbox and waited. She continued to wait for a reply that never came. After six months, she'd given up writing letters to Monya or expecting her to ever visit again.

They say the only constant in prison is *time*. For some, *time* travels fast. For others, it moves at the speed of a snail. For Cartier, she took it as it came. One year turned into three and when she thought she only had six months left, those months came and went. She had been in prison for five years now and was meeting the parole board for the second year in a row.

Over the past several years, she and Bam had become the best of friends. Miraculously, Bam was a new person. She went through almost three years of rehabilitation, and only had minor scratches from the beat-down from Donnie. Her speech and writing skills had improved tremendously. She wrote Cartier all the time trying to keep her spirits up.

Things had changed for Cartier. She and Jason finally developed a relationship, although she was in prison. He visited her twice per week, kept money in her commissary account, and kept the packages flowing. If she needed anything, he took care of it. Additionally, he helped out Trina and Prada, and declared to Cartier that he would always be there for them. Ryan was a thing of her past. He'd left Cartier the first night she got locked up and never came back around. Cartier had long ago stopped asking about his whereabouts. She didn't want to hate Ryan for doing her dirty, but she certainly didn't have any love for him.

When she met the parole board again, Jason, Trina, and Bam were right there for her. When the board once again denied her, she didn't understand. She began to wonder if the state would make her do the full fifteen years for killing Donnie. She was a model inmate. She had never been in trouble or even disciplined. She had managed to get her associate's degree and the prison guards were always complimenting her. She just didn't get it. She assumed she would be home, living a normal life three years ago. This letter read the same as the others, they felt she wasn't rehabilitated. As much as she tried to keep her head up, she felt the bottom was dropping out from beneath her.

"Keep your head up, baby girl," Jason said as he wiped her tears away in the visiting room.

"I hate to cry, but all I want to do is come home to you," Cartier stated.

Jason hated seeing Cartier like this and he felt especially bad today since he didn't have good news.

"Yo, baby," he began. "I went by your moms' crib last night and had to pound a nigga's head in."

"What? Who?" Cartier was distraught enough and couldn't believe this shit.

"Some young nigga too!" Jason began explaining. "As I'm walking up the stairs, all I hear is yelling and screaming. I knock on the door and it's taking like forever for Trina to open it. When she comes to the door, Prada is in the background screaming her lungs out and your mom's face is all fucked up. I look up and this little young nigga is trying to push past me trying to get through. I didn't even ask any questions before I hit that nigga with a two-piece combination. One hard left to the jaw and a quick right in the rib cage."

Jason demonstrated the hand and facial movements to Cartier. He was so animated. That was one thing Cartier loved about him, his protective nature.

He continued, "So I'm pounding on this dude and Trina is cheering me on. She's like, 'Yeah, fuck his punk ass up!' After I stomp him out and drag him out the building,

I go by there today to see if she wants to come up here with me and guess who's sitting in there with his feet up on the coffee table? He gave me a look like he'd won some sort of victory. I started to pound on that nigga again, but I just let him have his moment."

Cartier shook her head. "I know exactly who you talking about. His name is Reggie and he's only three years older than me. When I was little, he always tried to get with me and now he's sleeping with my moms. Like how embarrassing."

"Yeah, that's wack. I told Trina she on her own from here on out. I can't catch a case behind that bullshit."

"You right. Both of us can't be locked down. Besides, you're my rock. I don't know what I'd do without you."

Jason and Cartier looked deeply into each other's eyes. Softly, he rubbed her hands as they rested in his. As nerves began to take over, he whispered, "I've been thinking . . ."

"Thinking what?" Cartier asked.

"About you and me."

Cartier closed her eyes. She kept having a reoccurring dream that Jason would also stop visiting her. That he too would give up on her.

"Say it! Spit it out. I can handle it," Cartier said and snatched her hands from his.

"What are you getting upset about?" Jason asked, with shock and surprise on his face.

"I'm not upset," Cartier said with tears forming in her eyes.

"Then give me back your hands," Jason commanded.

Reluctantly, Cartier placed both hands back into Jason's.

"I was thinking that we should get married," he said matter-of-factly.

Cartier was now the one to be surprised and shocked. She didn't know what to say. This was the last thing she was expecting. Her heart filled with insurmountable emotions. The proposal was unsuspecting like an avalanche.

"You really wanna marry me?"

"I just asked you, didn't I? I didn't hear you asking me to marry you?"

Cartier laughed, "So when I get out we're—"

"Nah, baby, I don't want to wait until you get out. Let's do it now."

"In here?"

"Why are you making this difficult?" Jason facetiously complained. "You're fucking up my moment. I practiced this proposal all morning. I thought I'd ask you and you'd say, 'Of course I'll marry you. I love you. Why wouldn't I want to have your last name?'" Jason tried to emulate her voice to no avail.

"Baby, of course I'll marry you!" Cartier said excitedly. "You mean the world to me. I couldn't do this without you. I want to be your wife, but I don't want to be selfish. What if I have to do the full fifteen?"

"Then as your husband, we doing fifteen."

"I love you."

"I know you do."

"No, I really love you."

"And I said, I know."

They kissed briefly before the guard came over and told them they had to stop.

Jason continued, "You know we've been together for almost five years now and I tell you everything 'cause you my best friend, but I'm not the most faithful nigga around. You know I got needs and I started fucking with this chick from Albany—"

"Sabrina," Cartier surprised him. "Yeah, I know."

"How you hear about her? I thought I kept that on the low-low."

"You know ain't shit done in the dark."

"OK, true. But check it. I started to catch feelings for her—"

"Why are you telling me this? Do you think I want to hear that my man is loving another bitch?"

"Cartier, let me finish. Sabrina was doing everything in her power to make a nigga fall in love. I told her from the jump, like I tell all those bitches, that you my girl and when you come home that it's a wrap. And that bitch said something that made sense. She said that until I put a ring on your finger, then I won't know for sure who I'm gonna end up with."

Cartier listened intently, but internally, she wanted to bash all of Sabrina's teeth out her mouth. Sabrina was a pretty, educated girl from the Albany projects. She was a good girl who went to school every day and had enrolled in college with aspirations of becoming a lawyer. Cartier knew her whole resume. Cartier wouldn't say Sabrina was the sole reason she went to school to better herself, but at times when she wanted to give up, Sabrina fucking her man was the reason she forged ahead.

"So what are you saying?" Cartier asked.

"I'm saying I want to get off the market, because these chicks out here are like vultures, and since I know that it's you and only you that I love, I wanna make it official. Just say yes and make me the happiest man on this earth."

Cartier was always fulfilled when she left her visits with Jason. She was one of the very few women who still got visits from their boyfriends. With most inmates, the visits usually ceased within the first month or two of their incarceration. Jason rode with Cartier for years, and now he wanted to make it official. She shared with him that she had begun to dream of their marriage not long after she was locked up. What she loved most was that she and Jason could talk and tell each other everything.

She was on cloud nine. She was hyped. she went back to her cell and wrote out three letters: to her mother, Monya, and a love letter to Jason.

Cartier wore an all-white, silk wedding dress. Jason had on a black tuxedo. In attendance was Trina, Prada, Wonderful, Jason's best man, and Bam, who served as maid of honor. It hurt Cartier that Monya didn't attend, but she didn't let her absence temper the mood. As the young couple stood before the prison's justice of the peace and said their vows, the small room erupted into laughter and tears.

The prison allowed the family to bring a small portion of food and a wedding cake. They all sat around talking about the couple's future. Finally, Cartier and Jason sat in a small, private corner and began discussing their wedding night.

"It's going to take the prison at least three months to approve our trailer visits," Cartier began.

"I know. I can't wait for that—"

"You better wait! We're married now, so even though I'm in here you can't be out in those streets behaving like you're single."

"You don't have to tell me that. I took an oath before God to love and cherish you. Cartier, I would never do anything to hurt you, let alone break our vows."

Jason stared deeply into his bride's eyes and realized he'd done it. All his life he wanted Cartier and now she was his forever. He didn't plan on ever messing that up.

CHAPTER NINETEEN

———————⬤———————

Put a Ring On It

After Cartier and Jason went through a vigorous screening process to be allowed conjugal visits, which included being tested for any sexually transmitted diseases, the date was finally set for their first visit. The prison supplied the tissue, soap, sheets, pillows, towels, and condoms, and Jason bought the food and sexy lingerie for Cartier.

She couldn't believe how nervous she was. Of course, she wasn't a virgin and had sex on numerous occasions with different guys, but she and her husband had never been intimate. The immature side of her wondered what would happen if she didn't perform well. *Will he go back out into the streets and sleep with other women to satisfy his desires?*

The week prior to their conjugal visit, after each shower, Cartier would apply lotion to her body at least seven or eight times a day. She wanted her skin to be baby soft when he traced his fingers up and down her body. She also groomed herself as best as she could by trimming her pubic hair as low as possible, without being bald.

She knew the new craze for women were to have no or less pubic hair in order to give the man easy access when eating their pussy.

She smiled to herself. *Does Jason eat pussy?* It was the first of many thoughts that jumped in and out of her head. She thought about what positions he might like as well as positions she used to like. And she couldn't remember the last time she sucked a dick. She thought so much her head started to hurt.

The prison bus took her to the secluded, yet heavily guarded trailer park located on the prison grounds. Her trailer was number eight. She arrived at seven on a Friday and Jason arrived a couple of hours later. When he saw her, they quickly embraced.

"You smell so good," Cartier commented. He looked so handsome, clean and crisp. She could tell that he'd gotten a fresh haircut and was wearing new clothes, but she also detected nervousness. Or was that eagerness? She couldn't quite put her finger on it.

Jason responded by giving her a deep, sensual kiss. Immediately, his dick grew hard as he pressed his pelvis into her hypersensitive flesh. His hands began to explore her shapely body, kneading his fingers into her fleshy buttocks, his favorite asset on Cartier.

"Take off your clothes," he breathed, in a throaty whisper.

"No . . ." Cartier replied, coyly. "Not yet. We gotta wait."

"I've waited all my life for this. I don't want to wait a moment longer."

Cartier wanted to do the traditional romantic, girly thing. She had it all worked out in her mind. She would cook for him first, set the table, and they'd eat and tell each other how much they loved one another. Then they would take a shower together and wash each other off. After the shower, she would put on something sexy and dance for her man, her husband, and finally, they would make passionate love.

But it was obvious Jason had other plans.

"What about dinner?" she asked. "I've planned a romantic dinner—"

"Cartier, it's ten o'clock in the morning," Jason emphasized. "I'm not waiting until dinner to make love to my wife. We're not kids. We're a married couple. We got the whole weekend to have dinner and I don't know about you, but I want to spend my weekend making love. I want to leave you fulfilled and drained. I want my dick to be broken and out of commission until our next visit."

Cartier understood Jason's logic. She thought he had done a great job of putting things into perspective. Immediately, she dropped down to her knees and began to unzip his jeans. His dick stood prominently through his Calvin Klein boxers as her small hands pulled his meaty flesh out. Cartier closed her eyes tightly and began to nibble gently on the head. As she took him farther and farther into her mouth, Jason began to moan. His hands guided her head and encouraged her to take more of him. As Cartier licked, sucked and nibbled on his penis, she took one hand and began to masturbate. She was so wet and aroused she wanted Jason to enter her quickly. Instead, he walked her over to the bed and positioned them in the sixty-nine position.

"Sit on my face," he instructed the novice Cartier. It didn't take her long to fall into place. She sat on her husband's face and leaned over and continued to suck his plump dick. The sensations she felt as he ate her pussy were overwhelming. Cartier began to grind her hips into his face as his tongue darted in and out. Jason sucked on her clit as if it were his favorite meal. When he stuck his index finger inside her inflamed vagina, her wet juices came seeping out. As Cartier began to experience waves of pleasure, she tried to get up, but Jason wouldn't let her.

"Fuck my face," he encouraged. "This shit feel good, right ma?"

"Yesssss," she purred. "Oh, yesssss!"

"Yes what?" Jason asked and slapped her on her ass. The slap stunned her, yet it was very naughty and heightened her senses.

"Yes, daddy . . . it feels sooooo good," Cartier moaned.

"Tell me when you're gonna cum," Jason instructed.

Cartier felt strong waves enveloping her body and once again, she tried to get up, but was restrained by Jason. She began to suck harder on his dick as he concentrated on her clit. As Cartier came in Jason's mouth, he, in turn, erupted inside her mouth. The sour liquid exchanged by the couple only brought them that much closer. Exhausted, sweaty, and satisfied, they both collapsed in each other's arms and just reveled in the moment.

"Did you ever think that we'd be here . . . not in this place, but together as man and wife?" Jason asked.

"No. I never really saw myself with you."

"And why is that?"

"I guess because I thought we were too close as friends to ever cross that line, you know? Like I didn't ever want to compromise our friendship if it was only going to be for one night."

"One night? I got you for the rest of your life, so you better get used to that."

"I think I can do that," Cartier giggled.

Jason hopped out of the hard, full-sized bed and walked to the small bathroom, naked. Cartier admired her husband's physique. His plump dick hanging limply, broad shoulders and pillar thighs were extremely sexy. Cartier said a quick prayer to God thanking Him for bringing Jason into her life. Despite her circumstances, Cartier still found a reason, or reasons to be thankful.

After Jason relieved himself, he walked back toward the bed, rejuvenated. His eyes were speaking volumes as he crawled on top of Cartier.

"Now . . ." he kissed her belly, "that we got that out of the way. Let's make love."

Jason started at Cartier's feet. He slowly began to suck each toe, something no man had ever done to her. She experienced a sensation she had never felt before as he took each toe into his warm, wet mouth, and made his way up between her thighs, and then traced her belly with his tongue. He made his way to her side and then flipped her over and began to suck and lick the back of her neck. Gently, he whispered, "I love you. . . ."

Jason continued to baptize her body with slow, sensual kisses as he traveled back down, and took both his hands and spread her ass cheeks. His tongue was precise as he licked her anus, another experience Cartier had never encountered.

After Cartier was moist, he pulled her up and slowly entered her, doggy style. Jason began with slow, steady strokes as he gripped her shapely hips. As he began to speed up, Cartier had to brace herself on the headboard for support. As his dick brushed up against her G-spot, Cartier couldn't stifle her screams of pleasure. From her head to her toes, she was experiencing a tingly sensation that was foreign to her. Jason's dick had opened her wide and she moaned her appreciation.

Next, Jason lay on his back and Cartier got on top in the backward cowgirl position, and rode him until, once again, they both came together.

Just as Jason had asked, they made love throughout the weekend, only taking breaks to eat and sleep. When the weekend was over, they parted with huge grins on their faces. As soon as Cartier got back to her cell, she wrote Jason a letter reliving the weekend.

In her cell every night, Cartier thought about her future with Jason. When she returned home, she wanted them both to get as far away from the hood as possible.

She wanted Jason to stop selling drugs and for them to have a family. In less than a year, she'd go back before the parole board, and hopefully, she'd get released.

She began hearing great things about Atlanta and thought that would be a good place to start over. But when she mentioned the idea to Jason, and then Trina, they both vehemently opposed the idea.

"We don't got to run to Atlanta to have a good life," Jason began. "We can do that right here. We don't know nobody out there and I don't want to go there to have to come back."

Trina chimed in, "And you know I ain't moving out there. You know what they say about Atlanta? How am I supposed to find me a man if all the men out there like men?"

Cartier looked at her mother, who was pregnant with Reggie's child and shook her head.

"The last thing on your mind should be a man," Cartier said.

"Why? I ain't dead," Trina retorted.

Cartier realized with the two people she loved the most opposing leaving New York, she had to think of another way to leave the hood. She wanted to have a game plan, some kind of organization in her life. She didn't want to come home and feel lost. She knew Trina still had her money, technically, the Cartel's money, and Donnie's blood jewels. Cartier wanted to feel guilty, but that was water under the bridge. She couldn't bring back the past. She figured that she and Jason could put their money together and buy a house. She was thinking either Long Island or upstate New York.

That next morning, Cartier went to the library and researched homes and home loans. She told Jason to start building his credit by opening accounts in his name and paying at least seventy percent of the bills in full each month. He needed to establish a good credit history.

Diligently, Jason followed Cartier's lead. Meanwhile, she kept house hunting. She surmised the farther you moved out in Long Island, the cheaper the homes were. And in upstate, they had nice homes for as cheap as one hundred grand. Again, she brought the information to Jason and he wasn't having it.

"Look, that's too much driving just to go see my moms or say what's up to Wonderful," Jason objected. "You gotta find somewhere closer to the hood."

"If that's the case then, we might as well get an apartment on my block and live miserably ever after," she countered.

"Stop being dramatic," she replied.

"I'm not but it's like you won't let go," Cartier added. "If you keep it up, you'll stay stuck, and as your wife, you're going to pull me down with you. We got the means to get out of the hood. Why are you resisting?"

"Cartier, look, I'm a young dude," he explained, "and I don't want to be cooped up in the house out in west bubblefuck somewhere. Now if you want a house I'ma get you that. But I'm not going to sacrifice my fun and games in the process. That's not what I signed up for."

With every word spoken, Cartier almost felt defeated, but she was trying to program her mind to look at the glass as half-full, instead of half-empty. The happiest day of her life was when Jason proposed to her and told her he would shoulder her fifteen-year sentence as well. Why was she about to cause a rift over geography? Certainly, she knew how to compromise. She decided she could find them a nice place in Queens, which was close enough to his friends, yet far away from Brooklyn. At least, far enough away for her. Yes, they'd get less for their money, but she was sure that her husband would be happier there.

Cartier surfed the library's internet looking for the right house in Queens. She looked up zip codes and then surfed by streets. She was determined to find something. She deduced they could buy a two-family home in a nice neighborhood for $400,000. They could rent out one side as an income-producing unit, and remodel the basement so Trina, Prada, and the new baby could live there as well. She also hoped they could get another $60,000 for Donnie's jewelry, and Jason had already told her he had a $100,000. She knew with such a large down payment, their mortgage had to be low, something they could afford with regular jobs.

Cartier prayed every night that her hopes and dreams were not for nothing. As much as Jason talked about opening up a business and quitting the drug business, he hadn't done either. She worried about his safety. She knew that world and she knew the mean streets of Brooklyn. He could easily be murdered or catch a life sentence selling the type of weight he pushed. She prayed for her man each night and hoped he would think of something to do that was legal. Cartier felt that they were running out of time.

CHAPTER TWENTY

All is Fair in Love and War

Regardless of their disagreements about living locations, Cartier grew more in love with Jason as each day passed. She prayed for him at night, before lights out, and when she awakened every morning. She could see the future and she hoped the future was soon.

When Bam came to see her and told her something that could be very innocent, her gut twisted from disgust and her insecurities were exposed.

"Are you sure you saw them together?" Cartier asked.

"Cartier, I hate to be the bearer of bad news, but it just don't seem right for the two of them to be together, especially after the way she cut you out of her life."

Cartier refused to believe the news. "But are you sure you saw Monya and Jason together?"

"Yes, I'm sure," Bam replied. "And they both saw me too, so it ain't like I'm telling you something that should come as a shock to Jason. We all looked at each other and I just shook my head and kept walking."

Bam and Monya fell out while Bam was in the hospital and going through physical therapy. Monya

stopped coming to see Bam as she had stopped coming
to see Cartier. After Bam made a full recovery, she heard
all the awful things Monya had said about her. Monya
called Bam retarded and dead weight, and those words
hurt Bam deeply. As far as Bam was concerned, Monya
was a backstabbing snake. She knew in her heart if she
had seen Jason with anyone else, she probably wouldn't
have said anything.

"Well, maybe he was just giving her a ride home or
something," Cartier surmised.

"Look, you can make up all types of reasons of why
she was sitting pretty in the front seat of your husband's
truck, but before I did all that speculating, I would just ask
him. Be straight up. You can tell him I told you that I saw
them together. I really don't care."

"Nah, Bam, I won't mention your name. That ain't
right."

"He's gonna know where it came from anyway," Bam
said. "Jason ain't stupid."

"If from what you tell me, anybody could have seen
them together."

"Yeah, anybody could have, but I'm not anybody,"
Bam stated. "He'll know exactly where the information
came from and I don't ever want a man to think that I
can't hold my head up high and stand by what I believe
in. And besides, you shouldn't start lying in your marriage.
One lie will lead to many. Don't set that stage. Just be
straight up."

Cartier hugged her friend and thanked her for the

good advice. She was going to call Jason and ask about the situation, but decided it would be best to ask him face-to-face.

Monya, Cartier thought. *What were you doing with my man?*

C artier tried to convince herself she trusted her husband wholeheartedly, but when he missed his first visit in six years since she'd been incarcerated, her mind went wild. Her hands were wet and clammy as she waited in line for the telephone. She'd spoken to him last night and he assured her that he would be driving up.

"Hello."

"Whaddup?" Jason asked as if he didn't have a clue why she was calling him.

Cartier was quickly annoyed. "What's up?" she shouted. "What the fuck you mean what's up? Why didn't you come see me today?"

"Yo, who you talking to like that?" Jason retorted. "I ain't one of your little bitches in your crew. You better respect me."

"I'm talking to you! You getting on the phone acting all dumb."

"What the fuck was I supposed to fucking say?"

"If you had come up here to see me you wouldn't have to say shit. Where were you?"

"I had shit to do."

"Oh yeah? With who?"

"What do you mean with who?"

"Jay, don't play with me. You heard what I just asked you and you know what I mean!"

Jason chuckled, "Oh, I know what this is about. This is about Monya. Let me guess, Bam done ran up there and told you that she saw us together."

"You damn right she did! What the fuck are you doing with that bitch?"

"Wait, hold up," Jason said. "When Monya became a bitch?"

"Excuse me?"

"You heard me. All these years we weren't ever allowed to even mention her, but if we did you acted as if you didn't hold any grudges. Now all of a sudden she's a bitch? You girls kill me."

"You don't know shit about our situation!" Cartier had lost it. Her voice elevated to a unrecognizable pitch as she yelled into the phone. Her heart began to flutter from fear and she'd broken out into a sweat. "And why are you defending—"

"Hold on," Jason interrupted.

Jason put the phone down mid-sentence and began talking to his homeboy. Cartier listened as he carried on a full-length conversation about nothing in particular. He spoke about the weather, the new boots he wanted to purchase, the food at the new spot up in Harlem. Meanwhile, Cartier hung on the phone seething.

Finally, after about four minutes of disrespect, Jason said, "Look, I gotta go. I got shit to handle." And just like that he disconnected the line.

Anger swelled from the pit of her stomach and rose to form a lump in her throat. Cartier couldn't believe the level of disrespect she'd just received from the man she thought about day and night. Even if she wanted to, she couldn't contain her tears. They began gushing out as large droplets stained the front of her shirt and ran down her cheeks. His behavior hurt Cartier down to her soul. This was the first time in their relationship that Jason was ever mean to her and she hoped to God that it wasn't because of Monya. She tried to calm herself down by telling herself that even if Jason did push up on Monya, as a friend, Monya would never go for it. Just out of respect and for the respect of their friendship.

After Cartier whipped her tears, she went back to the telephone to call her mother. Trina would give her the wisdom she needed regarding the situation.

"What's up, ma?"

"Girl, you gonna live a long time," Trina said. "I was just thinking about you."

"Really?"

"Yup, sure was. What's wrong with you? You sound sad."

"I'm stressed out."

"Well, you don't have that much more time left in there."

"It's not that," Cartier replied. "Bam came to see me and told me that she saw Monya and Jason chilling together the other day."

"Now, why would Bam come and tell you some shit

like that?"

"Well, it's true. Jason didn't deny it."

"Whether it's true or not, she didn't have any right telling you that news when you're in no position to do shit about it."

"Bam did what she was supposed to do. I hope that if you had news that you wouldn't keep it from me, because I'm a big girl and I can handle it."

"You think so, huh?" Trina responded. "Is that why I can tell you've been crying? And don't lie to me and say you weren't."

The tears began flowing again. "I'm so stressed out . . ." Cartier cried. "That nigga just hung up the telephone on me."

"Don't cry, Cartier," Trina tried comforting her. "Ain't no bitch worth your tears. Jason married you and not Monya, so you don't have anything to worry about."

"What are you saying? Jason and Monya are fucking around?"

"Nah, I ain't saying that. I seen them together too and I asked around and found out that she started getting work from Jason. That's all I know. But if she was trying to get with him she'd be a fool—"

"You damn right she'd be a fool, because I would beat the brakes off that bitch when I got out!"

"No you won't!" Trina shot back. "She want you to do that, so that you could end back up in jail serving out the remainder of your sentence. Now you listen and you listen good. You gonna do the opposite of what I do. You see I know how to get a man, but my track record will show you that I don't know how to keep him. If you want to lose Jason, then you keep getting on his nerves and showing your insecurities. If he is fucking with Monya and you going all crazy, then he's gonna feel that she has something over you and put her on a higher pedestal than you. You sit back, gather information, and if he's dirty, then you leave him. But only if that's what you really want.

"While you're incarcerated, I don't want you to ever mention her name again. I'll keep my ear to the streets and see what I hear. Don't go crazy over Monya. She lightweight. You my child. I birthed you. I know your shortcomings and attributes, and believe me when I tell you that Monya don't got shit over you. You were always the brains behind that crew and you can surely outsmart her. She's just jealous of you—always has been. Always will be.

"And when Jason comes on those trailer visits you make it worth his while. You keep planning y'all future. Keep your toes and fingernails painted and your hair smelling clean. You show him that you're a good, educated woman, and I'll keep my eyes on that low, classless bitch!"

Cartier agreed with her mother. And she liked the idea of never mentioning Monya's name again while she was locked up. She knew it would be hard and almost kill her not to, but it was for the best. She didn't want to believe those two could swing an episode. The thought was repulsive. Monya knew Jason was all that Cartier had. Why would she want to take that away, especially after

Cartier had given up her freedom for her? This was how she repaid her ... Cartier was mortified.

CHAPTER TWENTY-ONE

A Sticky Situation

While Cartier was busy planning her and Jason's future, she never fathomed the future would include a plus one so quickly. When the prison's RN told Cartier she was ten weeks pregnant, she didn't know how to take the news. As much as she wanted to be elated about having Jason's baby, the fact remained that their future together was sketchy at best. Additionally, she had all but given up on ever being released from prison. She was tired of being denied at every parole hearing and always for the same reason. But her prison record was stellar; not a blemish in almost seven years. Now she was pregnant, adding to her fear.

Cartier did as Trina said, and never mentioned Monya again. She even speculated that her mother knew more than she was saying, but she decided to leave it be, especially now. If Jason was fucking Monya, she was in prison and she couldn't control or worry about it. He could always explain away their sightings as business.

When Jason came to visit Cartier for their weekly visit, she was visibly sick. Jason took one look at her swollen breasts and flushed face, and knew instantly.

"Are you pregnant?" he asked.

Cartier shook her head. "I just found out yesterday."

"How far along are you?"

"I'm ten weeks . . . how do you feel about that?"

"What's done is done," Jason replied nonchalantly.

Cartier was immediately sullen. It was as if she could do no right. She spoke with trepidation. "Are you not happy?" Her eyes displayed layers of hurt and anguish. She felt as though her whole marriage was falling apart.

Sensing her mood, Jason immediately perked up. "Of course I'm happy! You're having my daughter. I want her to look just like you." He gave Cartier a wet kiss on her forehead.

Cartier exhaled and actually smiled. It was the first time she'd felt good about anything in weeks. She knew the marriage was a huge mistake, but what was done was done. She wanted her marriage to work, even if it meant putting up with shit while she was still in prison.

"How do you know I'm not having your son?" she asked.

"I hope it's a girl," he said again. "What about you? You want a girl or boy?"

"Jason, I'm so scared," she said with genuine fear in her voice.

"About what?"

"The board denying my parole again. What will happen to our baby?"

"Stop talking crazy," Jason replied. He could hear the

worry in her voice. "All you need to worry about is eating right and doing exercise, so you can deliver a healthy baby. They gonna let you up out of this joint. You done went to school and got your education. You're a model inmate. They only hit you with extra time to shake you up. But trust, you coming home soon."

Cartier was happy for the encouragement from Jason. That day he showed a glimpse of the old Jason she had grown to know and love.

Two weeks later, Cartier was astonished to see Monya sitting in the visiting room waiting for her. From a distance, Cartier could tell she looked slightly larger than she remembered, but surmised that they were no longer teenagers. Cartier didn't know how she should feel toward Monya. Were they still friends? Why had she abandoned her when she needed her the most? More importantly, was she sleeping with her husband. Cartier had so many questions going through her head, but the overwhelming feeling of joy superseded any ill feelings. Cartier actually missed and still loved Monya.

Monya didn't bother to stand as Cartier approached. Cartier sat down and the two faced each other. Cartier had a slight smile on her face, inviting conversation, but Monya's face was stone. Cartier quickly adopted Monya's mood.

"What are you doing here?" Cartier asked. "What do you want after all these years?"

"I came to talk to you," Monya replied in a serious tone. "Woman to woman. We got a few things that need to be sorted out."

Instantly, Cartier knew the rumors were true. She cut through the bullshit and was straight-up. "You really fucked my husband."

"Yup, I really did."

"You were my friend. I never thought dick would come between us."

"Jason isn't just a dick. He's a whole package who takes care of me very well."

"OK, he takes care of you. He takes care of me. We could go tit for tat, but the fact still remains, he married me and you're the angry mistress."

Monya glared, "Correction. I'm his baby momma. . . ."

All the color drained from Cartier's face. She wanted to wrap her hands around Monya's throat and just squeeze. Immediately, she knew the reason for the visit. Monya came to provoke her. She knew Cartier was coming home soon, and Jason had probably told her that Cartier was pregnant. Cartier knew Monya wasn't lying. She could see the pregnancy all over her face and body.

"Congratulations, join the club," Cartier facetiously stated.

"Unfortunately for you, I'm in the first baby momma's club in a class all by myself. I'm nearly five months."

"And you came all the way up here to tell me that? You should have saved your gas money. I already got the memo. Jason told me," Cartier lied.

Now it was Monya's turn to lose color in her face. Jason told her he didn't want Cartier to know until after she came home. Maybe he broke down and told her beforehand . . . Monya wasn't sure what to think.

Cartier had on a poker face, which irked Monya. She thought her ex-friend would lash out and try to assault her. Scream all types of obscenities at her and denounce their friendship. Instead, she got a gleeful, well informed, bitch.

"Did he also tell you that he's filing for a divorce and we're getting married?"

"No, he never mentioned that. But he did say that you were delusional and gave good head."

"Great head. I give *great* head." The two adversaries eyed each other with hatred. Cartier wanted to ask Monya what had happened between them. How could the two of them, being as close as sisters, sit a few inches apart and loathe each other? If she had a hundred years to ponder the question, she was sure she still wouldn't come up with a viable answer. The situation had ripped Cartier apart internally, but she sat stoically until Monya abruptly ended the visit.

"I hope you got what you came for," Cartier yelled.

Monya just tossed up her middle finger and never looked back.

Inside her cell, Cartier purged her soul. She cried a wealth of emotions. She was confused and felt betrayed. Out of all the women Jason could have slept with, why did he have to sleep with Monya? And to sleep with her unprotected and get her pregnant. Another woman was having her husband's first born. Cartier felt trapped in a bad soap opera, only this was her reality. And for the first time since taking the rap, she wished she would have let Monya rot in jail.

That night, Cartier didn't feel like calling anyone. The next night she felt the same way. She just sat in her cell feeling sorry for herself. When Jason came for his usual visit, she had to pull herself together. Half of her didn't expect him to come. The other half of her was glad that he hadn't chosen Monya over her. Cartier kept her poker face on as she went and had a seat. Jason was extremely jovial. His demeanor plucked Cartier's nerve. But she was determined to keep it together.

"How's my baby?" Jason asked.

"Which one?"

"What you mean?" Jason asked, immediately sensing this would not be a good visit. He knew Monya had visited Cartier. When Cartier didn't call, he knew he was in deep shit. He wrestled with whether or not he should lie, but thought against it. He wouldn't fully admit too much, but if he lied now when he was busted, only to be caught again in that same lie when Cartier came home, would be senseless.

"I mean, which baby are you asking about? Me or our baby," Cartier smiled and broke the ice. She knew he was ready for an argument, but she remembered what her mother told her. Don't make Monya an issue.

Jason's smile stretched half a mile. He was tickled she didn't want a confrontation.

"Both my babies. You and little Cee Cee."

"Little Cee Cee? You've already nicknamed our baby and you don't know what we're having?"

"You're having my baby girl, because I always get what I want."

Cartier wanted to say so badly that his behavior spoke louder than his words, but she chose to remain quiet. Although she spoke with a smile on her face, her eyes told her true feelings. They were dead and flat. The news about Jason and Monya sneaking around, coupled with the fact that Monya was carrying his firstborn, had truly killed her inside. The smarter part of her told her to never speak to Jason again and raise her baby on her own. The competitive side was saying, *It's on, bitch*. At the moment Cartier didn't know which side would win. Her head or her heart.

For a while, as the baby grew inside her, Cartier began to withdraw. The nurses had to warn her that she needed to eat to put on weight and nourish her child. Cartier tried, but it was too much. She couldn't pretend the situation with Jason and Monya wasn't affecting her. How long would she have to smile in his face and say nothing while he was out gallivanting with his mistress? He was her husband, and he'd already broken their vows and fucked up in the worst way.

Finally, Cartier couldn't take it anymore. When Jason came for their weekend trailer visit, she decided to have a heart-to-heart. They had a lot of things to talk about, mainly, who would keep the baby until she came home.

"I was thinking that my moms could take care of the baby," Jason said, "until you come home and we could take over."

"No, I don't really know your mother like that and I would feel better if my mother cared for our baby," Cartier countered.

"She already got two kids that she's struggling with," Jason said with attitude. "Besides, she be having them young niggas up there, ain't no telling what could happen to my baby. And I swear to God I will kill your mother if she ever let anything happen to my seed."

"Calm down," Cartier screamed. "You always losing your cool for no reason and acting like a kid. We're adults and we need to talk through situations. You yelling and acting all dumb with threats ain't gonna solve nothing."

"You right, but I needed to make my point," Jason defended himself.

"It's still a point whether you scream it or speak it."

"A'ight, I got you. You don't gotta keep drilling me. So, what's up? Who's gonna watch the baby?"

"I still would prefer my mother," Cartier began explaining. "I've already asked her and told her she couldn't have company until I got home and that you'd give her money per month to help her with expenses. She said she thought that was a good idea."

"Is that what you really want?"

"Yes."

"Then, that's what it is."

"Good. Now we need to talk about you and your mistress."

That angle must have blindsided Jason, because his eyes stretched opened wide and he began babbling. It had been four months since Monya told Cartier about being pregnant and she never mentioned it once. Monya was due any day now and Jason actually began to believe Cartier wouldn't ever mention it.

"What are you talking about *mistress*?" he replied.

"Jason, please don't insult my intelligence. Your mistress. Monya. Your baby momma. We need to discuss that situation."

Jason exhaled. "What about it?"

"Before I step foot out of this jailhouse, you better end it," Cartier commanded. "I don't care when it started or why, nor do I care about her baby. But you better shut it down. Completely. If I come home and you're still seeing her, I will make you both regret that you ever betrayed me."

Cartier's words were filled with venom and laced with lies. She cared about it all. A part of her wanted to know all the seedy details. Who came on to whom first? Did they laugh at her? Were they in love? Did she fuck Jason better? She wanted to know that and more, but she wouldn't dare ask.

"Cartier, you right. And I'm sorry that—"

"Nah, it ain't that easy," she interrupted. "I don't want to hear your sorrys. I don't want to hear you beg and plead, and walk around here feeling sorry for yourself. I don't want you to make promises you don't intend to keep. You did that once before when you promised that you'd never betray me. Remember that?

"So I will never discuss this with you again. As I said, you will end that relationship, or I will. One way or another, your relationship with Monya will end."

Cartier was thinking crazy thoughts in her head as she sounded off about her husband's infidelities. As she spoke those words, she felt enough anger and rage to actually kill one or both of them for hurting her heart. At that moment, when she said shut it down or I will, she truly meant it.

This time, Trina was the bearer of bad news. Monya had had a healthy baby boy that she named, Jason Nicholas Payne, Jr. He was a *junior*. The thought repulsed Cartier. She didn't think the situation could feel any worse, but the news of the baby's birth was just as bad. She realized why Jason was pumping his fist for a baby girl. He already knew he was having a baby boy. Cartier wondered how she could love someone so much who hurt her so deeply. She had such big plans for their family and although she hated to admit it, Monya and Jason Jr. would be in their lives forever.

Whatever little tricks Monya was plotting would forever affect Cartier. Play dates, child support, sleepovers, daycare, birthdays, all would be compromised, because of her husband's infidelities. No matter how she sliced it, Monya would always remind Cartier she had her husband's firstborn and son. That was a double slap in the face.

That night, Cartier prayed for God to give her the strength to forgive those who hurt her most and to take away the regret she felt for standing up for Monya. She knew if the regret and disdain she had for Monya persisted, then it would kill her internally. It was already slowly tearing her up inside. She needed to let go of the past and begin to think about her future.

CHAPTER TWENTY-TWO

Baby Makes Three

The sharp pain shooting through her backside was new for Cartier. She had never felt this bad before. The pain was worse than any menstrual cramp she'd ever experienced. She doubled over, clutching her stomach in agony. Within seconds, she was perspiring profusely. "H-h-help . . . helpppp!" she managed to scream through her ordeal.

Her lower body felt as if it were on fire. Everything throbbed as she experienced sensations that were foreign to her. She wished her mother were there to rub her back and tell her everything was going to be all right.

She was happy when the guards showed up at her cell and took her to the prison infirmary. Now there was only the staff nurse and doctor, and they didn't tell her soothing words to comfort her or massage her aching back.

"You're a young girl. Push!" the nurse shouted, annoyed at Cartier's constant cries and complaints.

"It hurts!" Cartier screamed through her pain.

The nurse was disgusted. She didn't have any remorse for the convicted murderer getting knocked up in prison.

"It's supposed to hurt. You're birthing a child!" the nurse stated in a nasty tone.

Cartier couldn't understand where the nurse's anger was coming from, but she felt the disconnect with the elderly nurse. As much pain as she was in, she wished she could smack the bitch a time or two.

Eight hours later, Cartier gave birth to a healthy six pounds, five ounces baby girl. When the doctor placed her in Cartier's arms, she felt love. Her life finally had meaning and purpose. Cartier never expected to feel so emotional. Immediately, she began crying large tears as she continuously kissed the newborn's bald head.

"What shall I name you?" she asked her baby. The infant began to move around in her mother's arms. Cartier was so exhausted. All she wanted to do was close her eyes and go to sleep, but she couldn't. She only had a few hours with her baby before they took her away and she didn't want to waste one minute. Her heavy eyelids just stared at the little pink figure. Cartier studied her small fingers and toes, and examined her ears and the skin peeling from her body. Cartier tried in vain to see whom the little girl resembled, but it was too soon.

"What shall I name you?" Cartier asked again. After tossing around a few names in her head like Armani, Mercedes, Porsche, Cartier realized she didn't want to keep the tradition her mother had started. She wanted her daughter to be a good girl and have a chance at making a decent living. She was determined not to give her a name that would prevent her from having a professional job. She had seen the *60 Minutes* and *48 Hours* shows on TV about black folks being discriminated against in the professional workplace, because their names sounded too ethnic. And Armani and Mercedes definitely sounded black. Cartier smiled at her baby and thought that those names sounded more like a female swinging from a dancer's pole every night than one making business deals in a corporate boardroom.

"I bequeath you Christian Jane Payne," Cartier said to her newborn. Cartier liked the name. She liked that name very much, and she hoped that one day little Christian Jane Payne would like her name as well. It seemed like only seconds had passed before the nurse came in to take Christian away. Instantly, a deep depression set in Cartier's heart. She cried as the nurse nearly ripped the baby from her arms.

"I want my baby!" Cartier cried as she balled up her fists and then exploded in a fit of rage. She had to be sedated, which was something Cartier needed. The pressure had been intense for most of her pregnancy. At times, she wasn't sure if she would make it. She damned Jason and Monya for putting the extra stress on her during her pregnancy.

But as Cartier drifted off, she had good thoughts on her mind. She had delivered a blessing named Christian Jane Payne. Internally, she smiled as sleep called her name, a peaceful sleep.

CHAPTER TWENTY-THREE

2005 – What's Really Hood?

They say prayer changes things, and Cartier finally believed. She had been praying for months to have a healthy baby and be released from prison. When she met the parole board and outlined why she should be released, she was more vocal than other times she had met the board. Her compelling argument was that she was a mother and she wanted and needed to raise her child, so her child would never call any prison in the United States home.

When Cartier received the news she had been paroled, she could hardly believe it. When she received the letter the next day, it stated that she would be going home in two weeks. She couldn't wait to be with her family and primarily, back with Christian, who was almost two months old. She knew Trina was doing a great job raising her, but she surmised a baby needs her mother.

The long walk to the telephone was more a glide or an eager strut on this beautiful day. It could be storming or in the midst of the worst blizzard in the history of New York, Cartier didn't care. This day was a beautiful day.

Her first call was to Trina. Her smile stretched from

ear to ear as she dialed the numbers. Of course, Trina was asleep at ten o'clock in the morning.

"Ma, wake up. I got good news," Cartier screamed in the phone.

"Well, go on and say it," Trina's voice dragged. "I'm tired as hell. These kids done kept me up all night crying and then Crissy woke me up at six o'clock this morning for her bottle and wouldn't go back to sleep. I just got her to get some sleep."

"You won't be going through that much longer, 'cause guess who's coming home?"

Trina sat straight up in bed. "See! What did I tell you? My baby is coming home . . . praise God."

Tears of joy began to run down each woman's face. Cartier couldn't wait to hold Christian again and rock her to sleep or lay in bed with her daughter wrapped in her arms.

"You did tell me that they would cut me loose . . . truthfully I had my doubts. But it don't matter anymore. From here on out I'm going to start thinking and being positive. Ma, I'm tired of living the street life. When I get out I'm going to make something out of myself."

"I know you will," Trina agreed. "If I can't be the role model then you will. These kids need someone to look up too. Here, wait, Prada wants to talk to you."

"Hi Cartier. I miss you," her sister stated.

"I miss you too."

"I was playing with the baby and she was smiling. She's my niece. Did you know that?"

"Of course I knew that. OK, be a good girl and I'll see you soon."

Cartier hung up and called Jason immediately. When it went to voicemail, her stomach churned. Her stomach always did that if she called him early in the morning and he didn't pick up. Her mind went wild thinking he was in bed with a bitch. But Cartier told herself that Jason was a man and he had needs, but when she came home all that shit was going to stop. Since she just received her walking papers, she knew her future was going to be a bright one. She wasn't going to settle for less.

On the morning of her release, Cartier didn't take any of the items she had accumulated in prison, except her family photos. She didn't even take the letters and cards, for fear it would be a reminder of her days being locked away. She styled her hair, which was now nearly touching her butt, in a tight ponytail and painted her fingernails and toes. Jason had purchased her a nice designer dress and high-heel stilettos. She looked and felt great. Cartier was ready to take on the world.

The gates of the prison opened and Jason, Christian, Trina, Prada, and Fendi sat perched in Jason's Yukon Denali. He'd come a long way from driving his used Nissan Pathfinder. Jason walked over, embraced Cartier warmly, and kissed her on her neck.

Cartier then ran to the car and grabbed Christian. The little baby just stared into her mother's eyes. Cartier hadn't seen her since her birth. She didn't want anyone to bring her daughter to the prison. She didn't ever want her daughter to step one foot inside a prison. Cartier inhaled Christian's scent and fell in love all over again. This was one of the happiest moments in her life.

"Get in, let's get out of here. Haven't you been here long enough?" Jason asked after Cartier had embraced everyone.

"You got that right," she replied. "Where are we going?"

"Where do you want to go?" Jason asked.

"I want to go and have a real dinner. Some place nice," Cartier suggested.

"OK, but we gotta do that later," Jason added. "I got some business I need to take care of. I'm going to drop y'all off at your mom's house and come back and pick you up later."

"Why are we going to my mom's? You can drop me and Christian off at your apartment," Cartier snapped, annoyed with the bullshit.

"I ain't got no problem with you going to my crib—"

"Our crib," Cartier corrected.

"You right. What's mine is yours. You're my wife and that was always the plan. But I thought you wanted to spend time with your family. I said I was going to come back and pick you up and take you home."

Cartier thought for a moment. She did miss Trina and her sisters and wanted to spend time with them.

"OK, that's cool. Drop us off at my mom's and come

back later. But I'm really stressed out."

"Stressed out about what?" Jason asked.

"You knew I was coming home. Today should have been family day. You got a wife and a daughter to think about."

"Wait a minute. I've been thinking about you and only you when other motherfuckers abandoned your ass for seven years. Don't come out here lecturing me!"

"Other motherfuckers abandoned me? Who? Who are you talking about? Because the only motherfucker that abandoned me was your fucking baby momma."

"Oh here we go . . ."

"You brought it up. What? You ain't got shit to say now, do you?"

"Look, y'all need to stop all that fussing in front of these kids. It's too early to be arguing like that," Trina stated.

Both Jason and Cartier adhered to Trina's demand. Cartier felt betrayed and Jason was fuming. For Cartier, this wasn't what she imagined her first day out of prison to be like. She chose to shut the fuck up and enjoy the ride back to Brooklyn.

Jason had bigger problems than what Cartier was trying to conjure up. In Jason's mind, he was going to handle something that would affect the both of them. Two months ago, he messed around and slept with a stripper without a condom. Now she was screaming she was pregnant and needed him to provide money for an abortion. Jason didn't have any issues about paying for the abortion. But he was going with her to the clinic to make sure she actually went through with it. He couldn't afford another headache and he definitely couldn't think about what would happen if Cartier found out.

He decided to change the subject. "So where are we going to eat tonight?" Jason asked. "Or do you want to cook?"

"Didn't I say I want to go out?" Cartier said with anger and angst in her voice. "I just did a seven-year bid and you're already ready to throw me in a house and lock me down."

Jason knew she was flipping because she was angry that they weren't going to be together. But he was prepared to make love to her all night and take away all her frustrations.

Jason truly loved Cartier and really wanted to make it work. He wanted a cooperative marriage, whereas they both loved and encouraged each other to be better people. He didn't like to see her sad or stressed out, but as much as he tried, he couldn't stop doing dumb things in the heat of the moment. Jason knew what it would take for Cartier to fully trust him again. He understood women and their values, and women needed to understand men.

Cartier was unique in Jason's eyes, which made her special to him. He knew he wasn't the first to be with Cartier sexually, but he didn't know the other guys she had slept with. Unlike Monya. She'd slayed the whole neighborhood and then spilled out into other boroughs. Monya would always be a jump off, unfortunately for him;

she would also always be his baby momma. Jason knew women valued emotional support and adulation from their men. He was prepared to do all of that for Cartier.

Cartier kissed Jason and bid him farewell. "Be safe," she called out to him as he rolled up his window. Before she could even turn around, she heard an unrecognizable voice call out her name. With Christian perched on her hip, she stared at her former friend, Lil Momma.

"Is that really you?" Lil Momma asked.

Cartier didn't know how to respond. Lil Momma was standing there grinning warmly, which was a far change from the ice-grill Cartier remembered. One part of her wanted to keep the bullshit going and scream on Lil Momma for many reasons. But it was the past and she wanted to leave the past where it belonged. She chose to be the bigger person.

Lil Momma detected Cartier's hesitation. "Just for the record, I told Monya that that was fucked up what she did messing around with Jason behind your back."

"Really?"

"Yup. You know I never had a problem speaking my mind. I don't hold my tongue for nobody and right is right—wrong is wrong."

Cartier shifted Christian to her other hip. "This is my little girl, Christian."

Lil Momma peered over and looked into the infant's face. "She's gorgeous."

The proud mother beamed, "Thank you. Take care of yourself."

"You too."

Cartier had mixed emotions about Lil Momma and the Cartel. She had just done seven years of her life in prison, because she thought she was the leader and had to stand on the front line. But those years made her realize she was young. Hell, they were all young—trying to play in a grown person's world. She had made a vow to create a better life for herself and her child, and hopefully, Jason. The past needed to stay in the past.

"Cartier?" Lil Momma called out.

"Yes?"

"Take my number. Call me sometimes. Maybe we could do lunch or something. Talk about old times."

Cartier shook her head rapidly. "No, thank you."

Cartier walked toward the building where Trina and the kids were waiting for her. Trina nodded. "You did good. I wouldn't take that bitch's number either! I woulda told her to kiss my black ass!"

They both burst out into laughter.

"Yeah, I wanted to say all of that, but she ain't worth it," Cartier stated.

After walking five flights to the apartment, Cartier was amazed that everything still looked the same, except her bedroom had become Prada and Fendi's room. Her full-sized bed was now replaced with two twin beds and a crib. Barney, Strawberry Shortcake, and Dora flooded the room. It was a little girl's heaven. Cartier kicked off her heels and sat down on the sofa.

"You hungry?" Trina asked.

Cartier shrugged her shoulders. "A little bit." She paused. Though she was home, she was still trying to get her bearings. "It feels so strange to be back here after all this time."

"This is your home too, so I don't ever want you to think that you gotta put up with bullshit. You will always have a roof over your head if things don't work out with you and Jason."

"See, Ma, that's just it," Cartier began to explain. "I want to be fully committed to my marriage. I want to raise our child in a two-parent home and give her everything I didn't have. Jason has a good heart. That's evident with him doing this bid with me. He just fucked up, as men do and we gotta live with that. If every time we get into an argument, I come running home to Mommy, then he'll start to get used to that and take my absence as a way to fuck up even more."

"Chile, where you learn all that from? 'Cause I know you ain't get that from me."

Cartier smiled slightly. "I read a few self-help books while in prison after the Monya scandal. I needed to deal with it before I came home, because I swear the old Cartier would have beat the brakes off that bitch!" As Cartier spoke, her voice elevated to a high pitch.

"See now that's the child I know and love," Trina said proudly.

Trina walked into her room and retrieved Cartier's stash. Over the years, Trina had dipped in it here and there, but she used discipline. She didn't want her daughter coming home to nothing and having to go back out on the streets to make a living. Trina reasoned that Cartier not having anything led to her life in the streets and that led to her losing seven years of freedom. At least now, she came home to something and that would keep her from her past lifestyle.

"Here,"Trina said and shoved the box in Cartier's hands. "It's about five large short and the jewelry's still there."

Cartier exhaled as she opened up the box and looked at the crisp money folded tightly together in rubber bands. All at once, a flood of emotions came rushing back. She was such a dictator back then. It was no wonder most of her friends turned their backs on her when she needed them most. She was so bossy and always talked about the code. The same code she didn't abide by and made her less of a friend and more of a tyrant. She was ashamed of herself and of what she'd done. Although she didn't push the knife into Donnie's back, it was equally her fault that he was dead.

As she looked at the money and jewelry, she realized she could always be angry for taking the weight for Monya, but one day she had to even leave that be. Of course, Monya wasn't an innocent victim. Cartier knew if the police knew the facts, she would have still gone to jail. But Monya would have shared a cell and probably got more time. Cartier shook her head. The madness of it all.

She glanced over at Christian sleeping peacefully and then thought about Jason. What if someone took his life? Or took Cartier's life? Their child would grow up without a mother or father. That was exactly what Cartier and Monya did to Donnie.

"I don't want this blood money," she began.

Trina spun around. "What you talking about you don't want it? What does that mean?"

"It means just that. I simply don't want it. All that money will do is destroy everything bought from it and I don't want any more dark days in my life."

"I done struggled, sacrificed, and put your needs before mine," Trina replied. "All these years so when you came out you'd have some money to start fresh, and now you're saying that I could have used that money to provide a better lifestyle for me and these kids?".

Cartier was quickly annoyed. Her chest heaved up and down from stress. The day wasn't going how she'd envisioned all these years.

"Ma, you acting as if that's your money," Cartier responded. "You didn't do one thing to earn one dollar in this here box. This is blood money and I don't have to explain anything about its contents to you. I'm giving the Cartel their share of the money and that's all I have to say about it."

"The Cartel?" Trina was mortified. Images of fur coats and crocodile shoes began flashing through her head. She could have thought of a million ways she could have fucked up that money. Rage was boiling over inside of her and she didn't know how to react. Surely, she didn't raise no fool, but Cartier was acting as if she'd gotten hit with the dumb branch of the tree and Trina didn't like it one bit.

"Yes, the Cartel," Cartier said. "This money is rightfully theirs as it is mine."

Trina thought for a second. Her daughter was serious and short of fighting her for the money. She knew it was a good as gone.

"But part of it is yours too, so why can't you give me your share? It ain't like we in here living in the lap of luxury. We need shit too. Besides, the Cartel got enough drug money. They probably won't even take your little funky offering. And also, I think that you're beefing by giving them that money. After all they've done to you it will seem to them that you're trying to buy back their friendship. I don't know about you, but my pride wouldn't allow me to feel like that."

"Look, Ma, don't try and play those Jedi mind tricks. Ain't nobody on this here earth going to turn down green money. I don't care how much they got in the stash."

"But, Cartier, I expected you to do something with this money," Trina said honestly. "I was hoping you'd invest it into something that would bring more money and in the long run if you were all right financially, then you make sure I was all right. If you give that money away what you gonna have? Nothing. You'll be starting from scratch."

"Ma, I got a husband who will support his family until I'm stable enough to contribute. That's all I need. And you're correct and I need you to rest in my words. Once I'm financially stable, you won't want for anything. I promise you that."

Trina shrugged. There wasn't anything she could

say. She turned around away from the box of money and retreated to the quiet of her bedroom. She was done talking. Mostly, she was done looking in Cartier's face. Trina couldn't face stupid. At the moment, Trina reasoned that Cartier's first name was now *Stupid*.

C artier had dozed off to sleep on her mother's sofa and was knocked out. She didn't even hear the doorbell ringing, although she was just inches away.

"Cartier, didn't you hear the door?" Trina screamed, who was still sour about the money issue.

"I would have answered it if I heard it," Cartier said as she stood up, stretched, and wiped the cold out of her eyes. She knew Trina was still bitter and she wasn't about to feed into her mother's drama. She looked out the window and it was pitch dark. It felt late. Jason came strolling through as if it wasn't nearly eleven o'clock at night. Once Cartier realized the time, her nerves were irked, but she refused to curse his silly ass out. She decided that they would talk about it like adults once they were alone.

"What's up, baby?" Jason asked and pecked Cartier on her cheek. "I'm sorry I'm late. I got caught up in so much stuff tonight, you wouldn't believe it."

Cartier slowly shook her head up and down. "That's cool. Let me go and get Christian and then I'm ready." Cartier began packing up a few things, including the money in a small duffle bag, scooped up Christian, kissed Trina, and they were off.

Once safely inside the confines of his Yukon, Cartier started off slowly.

"I understand that all of this is new to you and that you're not used to having a curfew. But your daughter shouldn't be out here almost midnight waiting on her father to come and pick her up. Whatever you had to do could have waited until tomorrow. I'm not even going to throw my feelings in the mix."

"You right. I'm sorry. It won't happen again."

"Where were you?" she surprisingly asked.

"Huh?" Jason was clearly caught off guard by the question.

Cartier cut her eyes. She didn't want to revert to her old ways. She had to call on all her strength not to knock Jason upside his head. Nor did she want to mention the freshly implanted scratch running down the side of his face to his throat. No doubt a bitch.

"I said, where were you?" she asked again.

"Oh, I had some running around to do and money to pick up," he lied. "You know, shit like that."

"I thought you told me that once I came home that you were leaving the game and going legit."

"I'm working on that. I just got some more paper to stack so that you and the baby don't want for nothing."

"I think me and Christian will have more than enough as long as you're in our lives."

"What do you mean by that?"

"I'm just saying that if you stop doing what you're doing and come home at a decent hour every night, then that's all we'll need."

"Awww, that ain't shit. I can do that," he bolstered.

"I hope so," Cartier replied and touched the side of his face. She loved him so much but in her gut there was this eerie feeling of dread and doom lingering and she couldn't explain it away.

"Listen, I went to the jeweler today to pick you out a three carat, emerald cut ring."

"Why would you do that?" she asked.

"Because I want to replace that gold band you got on. My wife needs bling."

"I love my gold band," Cartier began. "You know what. Don't buy me that ring although I love you for wanting to do that for me. But I want a house. You can use the money you were going to use on my ring and buy us a house. Use that money as a down payment. I want Christian to have a backyard. That's always been my dream."

"You sure, because in a couple of months I'll be able to do both," Jason replied matter-of-factly.

"You mean a couple more months in the game," Cartier replied as she looked at him. "Stop it, Jason. Let's stick to our plans and not veer off. I want the house."

"OK, OK . . . geez . . . you're so bossy."

"That's what you love about me."

"You know it."

That night, after they made love, Cartier asked Jason about the scratch on his face.

"I was slap boxing with Kareem. That nigga is like a

bitch with his long nails. I told him that you were going to flip."

Cartier said nothing. She didn't believe one word of his alibi, but instead of telling him that, she snuggled up closer under his strong arms and went to sleep. No sense in arguing about something she couldn't prove.

CHAPTER TWENTY-FOUR

Reap What You Sow

The next day, Cartier got up early, made breakfast, and thought they'd spend the day together.

"I promise I will be back before noon," the excuse escaped Jason's lips. "And we all gonna spend the next few days together doing nothing but being a family and celebrating that you're home."

Cartier was heated. "Jason, I'm not going to tolerate this too much longer!" She sat at the table and watched Jason wolf down his breakfast in an attempt to get out of the apartment. She realized breaking him in and making a married man out of him was going to be tougher than she thought.

"Ma, calm down. I just said you ain't gonna have to take me handling my business too much longer." He kissed her lips. "I promise I'll be back before you know it."

When Jason embraced Cartier, they began to passionately kiss. Instantly, she felt moist and wanted to make love. Her hand went down to his jeans and she realized they had something in common. His dick was brick hard. Jason ushered Cartier to the kitchen table and sat her at the edge, positioning himself between her thighs. Quickly, he pulled her panties to the side and began to apply pressure against her moist, warm cave. Cartier began to rock her hips, inch-by-inch he opened her up until he had a good rhythm and his stroke was slow and steady.

"Fuck this pussy, baby . . ." Cartier purred into his ear as he leaned down and began to suck her nipples. As Jason sped up and the feeling began to intensify, Christian began to cry. They tried in vain to ignore her, but her crying persisted and eventually they stopped.

"Damn, see how spoiled she is?" Jason joked as he backed away and began to zip up his pants. "She don't want us to make another baby in here."

Cartier laughed and went to get Christian.

"A'ight, I'm out."

Cartier called a car service to take her and Christian back to her old neighborhood. She wanted to handle her business and get on with life. To move forward she had to go back to her past.

Her first stop was Janet's house. She knew Monya no longer lived there, but this was more convenient and she didn't want to beef with Monya. If she saw Monya, there was no telling what would transpire. She was trying to prevent that. She had already decided to give Janet Monya's share to give to her.

Cartier tapped on the door until she heard a familiar voice. It was Janet.

"Oh my gosh, Cartier. What a pleasant surprise," Janet clutched her chest, "And you brought the baby by to see me."

"Janet, I didn't bring Christian here to see you. If you wanted to see her you could have walked down to my mother's—"

"Cartier, don't get sassy," Janet snapped. "I don't have shit to do with what's going on with you and Monya."

Ignoring her comment, Cartier completed what she came to do. "Would you make sure she gets this? She'll know what this is about." Cartier handed Janet a small paper bag with nine thousand dollars and Donnie's Rolex and ring. After handing over the package, she left.

Next, she went to Shanine, who was equally surprised to see her former friend.

"What are you doing here?" Shanine asked.

"I won't be long. Here." Cartier shoved the bag containing nine thousand dollars in her hand.

"What's this?"

"Your half of our drug empire," Cartier answered.

"What?"

Cartier didn't stay long enough to explain. She still had two more stops, and Christian was beginning to get cranky. Cartier decided against walking up the steps to Lil Momma's. Instead, she rang the bell and told her to come downstairs.

Lil Momma wasn't sure what the unexpected visit was about. From the icy greeting she'd gotten from Cartier only days ago, she decided to be prepared for the worst.

She went to her top drawer and pulled out her razor and tucked it in her back pocket. She also tied up her sneakers tightly and put on a hoodie sweatshirt. She couldn't lie to herself and not admit that she was scared shitless. She was. Out of the whole Cartel, Cartier was the nicest with her hands, and Lil Momma knew she wasn't no match for her adversary. But Lil Momma was hardly a punk. Cartier bled just like she did, and no matter what, she could hold her own in a fight.

With her heart beating with trepidation as she jogged down the stairs, she was relieved to see Cartier holding Christian in her arms. Lil Momma's face softened.

"Hey," Lil Momma said as she stepped out onto the stoop.

"This is for you," Cartier handed her the bag. "It's your share of the Cartel money."

Lil Momma opened up the bag and peered down at the contents.

"We always thought that you'd spent this money," Lil Momma replied.

"Well, you thought wrong."

Cartier turned and jogged down the steps and Lil Momma called to her, "Why now?"

Cartier tuned her out. Methodically, she was washing her hands of her former crew and felt she certainly didn't owe anyone any answers. She'd made mistakes in the past; now she was rectifying them. No need to dissect who, what, and why.

Last, Cartier went to see Bam. She'd been the only

one out of the crew who remained loyal after all was said and done. Bam's eyes lit up as she peered down at the money.

"Cartier, you don't know how much this will help me. I'm swimming in credit card bills and college tuition. This money will be put to good use."

"I know it will," Cartier replied. "I'm so proud of you."

"And I admire you," Bam said. "Always have and always will."

The two embraced and then Cartier jetted home. If Jason's promise was solid, he'd be back home in less than an hour. Then they could finally begin making preparations for moving forward.

CHAPTER TWENTY-FIVE

2007 – Baby Momma Drama

The still summer morning was deceptive in the Payne household. Cartier got out of bed first and opened the blinds in their modest bedroom. The sun came beaming inside and blinded Jason.

"Ma, close those curtains," Jason moaned as he turned over and put the covers on his head.

"Nope. It's time to get up. You know Christian will be in here any moment asking about Dorney Park."

Jason laughed because he knew Cartier was right. Although Christian wasn't Jason's only child, she was the couple's only child; therefore, she was spoiled rotten.

"That little girl looks just like me," Jason said and grinned. Christian had his heart wrapped around her small fingers.

"So you say," Cartier replied and playfully threw a sock at him.

As Cartier went downstairs to prepare breakfast, Jason took that opportunity to turn on his cell phone. Immediately, it began alerting him that he had fourteen messages. He punched in his security code and began to listen. When he heard Monya's voice, he hit the delete button. He wasn't in the mood for her bullshit and didn't want any stress. Today was family day, and he wasn't about to allow Monya to ruin it with her antics.

Monya was the quintessential baby momma who brought drama by the boatload. It was her goal in life to make his life miserable. The only time she was somewhat happy was when Jason was sticking dick to her. When he was with her she was sweet as candy, but the moment he got up to leave to come home to Cartier, the bullshit started. She was never going to accept that he wasn't leaving Cartier.

Message after message, he hit the delete button. Every message was from his psycho chick—Monya. He knew he should have let her go a long time ago as he promised himself and Cartier he would. But she was a stone cold freak. Easily, the biggest freak he had ever been with. Monya could maneuver her legs in ways that no other woman could. She was extremely flexible and it turned him on. The only thing he didn't like about sexing her was she tried too hard to please him. She moaned too loud, sucked his dick too hard, and practically would do anything without provocation. If she wanted to eat his asshole, then she did it in a heartbeat—all without any prompting on his part. But her coochie had a lot of mileage on it. Her name rang bells throughout New York, and up and down I-95. And that wasn't a good look. Not a good look at all.

Jason finally jumped up and hopped in the shower.

As he lathered his body he thought about how his life was evolving. He opened a hand car wash and was turning a profit. It was in a prime location, Kings Highway in Brooklyn, and the most elite cars came through. He made the mortgage payments on time and was happy his honest work was affording him and his family a privileged lifestyle.

When he went downstairs to breakfast, Christian was already sitting in her high chair. Her round face was covered in bacon grease and scrambled eggs. His face always lit up at the sight of her.

"Give Daddy a kiss."

Immediately, Christian puckered up her small lips and said, "Mummm."

"Muah," he kissed her back.

"You two need to stop," Cartier joked. "Y'all love each other more than y'all love me."

Jason slapped her on her ass. "You my baby too. Give Daddy a kiss."

When the two kissed each other, Christian thought it was funny. She began laughing and clapped her hands. "Do it again," she cheered.

The young couple indulged their toddler and kissed again.

After breakfast, Cartier and Christian got dressed as Jason ducked phone calls from Monya. His stress level was nearing its limit.

"This is a stupid bitch," he said as he hit the *ignore* button on his cell. "She know a nigga is at home chilling."

Jason was talking out loud he was so frustrated with her antics. Finally, after ignoring thirty or more consecutive calls, he went inside the garage and answered.

"What the fuck you want?" he said heatedly.

"Why haven't you returned any of my calls?" Monya asked, equally heated.

"Yo, I'm not gonna keep going through this bullshit. You know I'm fucking home with my wif—"

Jason couldn't even get the word out before Monya went berserk. She always loathed it when he said the word *wife*. It was a pet peeve for her and the feeling was unsettling. She began a succession of inaudible words and Jason hung up. He couldn't take the foolishness. He turned his phone back off and took his family to Dorney Park.

On the ride home, he and Cartier began making plans about expanding their bedroom into a master suite.

"I think we could hire a contractor and get it done for around ten grand," Jason encouraged.

"I hope so, because I would really like a larger bedroom with a bathroom in it."

"And don't forget your walk-in closet. I know all ladies want a walk-in closet." Jason cut his eyes to the right and he could see Cartier grinning. "What you smiling about?"

"The house," she replied. "Our house and the upgrades we're going to do. After we do our bedroom, then we should do the kitchen and get all stainless steel appliances and granite countertops."

"Slow your role, spanky," Jason joked. "Put the brakes on. We gotta take this one step at a time."

"I know."

"Besides, the market ain't that great to be upgrading too much."

"But, Jason, it will be a good investment in the long run," she said convincingly. "And I want to stay here in our house forever. We live in a great community. We got our house at a steal and we have so much space in our backyard to continue to expand. I think upgrading could never be a bad idea. We just gotta make sure that the contractors are reputable."

"I will kill a motherfucker if they ever tried to take my money and fuck me—"

"I know that ain't Monya?" Cartier said in a pissed off tone, as she spotted a familiar looking car in their driveway—Monya's car.

"What the fuck that bitch doing here?" Jason said, not particularly speaking to Cartier.

"You tell me!" Cartier raised her voice. "How the fuck she know where we live?"

"I don't fucking know. I swear to God I didn't tell her," Jason tried explaining.

They both observed Monya perched outside of their house sitting on their stoop with her son, Jason Jr.

Cartier was so angry she couldn't see straight. She hopped out of the passenger's seat and did a beeline toward Monya, who was unfazed by the glare in her former friend's eyes.

"Yo, what the fuck you doing here in front of my house?" Cartier screamed.

Monya ignored the irate and screaming Cartier and directed her attention to Jason.

"Your son is missing his father," she said. "Spend time with him." Those were her last words as she left Jason Jr. sitting perched on the front steps with his thumb stuck firmly in his mouth.

When he saw his mother leaving without him, he burst into tears. His fat cheeks were stained with tears as his small hands reached out to a mother who wasn't affected by his outburst.

"Monya! Monya! Where the fuck you going?" Jason called out to Monya as he picked up his son. "This is some bullshit you on."

"Let that silly bitch keep walking," Cartier spat. She was glad Monya didn't utter one disrespectful word her way. She knew she would be locked up for whipping her ass. For years, Cartier wanted to kick Monya's ass, but she knew Monya didn't play fair. The moment the fight was over, Cartier was certain Monya would have her arrested.

"What's wrong with her? I'm telling you she's crazy," Jason shook his head. He didn't know what Monya was trying to pull but he didn't like it one bit.

Cartier went to the car and picked up Christian, who thankfully had slept through the drama. She couldn't wait to put the kids down to sleep, because she had some issues with Jason. Her gut was hardly ever wrong when it came to him, and this situation didn't sit well with her.

Finally, they were alone. Jason plopped down on the sofa, thinking everything was sweet, when Cartier let him have it.

"You still fucking Monya?" she asked, as her nose flared and her eyes shot fire.

"What are you talking about?" Jason asked innocently.

"I asked you a simple question. In fact, it's so simple it can be answered with a simple yes or no. Are you still fucking Monya?" Cartier was persistent.

"Nah, I'm ain't fucking with her. I swear on Cee Cee," Jason lied.

"No!" Cartier screamed. "Not are you fucking *with* her, but are you *fucking* her. Are you sticking your penis in Monya? I'm not talking about dinner and a movie."

"You can use all the word semantics you like, but I already answered that question. I said no. Now leave me alone with that bullshit and get out of my face—"

Cartier hauled off and slapped Jason so hard and swift that he was visibly stunned. He couldn't react like he would have expected himself to.

"I don't know who the fuck you think you talking to, but if I ever find out that you're still fucking her after all this time, I promise you I'm taking Christian and we're leaving for good."

"You ain't taking my baby nowhere!" Jason jumped up and got in Cartier's face.

"You heard what the fuck I said. Let me find out that y'all two are still fucking around and not only will I stomp a mud hole in that tramp, but I will cut you!" Cartier threatened. "And then I will still take Christian and leave your trifling ass!"

She walked away, not saying shit else to him.

CHAPTER TWENTY-SIX

Say Word?

Jason stood on the corner of his old stomping grounds, Marcy and Nostrand Avenue, smoking a cigarette down to the butt. The sun was scorching hot and it wasn't even noon. His man, Wonderful, stood next to him, listening to him cry a river. Every couple of minutes, Wonderful would nod his head in agreement and say, "True . . . true." Whether the statement was actually true or not was not relevant. Wonderful had been down the same path so many times before and was glad it was someone else who would be losing sleep tonight.

The white tee Jason had on was soaked in sweat. He took it off and exposed a trail of soft baby hair that lay smoothly on top of his six-pack. The ladies loved his body. He had bulging biceps and triceps, broad shoulders, and muscular legs. Those attributes, coupled with his handsome face and fat pockets, kept him on the top ten lists of all freaks.

"Yo, I feel like smashing my fist through her fucking face," he complained.

"Then do that shit," Wonderful encouraged.

"Nah, I don't be hitting on any women, you know. I got a daughter and that shit is foul. I wish a nigga would put his hands on my seed."

"True . . . true . . ."

"I'm the stupidest motherfucker walking this earth to fall for the okey-doke. 'I'm on the pill,' that bitch said. Now why in the fuck would I believe a trifling whore who I know want to break up what me and my wife got? Huh? Because I'm a stupid motherfucker!" Jason's voice began to elevate higher each time he called himself *stupid*.

"I hear you."

"But check it," Jason paused to wipe the sweat from his forehead, "when she gets here I'm going to tell her straight up that if she has this baby, then it's a fucking wrap between us. No more fucking. No more sneak trips. No more Prada bags and Gucci shoes. It's a fucking wrap."

"Yo, dead her, son," Wonderful advised, "there plenty other bitches out here. I don't know why you kept fucking with her."

"Because I liked fucking with her," Jason explained. "It's that simple."

"True . . . true . . . I feel you."

"And not for nothing. This baby probably ain't even mines. This shit could be Tupac fucking Shakur's for all I know," Jason joked, clowning himself. "You know how she gets down!"

"Word, son, I wouldn't take shorty's word on that one. Her resume is longer than my dick."

"I know. But remember I didn't want to believe that

she was carrying my son and I had her ass take a blood test and it came back that I was guilty as charged! I don't even want it to get that far with blood tests and shit. I just want her to straight up get rid of it."

Wonderful listened until he saw the white BMW pull up to the curb. Monya had on a pair of sun shades and lip gloss, but Wonderful could see her smile a mile away. Her hair was hanging straight, past her shoulders, and she had an I-think-I'm-cute expression plastered on her face.

"Here this bitch finally go," Jason tossed his cigarette to the ground. "A'ight, check you later. Let me go handle my business."

"Be easy, son. One."

"One."

Jason got in on the passenger's side, but not before he coughed up a wad of saliva and spit it on the ground. That was exactly how Monya was making him feel.

"Yo, turn down your music," he snapped. Monya had vintage Mary J. Blige blaring in the car.

"Nigga, please," Monya began. "You better lose the attitude if you know what's really good. Or shall I say what's really hood, 'cause I ain't the bitch to be going for your bullshit."

"You sound so fucking corny with your little slogans and shit," Jason responded. "Don't nobody got time for all of that. You ain't tough, Monya. And the moment you realize that the better off you'll be."

"Ask your girl how fucking tough I am," she retorted.

"My wife. Ask my wife? Why? She know you soft like

butter. Cartier ain't gonna say nothing different."

"Oh, you think so, huh?"

"I know so and if I even mentioned your name in our household, she would come and break your bony ass in half."

"You think I fear your bitch? You got me mixed up. I've been letting her fake ass get wreck off the work I put in for years! Everyone in the hood all shook like Cartier is a convicted murderer. That's only on paper. She ain't murder shit. All she can kill is a roach."

"What the fuck you beefin' 'bout?" Jason asked. "If Cartier didn't handle Donnie, then who did? You? Bam? Shanine? Lil Momma? Don't make me laugh."

"I took that trick's life and motherfuckers better start recognizing!" Monya shouted.

"Come again?"

"Nah, don't get stuck on stupid now," Monya replied. "You heard me. That's my work, and that lying bitch took seven years of your life while you were running up there to see her do time for a murder she ain't commit. And she locked you down with her lies. Your stupid ass is so dumb. You married a fraud."

Jason took in what Monya was saying and he didn't like it one bit. But not for the reasons Monya thought he would be angry. He was pissed at himself for holding down a low-life, skeezer bitch like Monya. How could he have been so stupid and hurt his wife the way he did by ever fucking with her in the first place? In that instant, his love for Cartier tripled and he didn't think he could love her more than he already did. Monya's mouth was still running, praising herself for murdering Donnie and belittling Cartier. He wanted to choke the life out of Monya for putting Cartier through all that she had endured. And yet, he couldn't understand her gripe.

Why had she turned on Cartier? The only true friend she had. Then he reversed the question and asked himself why had *he* turned on Cartier? They were both losers. Jason wanted to tell Monya how he truly felt, but her unexpected pregnancy was more important. That second baby would threaten to tear their marriage apart if Cartier were to find out. Jason was here to convince Monya to have an abortion and he didn't want to go off on another tangent.

"Look, what went down with you and Donnie is between y'all. I'm here to talk about this baby that I know ain't mine."

"You're a liar."

"Am I? How the fuck you get caught out there when you said you were on birth control? You set me up."

"Ain't nobody set shit up."

"You need to get off my dick and go and find another scapegoat, because I ain't the one."

"You don't do shit for your son—"

"OK, then why are you insisting on having this baby? Get an abortion and we can continue to fuck around."

"Continue to fuck around? You really think you got a gold-plated dick, don't you? After this baby I'm done with you. It's over."

"After this baby?" The realization that Monya was going to keep the baby, mixed with the fact that Cartier had held her down, put Jason in a foul mood.

"Yes, I'm having my baby," Monya stated bluntly. "You know I don't believe in abortions."

"Who the fuck you think you talking to? Tell a new nigga that bullshit. You done flushed more seeds than the toilet bowl man. If you want to have this baby, I'm telling you right now that you better erase my number. From here on out, you as good as dead to me. I'ma treat you like a dog on the street. I give you my word on that one."

"A dog, huh?" Monya pulled out her cell and began to dial numbers. Immediately, Jason got nervous and reached for her phone, but she pulled away. "Hello, Cartier—"

The knuckle slap was hard and swift. Monya's head snapped back and the telephone went flying to the car floor. Although he hated to hit a girl, in his eyes, Monya was the exception.

"You're too disrespectful!" Jason yelled. "Call my wife again and I promise you, you'll get worse than that! I will beat the life out of you! Do you hear me? You play too much."

"Fuck you! And fuck your bitch! I'm having this baby, motherfucker!" Monya went ballistic. She was screaming uncontrollably. In her eyes, she'd just gotten beat down over another broad, and she didn't like that one bit. She didn't consider that her act had provoked the events. "Get the fuck out my car!"

Jason obliged and slammed the car door. All he knew

was Monya better not call Cartier with the grim news. She'd better not follow through on her threat.

By three that afternoon, Jason had already drunk four Corona beers and ended up on 48th Street, the diamond district. He never did buy Cartier the wedding ring she deserved. He figured he had about seven months to make his marriage bulletproof before Cartier found out about the new baby. And there wasn't any time like the present to erase all his scandals.

The first thing he did was change his cell phone number. That would take effect within twenty-four hours. Next was the purchase of a huge diamond ring for Cartier. Lastly, he was going to take her on a romantic getaway, just the two of them.

"How about this one?" Manny, his jeweler pulled out a five-carat, VVS diamond setting that cost eighty-five thousand.

Not that Jason didn't have that amount of money, but he only wanted to spend about half that amount—maybe fifty thousand tops. Besides, he still had a lot of other things he wanted to do for Cartier. He wanted to continue upgrading their house and buy her a new car. It wasn't fair that Monya was parading around in a BMW and Cartier was riding American. Although Monya had hustled to get her own ride, Cartier was married to a hustler, so he needed to let motherfuckers know what time it was.

"That's a beauty, but my limit is fifty large," Jason responded. "Show me something around that price and not no bullshit Manny. Don't try to play me."

"You're one of my best customers," Manny replied. "Why would I disrespect you?"

Manny was slick and if he could pull the wool over somebody's head—he would. That was how he stayed in business. He'd just bought a beauty of a diamond for eighteen thousand that would appraise for double. He'd sell that to Jason for forty-five thousand and he was almost certain Jason would be pleased.

"I got just the perfect ring for your wife." Manny turned around and walked to the safe. He kneeled down and rifled through a few manila envelopes before settling on a small one with writing in red ink. He went in, retrieved the ring, and watched the expression on Jason's face.

"Damn, I like this, but how much?" Jason asked.

"Five grand under your max. At forty five thousand it's a steal. It's appraised for sixty."

"So, if I tell people I paid sixty grand for it, they'll believe me?"

"If they know about diamonds they will."

Jason shook his head and sealed the deal.

On his way home, Jason stopped at a local florist. Ronald, the owner, would always call him when they were about to discount the flowers and give Jason a good deal. Almost every week he bought Cartier roses or some beautiful arrangement. This week, there wasn't a discount, but he knew she would love the long-stemmed roses.

Jason was shocked to see the whole house was completely darkened. There wasn't one light on, nor was

Cartier's car in the driveway. He was good at sensing trouble. Wherever Cartier went, she would call him and let him know. That was proper protocol, especially when it involved taking Christian. When he called her cell phone it went straight to voicemail. He called several times later, and each time, directly to voicemail.

He called Monya.

"Did you fucking call my wife?" he angrily asked.

"Damn nigga, get off my shit," Monya replied. "If you want some pussy tonight come through, but don't be calling here with your stupid accusations."

"Did you call my wife, bitch?" Jason yelled. "Yes or no?"

"I didn't call Cartier yet. But don't get too comfortable, because by this time tomorrow, she will know!"

"Go ahead with that dumb shit you talking."

Jason hung up and felt relieved. He thought Monya was brazen enough to go along with her threat. Next, he called Trina.

"Hey, is Cartier there?" he asked when Trina answered.

"No," Trina snapped.

Not noticing the animosity in her voice, he continued. "Do you know where she is, because I'm home and I can't find her?"

"If she's not home, then that's not where she wants to be."

"What do you mean by that?" Jason asked.

"Jason, I don't got time to teach a grown man how to be just that—a grown man. I gotta go," Trina said dismissively and hung up.

Jason was heated. He didn't like riddles nor did he understand why he detected sarcasm in Trina's voice or where the hell Cartier and Christian were. And since Monya claimed she didn't call Cartier—which he didn't know if he should believe her or not—he decided to go by the one friend that she still had—Bam.

It was pretty late when Jason arrived on the block. He looked to see if Cartier's car was parked out front, but it wasn't. He began to panic. If he didn't find her soon, then he was going to the police and report her missing. As he approached Bam's door he could hear voices. Distinct and clear. It was Cartier and Bam, only he couldn't make out what they were saying. He felt mixed emotions: relief and anger. Why did she have her phone off all day and why was she at Bam's this time of night? He decided to ask those exact questions.

Jason knocked heavily on the front door. He postured and stuffed his hands deeply inside his pockets. The footsteps were faint and became increasingly heavier as they drew closer. The figure looked apprehensively through the peephole and then retreated. Again, he heard voices, now hushed and muffled.

He knocked again. And waited. Finally, his pressure was up. He began to bang on the door yelling out to Cartier. When there still wasn't any answer, he began to kick. The flimsy door began to give way on its hinges before it was finally flung open by a sour-faced Cartier.

She had her hands perched on her hips and a menacing look in her eyes.

Before Jason could open his mouth and begin cursing her out for making him worry, she charged him with all her strength, and began kicking and punching him all over his upper and lower body.

"I heard you! I heard all of it!" she kept repeating as he desperately tried to block each blow.

"Stop it," Jason pleaded. "S-s-stop!"

Cartier was relentless. She was emotionally drained and humiliated. She couldn't believe that her husband would make a fool out of her for the second time with the same bitch.

"You need to be castrated," she cried as she released her fury.

Jason had no idea what was going on. It was all happening too quickly. Finally, he was able to grab both her hands and restrain her. He grabbed her in a bear hug and wouldn't let her go.

In all the commotion, Bam never came out to intervene.

The young couple were sweating profusely and breathing heavily. Eventually, Jason got the situation under control.

"Ma, what did I do now?" he asked.

Cartier collapsed on the ground overflowing in tears. Her heavy weight pulled Jason down with her.

"How could you do this to me again?" she shrieked.

"What . . . you gotta tell me what I've done."

"I heard you today . . . on the phone . . . when Monya called me. I heard you two arguing about her having your baby and getting an abortion. You promised me that it was over."

Jason's heart began to beat fast. When he knocked the phone out of Monya's hand, it must have still been on. His first and only reaction was to lie.

"What are you talking about? That wasn't me."

Cartier cried even harder. She knew he was lying to her. She could hear the panic in his voice. She felt defeated. One part of her wanted to hear the lie, just so the pain would stop. But she knew she had to be a woman and deal with a situation she didn't have any input on creating.

"Just leave," she finally said.

"What? I'm not leaving you—"

"You better leave!" Cartier screamed like a crazy woman in a high pitched, unrecognizable voice.

Jason was visibly shaken. He'd never seen his wife like this.

The pain cut Cartier deeply. She looked like a helpless, wounded animal. He saw her pain first hand, up close and personal.

Jason felt so guilty for putting his wife through the torture and torment. He couldn't even think about what he'd do if he ever found out Cartier was with another man. Not only did Cartier find out about his indiscretions, but she'd have to constantly look in the face of two children as a reminder. She was more woman than he was man. He decided to go home and give her space. He wanted to go in and see Christian, but considering Cartier's state, he thought against it.

He tapped on the door and asked Bam to take her inside. Bam didn't even try to hide her roll of the eyes, but he knew he deserved the disrespect.

CHAPTER TWENTY-SEVEN

Hush

It was the first day of September, and Cartier was tired of playing the fool. She was tired of being Ms. Nice Bitch. She was going to beat the shit out of Monya and risk her freedom. Pounding on Monya's fragile body was going to be worth any time she would spend behind bars.

She sat parked three cars behind Jason's SUV and waited. She was no longer angry that Jason and Monya were still fucking. The moment she forgave Jason was the same moment he'd made the decision that he could get away with everything. It's no different than when a woman is being abused and the abuser says he's sorry. The moment she forgives him usually is the same moment he knows he'll hit her again.

Today, Monya would get her ass whipped for messing with another woman's man. For all Cartier cared Monya and Jason could fuck like rabbits. She was no longer felt emotionally attached to Jason.

Truth be told, Cartier fell in love with Jason out of loyalty. He stood by her when she did her bid, while brothas like Ryan kicked her to the curb. As she grew older, she knew she was wrong. And for that, she was pissed at herself. It took prison for her to realize the error of her ways. She made plans sitting in that eight-by-six cell every day for seven years. Now she was pissed at herself, because she actually could have done better by herself, without Jason weighing her down.

Three hours later, Cartier was still waiting. She didn't even care, because the more she sat, the more she thought about what she wanted to do to Monya. She sat back and remembered when they were younger, when she was the confrontational one. She was always quick to argue or fight. It was Monya who shied away from altercations. She always had to be pushed to argue or fight. Now, their roles were reversed.

Cartier really did her best to avoid getting into fights, and it seemed that fighting was all Monya wanted to do. Cartier knew what happened. Monya had smelled Donnie's blood. It had made her power hungry. She thought she was invincible, the *baddest bitch* on the block. Killing had a way of doing that to a person ... giving them that false bravado.

Eventually, Jason staggered out of Monya's apartment building, oblivious that he was being watched. He was so pathetic that Cartier actually despised him. She hated him so much she wanted him dead and she'd spit on his grave. But that was only wishful thinking. Sometimes a man can make you hate the ground they walk on, loathe the air they breathe, and actually wish death on them.

Cartier hated that Jason made her feel that way. She

had already planned her future, and they included a new start with her and Christian only. Jason wasn't and wouldn't be in her plans, so she told herself. But everything started after she handled her present business—beating the shit out of Monya.

If there was one thing Cartier knew for sure, it was that Monya would definitely open the door when she knocked. She knew Monya wouldn't play the punk, so she'd open up the door popping shit. And just as if she wrote the words to her own book, Monya opened the door.

"What the fuck you wa—"

The solid left hook was strong enough to knock out a bull. Monya almost dropped to her knees, but Cartier grabbed the bony bitch by her hair and pulled her back up. She continued to assault her face with a closed fist. Monya's screams could be heard for blocks. She was so dazed she couldn't properly defend herself. Blow after blow had weakened the sassy bitch, and Cartier never said one word. She tossed Monya around like a ragdoll, and then body slammed her onto her marble tiled floor. It felt like Monya's ribs broke in several places. Before she could fully scream from that blow, she was face-to-face with the bottom of Cartier's Nike's Air Trainers. Monya tasted and swallowed blood, and only prayed the abuse would be over soon. Inside her mind she was looking for where she could find a weapon. She wanted to stab Cartier for whipping her ass.

Winded and sweating freely, Cartier began to wind down. She was tired and her arms were weak. She needed to catch her breath and leaned against a nearby wall. She watched as Monya squirmed around on the floor in pain like the dog she was. Her face was unrecognizable, and although Cartier wanted to continue beating her ass after she caught her breath, suddenly she was afraid she might actually commit murder. Monya looked in bad shape. Her hair was soaked in blood and she was whimpering from pain.

"S-s-s-stop . . . I had the a-a-a-abortion," Monya stammered in agony. ". . . I s-s-swear."

Inexplicably, Cartier felt an overwhelming sense of remorse, mixed with a longing for the past. What had happened to their friendship? They were once close as sisters and now time had erased all the fond memories and replaced them with arguments, fights, revenge, anger, hatred, and dissention. She walked toward her archenemy, but not to deliver more blows. As she got closer, Monya slid away and cowered in the corner, unaware that Cartier actually wanted to help her this time.

"What happened to us, Monya?" Cartier began. "You were my sister and look at us. Why?"

Cartier didn't even realize she was crying. The tears were coming down at a rapid rate, almost blinding her. Suddenly, she slid down and collapsed on the floor and began balling her eyes out.

"Look at us," Cartier said. "I'm here trying to kill you. You're doing everything in your power to hurt me. It wasn't supposed to be like this. . . ." The tears continued to fall. She was a woman hurting and didn't understand why.

Besides petty envy and jealousy, her beef was never with Monya. She went to prison for Monya, to save her from being destroyed, and the very person she was trying to save had been trying to destroy her ever since.

"We were supposed to be in each other's weddings," Cartier continued. "Godparents to each other's children. Go on family vacations and be soccer moms . . . that's what I always wanted. I loved you! I loved you more than my own freedom and you betrayed me. What did I ever do to make you hate me?"

"I w-w-was always your sidekick," Monya shot back through the pain. "Y-y-you never treated me as your equal."

"I always respected you," Cartier responded.

"You always loved me. You never respected me!" Monya countered.

"But what does that have to do with your actions?" Cartier argued. "Isn't it better to be loved than respected?"

Monya tried in vain to sit up straight, but the pain was unbearable. Tears continued to roll down her smooth cheeks. "This isn't a mob movie. Why did I have to choose?"

"I did respect you. I did seven years out of respect!"

"I never asked you to. That was your choice. You'd made that decision. You never consulted me on how I felt about the situation."

"And you never stopped me," Cartier snapped back.

"Come on now, you knew it was already too late. You'd already pled to the case. What was I supposed to do? Stand up and say I did it and take twenty-five years? You would have forced my hand and that wasn't fair. They didn't h-h-have shit whatsoever."

"You were killing yourself with your hunger strike. The cops played you and you were too weak to believe in us, to believe in our friendship."

"Then you should have let me die . . . I wasn't asking you to fix m-m-m-me."

"As your friend I thought that's what we did for each other. We held each other down."

This was the first talk the two women had had in over eight years. In that time they'd grown apart and ultimately despised each other. The other alternative was that they could have expressed their true feelings and not held in the resentment that burdened their souls.

Cartier went and ran Monya a bath to clean her up. She was a bloody mess. Since she could barely walk, she had to lean on Cartier to help her get inside the warm tub. Cartier grabbed a cup from the kitchen and began to wash Monya's hair. As her strong fingers kneaded through Monya's soft hair, they shifted their conversation from bad times to good.

"Remember when Shorty Dip came on the block to fuck us up and our mothers were out there thumping with us? Trina beat fire out of Dip, didn't she?" Monya said, reminiscing on good times.

"My moms was so gangsta. I wonder if I'll be that way with Christian?"

"You could if you wanted to, but I don't think you'd want to," Monya replied.

"You're right. I've changed so much over the years.

Prison softened me up."

"You ain't that soft," Monya chuckled. "You just whipped my ass."

"Yeah, I did, didn't I?" Cartier laughed as well.

After Cartier washed Monya's back and body, she wrapped a towel around her and led her to her bedroom. Both women crawled inside the plush comfortable bed and continued their talk.

"Remember when we were in the third grade and we would beat up all the girls and make them give us their milk and cookies?" Cartier asked.

"What do you mean *we*? You did all that by yourself," Monya corrected.

"But your greedy ass was eating the cookies with me."

"Hell yeah! Those chocolate chip cookies were the shit, weren't they?"

Both women fell asleep in Monya's bed after talking until the sun came up. The next day Monya was still sore from her severe beat-down, so Cartier agreed to stay over and help her with Jason Junior. Meanwhile, Christian was over Trina's. As the two women rediscovered their friendship they both realized they'd been on an emotional rollercoaster for nearly a decade. From boosting, to selling drugs, to cohorts in a murder, to archenemies, and now back to friends. They'd both come full circle and it was like old times.

After Cartier helped Monya bathe, she sat down and began to braid her hair into two plaits. The house was still and was inviting more conversation, and both women felt talking through their differences was therapeutic.

"I don't know why I wanted to get with Jason so badly when I knew how he felt about you," Monya admitted. "Truly that was the lowest thing I could have done in my life . . ." Monya paused, almost afraid to go further, "besides, you know . . . Donnie."

Cartier shook her head. "Neither one of us are angels, but we shouldn't keep beating ourselves up about it. All we can do is make better decisions and try to be better people for our children."

"I know, but I was relentless in pursuing—"

"Look, it takes two. Jason could have easily resisted your advances. To me he had more of a duty to me than you."

"We're such horrible people, Cartier. Could you ever forgive us? Will you forgive me? I'm sorry . . . I'm truly sorry for hurting you. I truly must have bumped my fucking head."

"It's all good, Monya. It's the past, and I think I can get past it."

"You're more of a woman than I'll ever be," Monya concluded.

As the night progressed, the women grew close again as they reminisced on their past. When Cartier reached over and planted a soft kiss on Monya's lips, she didn't resist. Instead, she parted her mouth and welcomed the soft tongue of her former best friend. As their kisses got more intense, Cartier inched closer to Monya and began to remove her towel. As the towel feel to the bed, Cartier's hands began to explore Monya's battered body. Her strong hands began to massage every inch of Monya's body from her outer thighs to her small breasts.

Monya relaxed and welcomed the feelings as Cartier replaced her hand with her tongue. Soft, wet kisses traced Monya's outer legs to inner thighs until ultimately reaching her neatly manicured pussy. Hesitating only momentarily, Cartier parted Monya's nether lips and began to suck on her clitoris with steady, firm movement.

Monya moaned her pleasure as she gently rocked her hips back and forth. Both women wondered what they were doing making love to each other, but the feeling was too intense to stop. Cartier stuck her finger in Monya's inflamed pussy and hot juices seeped out. Cartier continued to finger fuck Monya until she pulled Cartier up and they began grinding on each other.

Monya then wanted to please Cartier and went down on her and began to taste her pussy. The two women were bent on pleasing one another as they experienced feelings that only a woman could invoke. Monya then took the lead and positioned herself on top of Cartier in the sixty-nine position. This took their pleasure to the next level and each woman experienced a mind-bending orgasm. They both lay there still, unwilling to talk.

Monya was trying to come up with words and then decided that actions would better represent any words. She jumped out of bed and went into her top drawer and pulled out her secret stash of sex toys. She had a massive, dark chocolate colored dildo that would enhance their lovemaking. Cartier smiled a devilish grin and Monya sauntered back toward the bed.

"I thought you'd like this," Monya smiled.

The two women brought each other to multiple orgasms until they were physically depleted. Within moments they both drifted off into a light sleep. Cartier awoke first a few hours later and tried to quietly leave, but Monya felt her rumbling in the bed.

"Don't go," Monya asked softly.

"I gotta go and get Christian."

"Who has her?"

"My mother."

"Then you can definitely stay," Monya shot back. "You know Trina won't trip."

"What about Jason? I know his ass will start calling soon. I've been missing for days."

Monya tossed her eyes up in the air at the mere mention of Jason's name. She didn't know if she should tell Cartier that he just left, before she arrived the other day. Although they didn't fuck, Jason did his favorite thing: ate her pussy like a champ and gave her some cash. She pushed that thought out of her head. That situation would have ruined what they both just shared, which Monya wasn't sure how to define.

"Can I ask you a question?" Monya asked.

"Maybe," Cartier replied, hesitantly. "It depends . . ."

"I mean it ain't that serious. I just wanted to know if you still loved Jason. I mean after everything he's put you through."

"Everything *y'all* put me through?"

"I'm not innocent in this, I know. But all I kept asking myself through all of our drama was why would you stay with him? You're too good for that motherfucker."

"And what about you?" Cartier came back. "You don't think that you're too good for him? Or is this your way of getting me to back off of Jason so you can have him exclusively?"

Again, Monya weighed her words and thought before she spoke. The hood in her wanted to snap and curse Cartier out, even after she just got her ass kicked. But after what they just shared she wanted to speak frankly and honestly.

"Even if you backed off I wouldn't have Jason exclusively," Monya replied. "He has way too many bitches to ever be faithful. Secondly, out of all his bitches—and I'm including myself, he loves you the most. I've done everything in my power to get him to leave you and he won't budge. But even though he won't leave you, that doesn't mean you can't leave him. I mean, look at me, I done fucked our whole borough, and you and I are competing over the same dude. Got babies by him and the whole nine. But what's fucked up is that you're a good girl and I ain't shit, now you tell me what's really good?"

"Monya, I feel you, but he's the father of my daughter."

"And?"

"And I don't want to break up our household even though I keep telling myself I would...that I should," Cartier explained. "I don't want Christian raised in a broken home as I did."

Monya shook her head. She really didn't get what Cartier was saying, but she decided not to push.

"Well, I'm not gonna fuck with him no more," Monya exclaimed.

"Stop lying, bitch," Cartier said, jokingly.

"I'm serious. He don't know how to fuck anyway and as you know his dick is so little and always want somebody to suck it."

Laughing, Cartier replied, "You too?"

"Hell yeah!" Monya began. "And after y'all fuck, do he be asking you, 'Was I enough for you?' I be wanting to say so badly, 'Hell motherfucking no!'"

At this point, both women burst out laughing. They were both tickled clowning Jason and his little dick.

"But all jokes aside, Jason is a good man," Cartier said. "I mean, he has a good heart, he's just a dog."

Monya couldn't understand how Cartier was coming to his defense, especially when she'd put up with all of his infidelities.

"I guess my definition of a good man is way different than yours. A good man in my book doesn't have numerous affairs and he certainly wouldn't sleep with my best friend and impregnate her. You have to see him for who he is."

Cartier thought about Jason, her marriage, Monya, and their children, and was confused. She wanted to block out Monya, but she couldn't. Monya began telling Cartier things she didn't want to hear, and no matter how she tried to put on a tough exterior, she was deeply hurt by Monya's words.

"I'm telling you, yes, he does love you, because he wouldn't leave you, but I don't think he ever respected you. He lay in my bed plenty of nights and just complained about you, and I loved every minute of it. You know I was a hater," Monya laughed. "I wanted to hear all the seedy details about how you were lazy and couldn't cook, and that you were boring in and out of bed. He said he felt like he had two kids, you and Christian, because he had to fully take care of both of y'all. He said if he didn't tell you what to wear each morning, you'd go naked. I told him what he was saying didn't sound like you at all, but he told me that you'd changed. That jail had broken you and that living with you was like living with a twelve-year-old kid."

Tears began to stream down Cartier's cheeks as Monya divulged all the seedy pillow talk between her and Jason. Cartier felt so low and confused. She thought she understood the pulse of her relationship, but as Monya rehashed Jason's thoughts, she realized she did lose herself in Jason's shadow. Being incarcerated had broken her spirit, and she just didn't want to fight anymore. She allowed Jason to be the breadwinner and head of the household. He was the king of the castle, and for years she was content with that. She thought she was content being cooped up in the house being a housewife. She thought he would appreciate her sacrifices. Instead, he mocked her to his mistresses and made a fool out of her.

Suddenly, Monya stopped rambling with her stories. She realized her words would hurt, but only superficially. Now she understood she was being selfish. She didn't want Cartier going back to Jason, so she opened up and gave her a snapshot of what Jason thought about her.

"I didn't mean to make you cry," Monya began. "He's not even worth your tears."

Cartier shook her head rapidly, but said nothing.

"You know, a lot of this is my fault. If I didn't stab Donnie and then let you take the weight, you would have never gone to prison and changed."

"That's not truly a fair statement," Cartier finally spoke. "I chose to plead out for a reason, and you couldn't have stopped me. I did it out of guilt. I made a lot of hardheaded decisions back then that wasn't fair to anyone. I had no right to put you in the middle of my crazy scheme. And I had also underestimated what you'd do under duress. Most of how my life unfolded was my fault and if you were the one doing the time, I would have died inside. If you and Jason think that I changed because I did time, there's no telling how I would have turned out if *you* did the time."

Cartier called Trina and asked if Christian could spend another night.

"Sure, you know that's no problem," Trina replied. "Why? You and Jason going out tonight?"

"Ma, Jason and I broke up," Cartier said matter-of-factly. "This time for good."

"What? What happened now? Does this have anything to do with Monya?"

"No, it doesn't. I'm just tired of his disrespectful ways

and all his cheating."

"Well, that's what men do, Cartier," Trina responded. "How many times do I have to tell you that the grass ain't always greener on the other side? Jason is a good man who loves you. The cheating will stop one day. He can't cheat forever."

"And I'm just supposed to sit around waiting with bated breath until he decides to stop?" Cartier snapped. "I can't let him have my happiness in the palm of his hands while he's deciding if he should do the right thing. I swear if I stay one more day I'm going to end up going back to prison. That's how angry he's making me, and I can't control my feelings or anger."

Trina got a little frightened when Cartier mentioned prison. She was approaching fifty and didn't have the energy to run back and forth to prison on visits, and lugging kids and packages. Trina wasn't sure if her advice for Cartier to stay put was the right advice.

"Well, ain't no man worth your freedom. You hear me?" Trina asked. "Husband or no husband, if he acting a fool, then kick his ass to the curb. He'll realize he messed up a good thing."

Cartier was glad her mother was on her side. She hung up, cut off her cell, and crawled back into bed with Monya. She knew the next morning she would have to deal with Jason. He had called over a hundred times, and left over eighty messages. His messages ranged from concern to panic to anger, but she didn't care.

In the morning she had lots of work to do.

Monya followed Cartier back to her house to retrieve her things. They waited until Jason left the house before they ran in like crackheads on speed, grabbing only the necessities. They tossed most of her clothes and all of Christian's clothes in large garbage bags and piled all of it into Monya's BMW. They used Cartier's car to pack Pampers, Christian's high chair, and a few toys.

Cartier took one look around and exhaled. She needed to be strong. She left a post-it note on the refrigerator that simply read: *Fuck You.* Next, she changed her cell phone number.

She didn't want to hear Jason trying to persuade her to come back home. She needed to leave him and pick her self-esteem off the floor.

CHAPTER TWENTY-EIGHT

Dirty Little Secret

Cartier and Monya's relationship took off expediently. They couldn't explain or understand their relationship. They both swore they weren't lesbians, although they made love almost each night.

"What are we doing?" Cartier asked.

"I don't know. Let's not define it," Monya began. "All I do know is that I don't want it to stop. You make me feel good and I'm finally able to be myself, flaws and all. When I'm with men I gotta put on this act and always be conscious about my actions. I gotta put on my sexy voice, toss my hair, keep my nails and toes painted, feed their egos . . . I mean, the list goes on and on. I have to act interested in their stupid war stories. I mean, I'm tired of playing dumb. With you, you know me. You know the real me and I don't have to pretend."

"Yeah, I hear you. But it's not like that with me and Jason. I don't put on any shows and neither should you. Don't let any man make you over. I know that I've put up with a lot of shit from Jason, but I was in a vulnerable position coming straight out of jail with a newborn baby.

Your situation is different. You had your own crib, your own money, and a stable of men willing to take care of you. I had a baby to feed without any money and I didn't want to go back out there and begin hustling again, and risk being taken away from Christian. I did what I had to do."

Monya shook her head. "Excuses. All you doing is making excuses. What happened to you? The Cartier I knew wasn't afraid of shit. She was a thinker who could put a plan together and take chances."

"I guess jail happened to me. I got soft because I didn't want to go back."

Monya tried her best to put herself in Cartier's position, but that was tough to do.

CHAPTER TWENTY-NINE

Money, Hoes, and Clothes

Jason crept down Fifth Avenue toward the 40/40 Club. The line was wrapped around the corner and it was nearly two in the morning. He'd already snatched up Pinky, a stripper at Club Desire in the Bronx. He had to promise her a night's pay if she left with him. His intentions were to take her straight home, so she could do a private dance for him. However, once they were rolling, he realized he wasn't ready to go in yet. He no longer had a curfew. When Cartier was home, she always told him what time to be home, usually before the sun came up. If the sun came up, then Cartier would lock his ass out. He did his best to push her out of his mind. She was the past, and so was his marriage.

He peered at the sexy, young stripper and wondered how old she was. Her dark-chocolate skin looked shiny from the stage and felt like silk when he glided his hands down her shapely thighs. He couldn't tell whether her hair was real or a weave, and he liked her voice when she spoke—soft and flirty.

"How old are you?" Jason asked.

"I'm nineteen," she began. "I've been doing this shit for a year to pay for school."

Jason had heard that lie before, but he decided not to judge her. He knew how hard it was out here for women having to use what they had to survive. "What school you go to?"

Giggling, she replied, "I'm not in school, yet. I'm thinking about going to Hofstra for accounting."

"If you're not in school, then how are you stripping to pay for college?" Jason nosily asked. "Did I miss something?"

"Nah, what I meant is that I'm saving up all my money and then I'll enroll in college. I can't concentrate on college and dance as well. So, I'll do this for another year and then quit all together. I don't want to stop and then have to start again. Shit, I got bills and when I enroll, I'll also need money to pay for my living expenses."

"Don't they got financial aid for all that?"

Again, she giggled. "I guess . . ."

"What's so funny?" Jason asked, annoyed.

"I don't know," Pinky replied, as she slid her small hand up toward Jason's flaccid penis.

It took his dick more than a quick hand movement to get hard. He was thirty-one years old and a heavy drinker. But he still appreciated the gesture.

"Why do they call you Pinky, and not Blacky?" Jason wanted to know. He wasn't trying to be rude, yet didn't care if she got offended. He loved dark chocolate girls. The darker the berry, the sweeter the juice.

Yet again, she giggled and Jason became slightly annoyed.

"Because my pussy lips are so pink," she retorted.

Jason, with Pinky trailing behind, walked directly to the V.I.P. line and immediately caught the head bouncer's, Big Mike, attention. The rope chain was instantly opened, and Jason and Pinky were led through. Jason gave Big Mike a pound with two crisp one hundred dollar bills folded neatly.

Inside the club was a jungle gym. It was hot, sweaty, and overflowing with young men and women. The 40/40 Club had definitely turned into a twenty-five and under club, and although Jason was over thirty, he loved checking out the young girls dressed so scantily. He realized the young women he fucked didn't come with the baggage like his former mistress, Monya. They were easy to maintain, because they didn't have shit, and didn't want much, so no overhead. He could buy them a pair of sneakers or jeans, or just toss them hair and nail money. Meanwhile, older women had rent or mortgage payments, car notes, daycare expenses, and credit card bills. Additionally, they didn't have any qualms asking him to take care of one or all of their damn expenses. Plus, he could tell a young girl any dumb shit that popped in his head and they'd believe him.

Jason only stayed long enough to have a couple shots of Hennessy. He knew in New York the cops had cracked down on drinking and driving. They had roadblocks set up outside of all the popular hot spots, and he couldn't afford to catch a bullshit case.

"That was fun, right?" Pinky exclaimed.

"Not really."

"No?"

"What the fuck did we do?"

"I think the music was good." Pinky could tell he was annoyed, but she played it off. As long as the money was right and long, she was cool with his attitude.

Jason started the car, but kept it in idle. "I got better plans to have fun. You're coming with me tonight. Do you have a problem with that?"

"My time is yours," she giggled. "But my time costs."

Instantly, Jason stomped on his brakes. "Let's get this straight, baby girl. I don't pay for pussy. Now I said I'd give you a couple dollars for leaving work early, but don't get carried away. I don't give a fuck about you! I mean, you look a'ight, but don't sit up here like you fucking Queen Sheba. I fucked better bitches than you and you're not doing me any favors. You can get the fuck out right here and don't let my car door hit you on your way out."

Pinky was startled by his outburst. The gentleman she'd left the club with had left the car. She was now with a man who had a temper and spooky eyes. She felt that perhaps the last line about her time being costly was a bit overstated. She was tired of getting used and fucked for free. Since Jason seemed like he could afford to spare a couple dollars, she went for it. And although she knew she wasn't the cutest chick in the world, she knew she had a wet, tight pussy, and knew how to work her hips. She told herself that after they fucked and he got a shot of her pink pussy, she'd crack on him for some dough.

"I'm sorry, baby," she crooned. "I was being silly. I want to go home with you."

Jason began drinking heavily after Cartier and Christian moved out. At first he pretended to enjoy his newfound freedom, staying out late most nights and making it rain money in all the high-end strip clubs and trendy hotspots. But after two weeks of blowing through money and rolling in and out of different women's beds, the nostalgia was over and he wanted his wife back. Only he couldn't find her.

He didn't believe Trina when she said she didn't know where she was, but after stalking Trina and Bam, there wasn't any sign of Cartier. And finally, when he couldn't get any pussy from Monya and she wouldn't return any of his calls, he realized he had finally been dumped by both his wife and mistress.

He decided to drive back over to Trina's for his daily harassment. As he pulled on the block, he saw something that almost stopped his heart. Monya's white BMW was parked in front of Trina's building, and Cartier, Monya, Jason Jr., and Christian were getting out. The visual damn near turned his hair white from shock. Inexplicably, he was enraged. His actions of sleeping with both women were supposed to drive a wedge between Monya and Cartier, and now it seemed as if they were best friends again. *How? Why?* His mind searched for answers.

Enraged, he jumped out of his jeep and approached the

passenger's side, startling Cartier. "Yo, where the fuck you been all this time?" he asked in a huff.

Calmly, Cartier continued to unlatch Christian's car seat as Monya gathered Jason Jr. and quickly went to stand by her friend's side. Slowly, she pulled out her cell phone and called Trina. "Ma, come downstairs and get Christian."

"Nah, she not taking my daughter no-fucking-where!" Jason's eyes were darting from Cartier to Monya. If he'd had an ounce of liquor in his bloodstream, he would have gone off and attacked both women. He was that angry. His sober mind allowed him to keep everything in the right perspective. Both his kids were there.

"Don't start acting a fool out here," Cartier threatened.

"Who you think you talking to?" Jason continued to raise his voice. "You gonna take my daughter from me and I don't know where you've been at for weeks?"

"I told you that I was out and that I wanted a divorce," Cartier responded. "If you want to see your daughter, you're going to have to do what regular people do, which is file for visitation rights with family court. And I will be seeking full custody and child support."

Jason could hardly believe his ears. This was the hood, and nobody got a legal divorce with proper paperwork. They just separated and lived out their lives. Secondly, visitation rights and child support? She was talking like a suburban housewife. Cartier needed to look in the mirror and see her black face, because right now she was acting as if her name was Becky.

"Save that bullshit act you putting on, OK. I don't know who you trying to—"

"What's going on out here?" Trina said as she trotted down the steps toward the small commotion with Fendi trailing behind her.

Cartier handed Christian to Trina, who was confused. She saw Monya and Jason and Cartier, and knew something was about to go down. Trina knew Cartier could whip Monya's ass any day, but she really didn't want them fighting over Jason. She had so many questions she wanted to ask Cartier. Primarily, where she had been the past couple of weeks. But Cartier had other instructions.

"Nothing much, Ma," Cartier answered. "Just take Christian upstairs and I'll be up there shortly."

Monya wasn't leaving Cartier outside by herself with Jason acting crazy. She walked past Jason and asked Fendi to take Jason Jr. Upstairs too.

Trina was really confused, but she wasn't fucking with Monya. "No," she yelled, "take him to your mother!"

"Ma, no, take him upstairs too," Cartier intervened. "It's all right, I'll explain later."

Now Trina's mind felt like scrambled eggs. She realized not to ask any more questions, because she wasn't about to get any answers. All she could do was take the kids upstairs and wait.

While all this was transpiring, Jason had his hands stuffed in his pockets to prevent himself from flipping out. When his kids were out of earshot, he started in on Monya.

"What the fuck you staying around for?" he shouted. "You need to carry your ass on too. This is about me and my wife!"

"Don't front now like you the family man, 'cause she already knows everything! And I mean, *everything*," Monya taunted. She loved watching him squirm. It was in that moment Monya knew she would never be a man's mistress again. She was too good for that.

At Monya's threat, Jason's disposition changed. He decided to use another approach to get his wife back. His voice was now a plea. "Ma, I want you to come home. Let's straighten this out, just you and me. You know I love you. I love my family and I don't know how we got here."

"I'm not going back," Cartier began. "I gave you all the chances I could and now I'm done. I want out."

"Nah, I'm not letting you go," Jason protested. "What do you want me to do? Beg? OK, I'm begging you to come back."

Monya inched closer to Cartier to remind her that she was still there. "Cartier, don't believe that bullshit."

"Monya, I will beat the fuck out of you out here," he threatened and stepped closer to Monya. Cartier held out her hand in defense of Monya.

"Stop bugging out!" Cartier exclaimed. "This ain't her fault."

"This bitch don't give a fuck about you!" Jason screamed. "She's playing you right now. She's just jealous of what we shared and mad that I don't want her ass."

"You want my pussy though," Monya shot back.

Jason was so humiliated and aggravated that he swung on Monya, only missing her head by inches. Cartier and Monya both reacted and swung back on Jason, who was able to block both blows. Stunned at Cartier's actions, he staggered backwards toward his vehicle. He needed time to clear his head, because at the moment, he felt like he was in a bad movie. He noticed an exchange between the two women and couldn't understand what was going on. It seemed eerie the way they were protecting each other. Then he remembered that they once had a special bond. Cartier even did a bid for Monya.

Jason didn't know what he could do to make Cartier feel the same pain he was feeling. He thought about running upstairs and snatching Christian, but then he thought about his freedom. Who would watch the baby later on tonight when he wanted to run the streets? And besides, it was better to keep Cartier tied down with a baby, just in case she'd met a new nigga. Jason had already told himself if he found her fucking with another nigga, he would beat the shit out of her. He also knew he was going to find out about that Harlem nigga she used to fuck with named Ryan, and see if they were fucking around behind his back.

He was indomitable. Nothing could keep him down.

As the weeks passed, Jason continued to call Trina and beg her to tell Cartier to come home. Each time, she refused. Jason was sick to his core. He stopped eating properly, caring about his attire, and refused to get a haircut. He'd fallen into a deep depression and there wasn't a party, woman, or homeboy that could pull him out of it. He was used to waking up, hugging his wife's shapely body, and kissing the back of her neck. He missed her making breakfast in the morning or waking up with Christian between them and baby toes in his face.

Jason concluded that he was the biggest idiot on the planet. He gave up his stability for Monya, someone he wasn't even in love with, even after his wife had warned him to stay away.

CHAPTER THIRTY

Confessions

Jason still found it hard to believe Cartier had left him and taken their daughter with her. The most disturbing thing was he didn't have any idea where they were. He knew Monya had something to do with the breakup. He kept telling himself that was why he left her ass alone, but he knew it was the other way around—she stopped fucking with him. In many ways, he was a broken man, but it wasn't something he would admit. To admit it meant he had failed, and there was nothing strong about that. Cartier was his love, Monya was his pussy, and he didn't have either. Losing your woman and your pussy on the side made a strong man weak. He didn't like that shit. And to add insult to injury, they both changed their cell phone numbers.

It was mink weather in New York and Jason had on a velour sweatsuit and goose down jacket. Hennessy warmed up his body as he stood outside of his jeep smoking a cigarette and talking shit to Wonderful.

"Yo, when I see that bitch, I'ma put my foot dead in her ass for taking my seed from me," Jason complained.

"Yo, that was some foul shit she did," Wonderful agreed. "I can't believe you ain't heard from her in months, dog. That's some gangsta shit she on."

"You know Cartier ain't no punk," Jason responded. "She got a lot of hurt inside her, and she knows the best way to get at me is through my daughter."

As they were talking, Wonderful spotted the jeep first. "Speak of the devil. Ain't that Monya's ride right there?"

Jason looked toward the white BMW as it stood at the light. After a few seconds, his eyes focused on the passenger. Their eyes met and he dropped his cigarette and began to walk toward the curb.

Now Monya was staring at him and instantly, he raced toward the car. Only Monya didn't stop. She stepped on the gas and bounced. Jason quickly jumped in his SUV and gave chase.

He hadn't seen either one of them in months. His mind was boggled that these two were together again. What the fuck was going on? Why didn't he check Monya for Cartier? Never in his wildest imagination did he think they'd be living together. Were they living together? He didn't know, but he was going to find out. As each car weaved in and out of traffic, Jason now had plans to beat both women down. Monya was running from him and Cartier for leaving him sick.

By the time Monya hit Atlantic Avenue, Jason decided to fall back. He realized he was riding dirty and if he got pulled over, he'd do a couple years for the burner he had in his glove compartment. He let her get away and decided he'd catch them both in front of Monya's building. Jason made a quick left onto Howard Avenue and peeled off. He knew if he sat and waited for Monya to pull up, they'd spot him and take off. He thought he'd simply wait until early morning, park down the street, and catch them when they were walking out. That was his plan, until his pride crept in.

Why the fuck was he trying to find someone who didn't want to be found? Wife or no wife, Cartier making Monya step on the gas and fly through the streets of Brooklyn like he was some sort of stalker had him vexed. Did she not realize he wanted to see his daughter and she didn't have any right to take Christian away?

He remixed his plans and decided that first thing in the morning, he would file a police report, file for divorce, and also file papers with family court for full custody. If she wanted to play, he would go hard and show her who she was fucking with.

Cartier received the certified letter demanding she appear in Family Court on January 17. The next day, a petition for divorce was served from a court process server. Both documents were sent to Monya's address and caught Cartier off guard. She never expected Jason to serve her with papers, and worse, she was inexplicably hurt that Jason didn't come and try to take her and Christian back. He refused to fight. He decided to go legal. She knew she had to get her act together, but the thought of Jason knowing where she was and didn't put up an effort to get her back plucked a nerve.

Each day that passed, Cartier thought she was finally over him. But the legal ramifications brought memories rushing to the surface. It was indifference on her part. Jason had treated her like shit, but he was a good provider. Did she really want her marriage to be over? The finality of the paperwork had scared her, and Jason was going to call her bluff. Cartier stuffed the papers into her pocketbook. She needed to speak to someone. She needed to talk to her mother. She called Trina.

"Ma, what are you doing?"

"I'm on the other line with Jason," Trina said.

"What? Why?" Cartier asked with shock in her voice.

"Hold on, Cartier, because he's making some accusations I need to address with you," Trina responded.

Trina clicked over and had Cartier on hold for close to five uncomfortable minutes, before she came back on the line.

"Hello, you still there?" Trina asked.

"Yeah, Ma, I'm here. Now what Jason talking about? Did he tell you that he's suing me for divorce and joint custody?"

Trina heard the panic in Cartier's voice. "He told me something more disturbing. What's going on with you and Monya?"

Cartier heard the suspicion in Trina's voice. "What do you mean?" Cartier said weakly. Her voice was telling as well. Her tone had raised an octave as her hands began to tremble.

"He said he's been hearing about some freaky shit going on with you and Monya, and I told him no fucking way. There's no way my daughter is a dyke!"

The mere word made her feel dirty. And worse, she had to hear the word from her mother. What was she doing with her life? Since day one, she'd made a series of bad decisions. How could she raise her daughter in the living environment with her and Monya?

"What? Where did he get that from?"

"He said it's the talk in the streets and he's heard it from more than one person. Cartier, he's upset and so am I. What are you and Monya doing under her roof? And why are you and her friends again, anyway? After everything she put you through. I don't trust her. I saw the pain in your eyes when she stopped coming to see you in jail. And I saw the pain in your eyes when you found out about her and Jason. And I saw the pain in your eyes when she gave birth to his son. How much more pain you gonna let her put you through? If Jason moves forward with the divorce and custody, you could lose everything, including my grandchild."

Trina was fearful for Cartier and didn't trust Monya as far as she could throw her. But she knew one thing, if Monya ever hurt her daughter again, she would personally give her a beat-down she wouldn't forget. And if Janet wanted to get in it, she could get it to. Trina figured she might be older, but she knew for a fact that she hadn't lost her ability to throw a solid punch.

"Ma, you know me better than that," Cartier began. "I did seven years in jail and ain't none of those bitches ever turned me. You think I'm gonna get out here on the street and flip the switch? Monya and I are just rediscovering our friendship. She's truly sorry for what she put me through," Cartier lied. She was glad she wasn't face-to-face with Trina. She knew her reaction and facial expression to Trina's allegations would have given her away.

"Well, that's what I told him, but he ain't hearing me."

"He's just mad, that's all," Cartier surmised.

While Cartier and Trina spoke, Cartier's cell phone began ringing. It was Bam. "Ma, let me call you back. It's Bam on the other line."

"Hey, Bam," Cartier sang. "What's up, girl?" Cartier was happy Bam rescued her from telling Trina more lies. Her stomach was churning and her heart was hurting from listening to Trina's possible disappointment in her.

"Shit. Listen, where you at?" Bam asked.

"I'm on the low over at Monya's, hiding from my baby daddy," Cartier joked. "Why? What's good?"

"Is Monya there with you?"

"Nah, she had to run a few errands."

"Good, because between me and you, I got something to ask you, but you got to promise not to tell Monya."

Cartier's heart dropped, but she made the promise.

"I got at least eight calls today asking me if you and Monya are swinging an episode," Bam stated.

"Why the fuck are people bugging?" Cartier screamed. "My moms' just told me the same thing. I mean, are people stupid or what? Where are they getting that from?"

"Well, as I said, you ain't heard this from me, but people are getting it from Monya," Bam replied. "That, coupled with you two being inseparable for the past couple months after being archenemies, is all they really needed."

"From Monya?" Cartier's pressure rose. "Why would Monya say something so stupid?"

"You tell me?"

"I don't fucking know. I'm not a fucking lesbian," Cartier screamed and Bam got nervous.

"Look, chill," Bam said. "I'm just passing information. Don't kill the messenger. All you need to do is talk to Monya and get your shit straight. That don't look good out here in the hood. You feel me?"

"Yeah, I feel you."

Cartier couldn't wait for Monya to come home and have it out with her lover. She couldn't understand why Monya would go around blabbing her big mouth about the two of them, unless it was to spite Jason. And she wasn't cool with that. How could Jason be history if Monya was still trying to throw mud in her face? Cartier was anxious when she heard the key in the door.

"Hey, babe," Monya sang.

Cartier wasted no time in getting right to the point. "Monya, I'm very upset."

"Why? What happened? Is it Jason?"

"No, it's you," Cartier corrected.

"Me?" Monya began. "What did I do?"

"You can't keep your mouth shut!" Cartier said upset.

"I'm insulted," Monya responded. "Why are you yelling at me?"

"Are you going around telling people that we're a couple?"

"Yeah, I told a few people—"

"What? Why would you do that? What's wrong with you!"

"I didn't know that we had anything to hide. We've been together now for months—"

"I can't believe this," Cartier yelled. She was humiliated. She physically wanted to vomit. "Who did you tell? I need to know."

Monya couldn't understand why Cartier was freaking out. They loved each other and she didn't think they needed to hide anything. She was happy with Cartier and felt Cartier was happy with her. In fact, she'd just told Jason only minutes ago. "Well, right before I came in, Jason called me and asked were the rumors true. When I told him they were, he asked if we would do a threesome with him. You know I cursed that little dick motherfucker out."

Cartier blinked a million times hoping she could blink away the reality of the situation. She didn't know if Monya was stupid or spiteful.

"I'm very upset right now," Cartier exclaimed. "You had no right to tell people that I'm a lesbian."

"But we are together," Monya reasoned.

"But I'm not a lesbian!" Cartier screamed like a crazy woman. "Look, Monya, I don't know what we're doing here, but this isn't permanent. You and I are only a temporary situation. We can't live like this forever and raise our kids."

"Cartier, I love you," Monya said. She was still holding the groceries she brought in and finally placed them down. "I thought you felt the same way."

"I do love you, Monya, but I'm not a lesbian. You need to understand that."

Now it was Monya's turn to yell and scream. "Stop labeling us! We are what we are and we shouldn't have to define it or apologize either. What are you afraid of? Rumors? Gossip? Who the fuck cares about those miserable motherfuckers? They should only wish that they had what we have."

"Monya, why did you have to tell people before speaking with me first?" Cartier sounded defeated. So many thoughts were running around in her head. From her mother, Trina, to her husband, Jason, to her friend, Bam, and all of Brooklyn, she thought she would be too embarrassed to face anyone, let alone explain her actions or new lifestyle.

"Look, I'm sorry. Don't be mad with me, but I've been so happy lately that I couldn't hold it in any longer." Monya softly touched Cartier's face. "I've finally found someone who loves me and not just my pussy. All these years, men have used me like a slave. Fucking and sucking for a few dollars and a temporary companion. They all treated me like I wasn't shit. As if I wasn't worthy of a real relationship. They had me all wrong and didn't bother to get to know me. The real me. Cartier, I love you because you love my flaws and all. I was wrong and I made a mistake. If you care about what people think, then let's move away. Leave all this bullshit behind. We don't need these two-faced miserable people."

"Leave and go where?" Cartier asked. She was spent.

"I don't know. We could go to North Carolina or Atlanta and buy a house. We could get jobs and make new friends and start a new life," Monya stated emphatically. "Let's just leave the baggage behind."

"A house, huh? With what money? Maybe I can just call up Jason and ask for thirty grand to put a deposit on a house. I'm sure he'd love to give it to me." Cartier's comment dripped with facetiousness and defeat. She didn't know if she was coming or going.

"Fuck Jason," Monya spat. "I keep telling you we don't need that motherfucker! I got connections. I still got my Cartel connections. I could make a couple more runs and come up with at least fifty large."

"Are you crazy?"

"What's the problem?"

"You can't go back out there hustling. It's too dangerous and totally not worth it. You have your son to think about. Don't think about me, because I'm not worth it either."

"But I don't want you to leave me," Monya said. Her voice was trembling and bursting with fear. "I love you, Cartier. Please don't leave me."

Cartier and Monya made love that night. Cartier

brought the heat, as passionate as they had ever been together.

The next morning, Cartier got up and prepared to leave Monya for good.

CHAPTER THIRTY-ONE

Back to Basics

J ason had moved on as much as he could. He missed Cartier and Christian. For him, it was hard to think about one without thinking about the other. But at night, and even in the morning when he rolled out of bed, it was Cartier that was on his mind. He had just stepped out of the shower and looked around the bedroom. He didn't like what he saw. The house was in shambles. Panties, bras, boxers, socks, jeans, and boots cluttered his world. And worse than the bedroom, the bathroom and kitchen were both filthy as hell. He hated this shit and that was an understatement.

He was pissed at himself, but who could he tell? His road dog, Wonderful, was tired of him complaining about this and that. Wonderful wanted him to handle his business—either break down and get Cartier and his seed back or make a go of it with Pinky, his new live-in girlfriend, who didn't measure up to Cartier.

And that was the problem for Jason. Pinky didn't measure up. In bed, she was all that. She sucked his dick like a champ, including swallowing every damn drop of his nut, and fucked him as if he had the best dick in the world. But she was a trifling, lazy-ass bitch. When he let her move in, he didn't know she was that damn nasty. Taking a shower after sex was a must for him, but she refused to do that.

Jason missed Cartier. She kept a clean house and kept shit in order. He had no worries with Cartier. Even with all the junk he did, he never had to worry about another brotha invading his territory. He wished he could say the same thing about another woman, Monya in particular.

It wasn't cool in the streets for another bitch to take your woman. He heard the whispers and knew the fairy tales about a woman taking your woman meant you weren't hitting it right or didn't have her talking in tongues. It was embarrassing, but he didn't give a damn. Every day, he hoped Cartier would be walking through the front door, saying *I'm home*.

"You not going to get in the shower?" Jason asked loud enough to wake Pinky up from her deep sleep.

Pinky struggled to focus on her surroundings. She was still getting used to her bearings, waking up in Jason's house and not her mother's.

Her dry, pasty lips were practically sticking together. She almost had to pry them open to speak. Yawning and stretching at the same time, she finally spoke.

"You talking to me?" she giggled.

He looked at her and thought, *What a complete fucking idiot*. He was tired of her dumbass and equally tired of all the damn giggling. He snapped, "Who the fuck else would I be talking to?"

"Why you gotta be yelling? I can hear you."

Jason was spent. He didn't even know why he bothered.

"I said are you getting in the shower?" Jason said irritated.

"Why? We going somewhere?" Pinky stood and was still naked.

"Is that the only reason you'd get in the shower?" Jason asked. He couldn't understand how she could allow herself as a female to be so nasty. He had to practically threaten her to wash her ass like she was a child. Not allowing her to answer, he continued. "OK, then. Yeah, we going in the living room so you could clean the fuck up, so jump your funky ass in the shower and I'm not going to tell you twice!"

His voice had risen from monotone to the brink of screaming. Startled, Pinky began to cry.

"I just worked my ass off sucking your dick in here earlier. Why I gotta clean up? I'm tired. You know you could help clean up around here some times. I'm not your maid. Shit, you don't pay me enough to be fucking you *and* cleaning up."

Jason looked at the pitiful sight incredulously. What had he gotten himself into? She was a lazy, ignorant air head who sat around drinking and eating up his food all day. She didn't work nor was her ass going to college as she had so adamantly professed in the beginning of their relationship. His mind fast-forwarded ten years from now when her body wouldn't be as tight and her pussy wouldn't be so wet, and got turned off. There wasn't any way he was going to get caught out there. They didn't have any attachments and her tears weren't going to save her.

"Are you retarded?" he asked. He honestly thought that she could be a little touched.

"I'm very smart," she rebutted.

Before he could reply, his cell phone rang and the number didn't look familiar, but he answered it anyway. Any distraction was welcomed.

"Hello," he barked.

"Jason? What's wrong?" Cartier asked.

"Who's this?"

There was a pregnant pause, "Your wife. . . ."

"I see you got the papers," he facetiously asked.

"Yes, I got them," she responded. "And we need to talk."

"Talk about what?"

"Us?"

Jason's heart began to palpitate. He looked at Pinky, who was still waiting to finish their argument. "What about us?" he said to Cartier.

"I want to come home," she pleaded.

Jason could hear something in her voice. He didn't know if it was love or desperation. Again, Jason looked at Pinky, who now suspected he was talking to a female.

"Who's that on the phone?" Pinky's voice was loud enough to be heard through the phone.

"You there with a bitch?" Cartier asked quickly.

As both women slung questions at Jason, his mind raced to handle both women. His heart melted when he heard Cartier state that she wanted to come home. He wanted nothing more.

"Yeah, I got a little situation," Jason said to Cartier. "Not anything that can't be handled."

"Well, you better handle that situation before I come over there and handle it for you. Please don't make me catch a case over some bullshit! You better kick that whore out now!"

Cartier was back on her gangsta. She was like a lioness protecting her territory and Jason liked every minute of it. Of course, he'd never let Cartier get her hands on Pinky. She'd rip Pinky's fragile ass into pieces and Jason didn't want that. He just wanted her out.

He was tempted to tell Cartier to back the fuck down, since she had been licking and bumping pussy with Monya, but he let that pass. He missed his lady and he wanted her back. He knew it would be nice to have Cartier and Christian back where they belonged.

"You got it, ma," was his reply to Cartier. "I'll get that taken care of—"

"Oh, you are talking to a bitch!" Pinky yelled as her nostrils flared. She bent down and tossed one of her stilettos at Jason's head. Luckily, he ducked just in time. "You disrespectful motherfucker!"

Jason dropped the phone.

"Yo, what the fuck is your problem?" Jason shouted.

"You lucky I don't hit females, because I would have busted your shit open. I'm talking to my wife!"

"Fuck that bitch!" Pinky shouted back. "She don't mean nothing to me! She fucking left you and now I'm supposed to respect her. Where was she when we were fucking earlier? Huh? Riddle me that, motherfucker." Pinky was livid. How dare Jason scream on her to impress his wife. She'd never been so humiliated in her life. It was bad enough that he wouldn't get rid of his wife's clothes that still hung in the closet, or destroy her pictures. She wasn't even cute to Pinky. "Her ugly ass!"

Pinky walked over toward Jason and dashed toward the dropped phone. He tried to get to it before she did, but her agile body and youth beat him to the punch.

"Give me the phone," he yelled.

"Hello, who's this?" Pinky asked.

"Bitch, you already know who this is," Cartier snapped back. "This is his wife!"

"He don't want your ugly ass!"

Jason thought about wrestling the phone from Pinky, but decided Cartier could take care of herself.

"Let me say this to you clearly," Cartier began. "It will take me approximately thirty-seven minutes to get over there from where I am. I'm walking toward my car as we speak. It will take me approximately eight minutes to beat you down to a pulp. When I get there, I promise you that I will stomp your teeth out of your mouth and rip each strand of hair dangling on your head. You won't be able to see out of both eyes and will be unrecognizable to all your family and friends for weeks. Now ask yourself if fucking with my husband is worth it. If it is, then great. Have your sneakers laced up tightly and your fighting gear on. If not, then you have about thirty-four minutes to vacate the premises."

The phone clicked and Pinky held onto it for a few seconds longer, trying to think what she really wanted to do. Was she really ready for battle? She had heard about Cartier and knew she used to be a vicious bitch. And she sounded like she was still just as vicious. She would be stupid to still be there when Cartier arrived. But she had to leave with dignity. She began to front for her one-man audience. She refused to go out like a punk. "Bitch, fuck you, Don't nobody want this fucking loser. I got so many men I can't count. You can have him!" Pinky tossed the phone and began to run around frantically grabbing her clothes and shoes in an effort to leave before Cartier showed up.

Jason watched in amusement and relief. He couldn't wait to have his wife back.

Cartier pulled up ten minutes after Pinky had departed. She had sped the whole way over. She was ready to whip ass as she stomped up the driveway. Jason opened the door with only a pair of sweatpants on and a huge smile. He didn't even speak. He just grabbed Cartier in a bear hug and dragged her into the house. They began kissing passionately and groping each other. Cartier surmised the slick talking tramp had vacated the premises.

Cartier dropped the matter. The bitch left. It wasn't worth mentioning. She had messed around with Monya and how could she expect any man to go without pussy for several days, let alone several months.

"I love you, ma," Jason kept repeating through each kiss. He truly meant it. Whether his actions showed it or not, Cartier was the love of his life and he was miserable without her.

For so long he wanted her and when he got her he didn't give her the respect she rightly deserved. Part of that was because he was a street dude and they didn't always play by the rules. And because he was still young and growing into a man each day. His father wasn't around when he was growing up to teach him how to be a man, so he let the streets dictate his actions. All his friends did fucked up shit to their women, fucking their best friends and whatnot, so instead of him being a leader, he followed other's lead. And that path wasn't putting a smile on his face. Holding and kissing his wife was what he realized made him happy. He hoped that they could redeem their relationship and make a new beginning.

"I love you, too," Cartier replied.

Jason realized tears were streaming down Cartier's cheeks. He'd truly put their marriage in jeopardy and he knew that he'd hurt her deeply.

Jason pulled Cartier into their bed, the bed he'd only moments ago shared with Pinky and they began to make love. He ate her pussy until her legs trembled and she called out his name over and over again. The way she wrapped her legs around his waist and he sank deeper and deeper into her vaginal walls, connected the couple without words. They realized they had both made mistakes. But for now, those mistakes were left buried, underneath the surface. It was the blissfulness of the moment—a bliss they hoped wouldn't end.

After hours of lovemaking and sleep, Jason was the first to speak. "Ma, I'm so sorry for all the hurt I put you through. I know I've fucked up time and time again, and each time you forgave me. I didn't know that you could, and would, finally get sick of me. I took you for granted and I realize that now."

"You made it so hard to keep loving you," Cartier began. "Each time I forgave you and opened my heart to you, you would hurt me again, and I'd feel like a fool. I'm so afraid to try again, yet, my heart won't let you go. I gotta know if we give it one last try that I can trust you not to fuck me over."

Jason had made up his mind. No more cheating. Ever. "You can trust me," Jason said and began to suck each of Cartier's fingers. "You're the only woman for me. I was sick without you and Christian. Promise me you won't ever leave me again."

Jason looked deeply into Cartier's eyes. He wanted confirmation.

"I promise," she replied and they kissed again. As Cartier lay on his chest, he softly stroked her back.

"Are you and Monya through?"

The question made Cartier uncomfortable, but she

knew it was coming. She just nodded her head and that was enough for Jason. He squeezed her tighter and they both drifted off into a peaceful sleep.

CHAPTER THIRTY-TWO

———◆———

Rock-A-Bye, Baby

Monya had to admit that she was desperate. Cartier had left in the wee hours of the morning with just a Post-it® note that read: I'M SORRY. SOME DAY YOU'LL UNDERSTAND MY DECISION.

Right now, all Monya could understand was getting up enough money to move her and Cartier away from New York, and the judgmental glares from people in their hood. Monya felt that not only was Cartier embarrassed by their relationship but she was also afraid that Monya wouldn't be able to support her as Jason could. Monya had a lot on her shoulders and a lot to prove. She needed Cartier to know that she was capable of getting that paper just as a man could. It didn't take much maneuvering for Monya to call Jesus, the Puerto Rican cocaine supplier she'd used for years. Monya had fucked him a few times in the past, but he wasn't ever going to wife her. He was too loyal to his Puerto Rican women to let a black chick be his main and only girl.

"Jesus, what's good, papi?"

"Oh, Monya, mami, long time, no?"

"*Sí*, daddy. Look, I need to hold something. I got moves to make. *Comprende?*"

Jesus knew exactly what she was referring to and was glad she wasn't stupid enough to talk over the telephone. He told her to come through his stash house on Chestnut and Liberty Avenue in East New York, Brooklyn. Monya was excited about the prospect of making her own money again. Jesus had the lowest number around town, and his shit was pure white, Columbian uncut cocaine. The competition was selling a kilo for twenty-one five. She was going to monopolize the game by selling at nineteen. Jesus was giving her the keys on consignment at seventeen per brick, so she stood to make two large off each key.

Monya dusted off the 1998 Ford Taurus stash car and went and picked up Shanine to make the run with her. They had to make two stops. The first stop was to meet Ryan, Cartier's old beat in North Carolina. Word was he was getting a lot of paper in Raleigh and was doing great for himself. He supposedly bought a large enough house for a half a million that motherfuckers were calling it a mansion. Five hundred thousand in New York bought you a dump with rats and roaches. Monya was definitely looking forward to moving her and Cartier out of town so they could live in luxury.

"What's up, bitch?" Shanine joked as she got in the passenger's seat. She had an overnight duffle bag she put in the trunk, and a few books were strewn throughout the car to look the part, just in case they got pulled over on the highway.

"Money, that's what's up," Monya said.

"I feel you," Shanine replied. Things had gone south for her since they'd stopped hustling. She'd spent up her stash money and was struggling day to day to pay her bills. Monya had called right on time. She was about to go down to the welfare system and apply for assistance and food stamps. "You got the car inspected?"

"Nah, we fin to go and do that now, that's why I'm here so early."

"OK, cool."

Monya knew getting the car inspected was a must. It was mandatory the brake lights worked properly, as well as the brake line and oil pan didn't leak. The worst thing that could happen when riding dirty was getting pulled over by the cops because a brake light was out or something else broke down. That wasn't a good thing on the highway with a car full of drugs. There were too many stories to tell of stupid motherfuckers getting locked up, because they didn't ensure their ride was working properly before filling it with drugs. Plus, the cops were on to the secret compartments on these cars, so they had to play the part to the hilt when cruising down I-95. Their freedom depended on it.

After they got a clean bill from the mechanic, they headed toward Jesus.

"So, what's the plan?" Shanine asked. "You didn't go into details over the phone. Who we hitting off and how much we making?"

"True. OK, we about to get paid," Monya explained.

"Ryan is in North Carolina right now, doing lovely. He wants eleven keys at nineteen each. We're gonna make twenty-two large off that. Then, Big Mike wants nine keys. He wants us to meet his man in South Carolina and then we head back home. We stand to make eighteen off him."

"What Ryan? From Harlem? Cartier's old beat?" Shanine was inquisitive. She didn't like the sound of this.

"Yeah, him," Monya replied. "He heard I had product for a good number and he reached out."

Shanine was skeptical. "I mean, I know who he is, but he ain't ever copped from us before. What if this nigga try to rock us to sleep?"

"He good peoples."

"And why do he want so many?" Shanine's bullshit meter was on high. This whole joint didn't smell right to her.

"Because we got the lowest number on the streets," Monya proudly replied. "Everybody else is coming in at twenty-one five. Do you know how my phone is ringing off the hook? We both gonna make twenty large each in two days time. After this one more run, I'm out the game for good this time."

"Bitch, you said that eight months ago and you're back. You keep coming back because the money is fast. Fast money spends just as fast, so if you ask me, we got a few more years of this shit unless either one of us hits the lotto or meets a ball player stupid enough to marry one of us," Shanine joked.

"Nah, I'm serious," Monya said and her tone changed. "I'm out for real. Once I save up fifty, I'm taking my son to Atlanta and chill out, buy a house and get a real job."

"You seriously gonna leave me?"

"Shit, you can come too. Ain't nothing stopping you. You don't have a steady man nor any kids, so you should think about it too."

"But what made you decide this? I thought we were Brooklyn forever. Do or die in this motherfucker."

"We're not kids anymore," Monya exclaimed. "I'm damn near thirty years old. I gotta think about my future. Don't you ever want out?"

"Out of what?"

"The game. Poverty. The bullshit."

"Monya, I was born and raised around the riffraff. I think I'd feel out of place in some hick town around a bunch of country motherfuckers saying shit like, 'Yessum.' That's just not my style. I'm used to the gunshots, fights, designer clothes, the struggle, keepin' it real, I'm a full-fledged Brooklyn Bitch and I don't want change."

Monya nodded. Although she didn't agree with Shanine, she certainly understood.

"I guess I feel you, but one day you might change your mind and when that day comes, you better come and check us out in Atlanta."

"Who're us? You and my godchild?"

Monya hesitated. "Yeah, him. And Cartier . . ."

Shanine cut her eyes toward her friend. "So it is true? Y'all really fucking around?"

Monya's wide smile confirmed it all.

"Damn, I wanted so badly to ask you if the rumors were true, but I didn't want you cursing me out. How the fuck that happened?"

"It just happened."

"Well, not to be disrespectful, but please spare me the details. In fact, let's change the subject."

The thought of Monya and Cartier fucking gave Shanine the heebie-jeebies. She definitely didn't want any parts of Atlanta now that the situation became clearer.

Monya took her time as she arrived on the street of Jesus's stash house. She thought it was clever as hell to run a multi-million dollar drug operation out of a dilapidated neighborhood. The houses looked to be eighty years old and every two feet, the streets had large potholes or broken pavement.

At the house, security cameras were everywhere and the place was guarded by enough bodyguards packing heat. Monya backed the Taurus in the driveway of the gated property. Monya and Shanine went in through the side door, expecting to see Jesus, but he wasn't available. They stood face-to-face with three Spanish speaking men, holding and pointing guns directly at them.

Jesus being unavailable had unnerved both women. They were used to him being there. Jesus made them feel safe.

Monya spoke. "We're supposed to pick up twenty keys on consignment. Jesus said it was OK. Why isn't he here?"

"Don't worry mami. He say give you good stuff. He like you he say. We have it here," one of the gunmen said. He turned toward another gunman, "Vamoose."

Within seconds, they were bringing out twenty neatly packaged kilos of cocaine.

"Where do you want these?" the leader of the henchman asked. "The trunk of car?"

"Umm, well no. We got a stash car," Monya explained. They understood perfectly. They also had stash cars. Most of their customers owned and used stash cars. Although it wasn't foolproof, it was a deterrent. The gunmen began loading the keys into Monya's secret compartments on her Taurus. Before they left, it wasn't without warning.

"Jesus say you have three days to bring him three hundred forty thousand dineros. He say to tell you if you fuck around, you dead. OK, mami? You understand?"

Monya exhaled. Not that Jesus wouldn't have given her the same threat, he just would have been a little more tactful in conveying his message.

"*Sí*, I understand."

Monya and Shanine hopped in the car with Monya jumping in the driver's seat. They would switch driving every five hours until they reached their first destination. Monya popped in vintage Notorious B.I.G and they sat back and relaxed as their car glided down the highway.

Big Mike was antsy and called Monya's cell phone incessantly during the ride 95-South.

"Yo, how long y'all gonna be?" Big Mike complained. "I got peoples that need those joints."

"I said I gotchu, nigga," Monya said, weighing her words while talking over the telephone. "We just got to make a quick stop in N.C. to hit off Ryan from up top and then we gonna come through and meet your man."

"What Ryan? With the blow-out?"

"Yeah, that nigga."

"A'ight, do you. But hurry the fuck up!" Big Mike disconnected the call.

They took their time reaching North Carolina, making sure to do the speed limit and stopping to eat. The drive took twelve hours and Monya called Ryan several blocks from his crib.

"What's good, ma?" Ryan said when he answered the phone.

"It's all good. We here."

"Who're *we*? You know I don't fuck with a lot of peoples." Ryan was agitated. He didn't have any idea who Monya had with her, and in this business no one was to be trusted.

"Nah, calm down. It's just me and Shanine. She's my road dawg. She's cool. You remember her, right?"

"Oh, yeah, yeah, I remember shorty. OK, it's just y'all?"

"Look, I just told you who I'm rolling with. We're tired as hell and you're acting paranoid. Are we gonna do this or not? I don't want to be out here like this. . . ."

"No doubt. Do you know how to get to my place?"

"I don't know this fucking town," Monya replied.

"Give me the address again and I'll put it in my GPS on my cell phone."

Ryan hesitated. "Nah, don't do that. I don't like loose ends when shit ain't right, you know? Stay on the phone and I'll direct you from where you are."

Ryan remained on speakerphone and guided the women to his remote location. When they arrived, Shanine opted to stay in the car.

Monya thought about it and agreed. "You're right. I'll be out in a few minutes."

Ryan approached the car and peered in. Both women looked at the neatly dressed man and both had the same thought. Ryan was definitely eye candy. But he'd done Cartier dirty and left her when she needed him most. Monya decided not to tell Cartier that she and Ryan had done a business transaction. She didn't know if the mention of his name would irritate Cartier and bring back bad memories.

"What's up, ladies? Y'all look good," he began. Instantly they both showed Colgate smiles at the charming drug hustler.

"Thanks. You ready?" Monya asked. She was truly tired and couldn't wait to get her hands on the quick money and continue to the next town.

"I was born ready. Come on," Ryan said and opened up Monya's door. She jumped out and began to follow Ryan into the house when he noticed Shanine wasn't following. "She not coming?"

"No, she's going to stay inside the car," Monya

answered.

"Oh, that's what's up. Where's the shit?"

"Inside the stash."

"What the fuck you waiting on?" Ryan snapped, which startled Monya. She shook off the feeling and decided to lay down the law.

"We don't do business like that," she explained. "I'll come in and make sure the count is correct and then I'll give Shanine the paper and bring you the product. This ain't brain surgery, Ryan. It's a drug deal. I'm sure you've done plenty of transactions before."

"Shit, listen to you, all sassy and shit." He laughed. "How you know this ain't my first time? You might have to show me a few moves."

"Oh, please," Monya giggled.

"You look like you have a few moves to show a nigga," Ryan said, eyeing Monya up and down. She knew he was flirting and switched her tiny hips a little harder. She didn't want to swing an episode, but she was a woman and wanted to be wanted.

"I don't know about all of that," Monya flirted back.

"So from here where y'all headed?" Ryan asked. "Back to NY or do y'all have more stops?"

"We got one more stop."

"OK, then I better get you up out of here quick."

Ryan led Monya into a small two-story foyer. It was a nice sized home in a residential area. It had to be close to three thousand square feet.

"Is this your house?"

"Yeah, I own it, but I don't lay my head here. I just use it for business."

Monya knew this wasn't the huge mansion that everyone was speaking of. But she would have been just as happy living in that house. It was the nicest home she'd ever been inside, and it probably cost peanuts. She couldn't wait to do the next few runs and buy her and Cartier a huge home in Atlanta.

"You living large, ain't you?" Monya asked.

"I'm doing all right," he began. "Go and take a seat inside the living room and I'll go get that paper."

Monya walked and had a seat on the plush sofa. She really wanted to kick off her shoes and take a nap. She was tired as hell, but riding up and down I-95 was part of the game. That's how she made her money.

She heard some rumbling upstairs and looked down at her watch. Ryan was taking too long to gather that dough.

"Yo, hurry up," she yelled. "I got shit to do." Monya yawned a few times and was interrupted by her cell phone. It was Shanine.

"What the fuck is going on inside there? You a'ight?"

"Yeah, I'm good. I'm just waiting for him to count that paper. I should be out soon."

"You want me to hold on the phone until you come out?"

"Nah, I'm good. If I'm not out in ten minutes, then call back. Matter-of-fact, get in the driver's seat and be on alert. Anything funny, just jet and call 5-0. But don't get alarmed, I'm not feeling any static."

"OK, one."

Monya continued to wait impatiently and suddenly just before she dosed off, Ryan appeared. He had a duffle bag and Monya was relieved. She was ready to get on the road and make her next stop. Ryan plopped on the sofa next to her and tossed her the bag.

"This all me?" Monya questioned.

"Count it."

"Oh, no doubt. That's the first thing I always do. I ain't new to this."

"Stop talking like you a gangsta," Ryan began. "If you were a real gangsta you wouldn't have walked into this."

Monya felt a strong nudge in her side as she opened the bag and realized it was filled with newspaper.

"What the fuck is this?" her voice exuded fear as her hands trembled.

"You already know what it is." Ryan's voice was icy cold and his demeanor had changed. "A, yo!"

Ryan called and two more gunmen appeared, wearing black hoodie sweatshirts, jeans, and boots, brandishing weapons.

"Ryan, you gonna play me like this?" Monya asked as her eyes pleaded with Ryan. He was unaffected. Monya didn't have any idea what they were going to do to her, but she hoped Shanine did as she was told and call back, be on alert, and hopefully, get away and call for help.

"Bitch, shut the fuck up," Ryan shouted. "Get your

silly ass up and if you make one sound, I'ma put a bullet in your head."

As everyone surrounded her, Monya thought about her son. Was she really going to die? Would Ryan really go out like that? For all she cared, they could take the drugs and she'd handle Jesus when she got back. But even as she tried to rationalize her thoughts, she knew that there wasn't any way they'd just take the drugs and leave them alive. Monya began to cry and plead.

"Ryan, you don't even gotta go out like this," she pleaded. "You can take the whole car, just don't hurt us. I got a son that needs me."

Ryan shook his head.

"Damn, Monya. I ain't even like that. I'm mean, shit, we are gonna take your shit, but we ain't no murderers. Just don't go acting stupid and it's all good. Now get the fuck up."

Monya was glad he was leading her out of the house. She thought that she would end up duct taped in the basement with a bullet in her head. Suddenly, she tried to be optimistic. The two gunmen fell back as Ryan and Monya walked toward the car. Just as planned Shanine was in the driver's seat. She looked at Monya with the duffle bag in her hand and exhaled. Had she looked deeper at her friend's expression, she would have seen her panic stricken eyes.

Shanine rolled down the window. "About time—"

Ryan was quick and brief. He pulled out the burner and pointed it toward Shanine. She was about to scream when Ryan began barking orders.

"Shut the fuck up or you're dead. Do you understand me?"

"What's going on?" Shanine voiced weakly.

Before the girls knew what was happening, they were being surrounded and hustled into the car. Shanine was instructed to slide over into the passenger's seat and Monya sat in the back, next to one armed dude she didn't know. The other dude hopped in a Toyota Camry and followed. Ryan took the wheel and began driving. For a while, no one said anything. The car was silent as wild thoughts ran rampant through each girl's head. Shanine began to pray silently as Monya thought of a way to get out of their situation. The only thing she could think of was compassion.

"Ryan, you promised that you were going to let us go, right?" Monya asked with fear in her voice. "You know I'm only out here doing this so that I could feed my son."

Ryan remained calm. He was making sure he obeyed all the traffic laws. As he drove to the remote location, both women began to cry louder. Their deep moans of agony didn't faze the men. Ryan figured women in the game should know the repercussions of the game. If they wanted to act like men, then they got handled like men. He heard about the Cartel running through the streets of New York, selling drugs, fighting, and even killing motherfuckers. He'd heard about how they did Donnie dirty and couldn't believe the hypocrisy.

They could take a life and then beg for theirs? *What*

about Donnie's kids? Ryan rationalized. Though he didn't give a fuck about Donnie; he didn't even know the motherfucker. He just couldn't believe that they actually thought the drug game was sweet. It was ruthless and he was a ruthless motherfucker. He'd been robbing and murdering niggas since he was seventeen and running up in stash houses on Riverside Drive. If they couldn't handle the heat, they should have stayed in the kitchen, baking cookies or some shit like that.

Finally, he reached his location. He pulled over to the side and looked in his rearview mirror to see if Chopper, his man who was following, was close behind. He pulled over too.

"Pop open the compartments," Ryan said to Shanine. With trembling hands, she opened the glove compartment and hit a switch. The trunk popped open and the secret compartment slowly opened.

Chopper, who was now standing over the trunk, smiled. He then walked toward the driver's side and approached Ryan.

"Damn, that shit look pretty," Chopper smiled and revealed a row of rotten gold teeth. "It looks like Christmas back there. They brought more than you ordered."

"It's all good, motherfucker," Ryan said. "Start loading that shit in our car."

"Yeah, no doubt," Chopper stated and began transferring the cocaine into their stash car.

Shanine sat wringing her hands together. She was crying so hard she couldn't see past her tears. Snot had oozed down her nose and she didn't bother cleaning herself up. She knew her life was in someone else's hands and she didn't know whether Ryan had already decided their fate. When Chopper slammed the trunk closed, both women yelped.

"You gonna let us go, right, Ryan?" Monya asked again.

Ryan got out of the car and Mikey, the other passenger, did the same.

Ryan leaned over into the car, "Close your eyes!" he commanded.

"Ryan, no!" Shanine yelled, but the bullet piercing through her head had silenced her. Monya didn't have a chance to react before she was slumped over in the back passenger seat with a bullet lodged in her head.

"Yo, let's be out!"

CHAPTER THIRTY-THREE

Hard to Say Goodbye

The news hit Cartier like a Mack truck. Her whole body went limp as she collapsed into Jason's arms. He too was hurting inside. No matter what he and Monya went through, she didn't deserve to be done dirty that way. She was the mother of his only son.

"What happened?" Cartier asked between tears.

"Cartier, I don't know," Jason replied. "Her and Shanine were found both shot in the head in North Carolina. That's all I know. You gotta call your mother."

Cartier was distraught, but managed to call Trina. "Ma," Cartier cried, "who could have done such a thing?"

"The police don't know shit, but you better meet us at the airport. Janet and I are on the first plane flying out."

"OK, I'm there."

Cartier grabbed her family, and she and Jason drove to LaGuardia Airport, where they met Trina, Prada, Fendi, Janet, and Jason Junior. They all had a two hour wait until they boarded the next plane to Raleigh-Durham.

Janet was a nervous wreck. "They tried to kill my baby," she kept repeating.

"She's strong," Trina soothed. "She's gonna make it. She would have already let go. You know that chile is a fighter."

Monya was shot in the head, but she didn't die on the scene. Shanine wasn't as lucky. Her body was being transported from North Carolina to New York, so her mother could give her a proper burial.

As they sat in the airport, everyone had conspiracy theories on who murdered and tried to murder the girls. It wasn't a secret they'd gone to North Carolina on a drug transaction. Everyone up north knew that, but Janet didn't disclose that information to the police. She didn't want them writing Monya off. She wanted the perpetrators caught. When they finally arrived at the hospital in Raleigh, the news was grave.

"Ma'am, I'm afraid your daughter's brain dead," the doctor stated. "Critical levels of oxygen have stopped reaching her brain, rendering it useless. I'm recommending you let her go to be at peace."

"You mean pull the plug?" Janet screamed frantically. "You want me to murder my baby?"

"Ma'am, calm down, please," the doctor said in a soothing tone. "She's already dead."

"No-o-o-ooooo!" Janet cried and all the children burst into tears. They were frightened at the loud commotion taking place. "I can't do it."

Trina ran and embraced Janet, and rocked her back and forth in her arms as Jason cradled Cartier. Everyone was devastated. They all felt that they were in a bad dream.

The police stood to the side, waiting to speak to the frazzled mother. The crime was so abhorrent that they wanted to see if the New Yorkers had any clues where they were going or who they were meeting.

Unfortunately, no one knew a thing. They were clueless.

CHAPTER THIRTY-FOUR

Ashes to Ashes

On the morning of Shanine's funeral, Cartier couldn't pull herself out of bed. She didn't know if she could see her friend in a casket.

"Ma, you gotta get up," Jason soothed as he rubbed her back. "You gotta be strong. Shanine is counting on you."

When they pulled up in front of Baptista Funeral Home, Cartier could barely see the front entrance. It was jam-packed with family and friends. She was overwhelmed with emotions and couldn't hold it in. Monya was still laying brain dead in a hospital with tubes running in and out of her nose and mouth, with a respirator breathing for her. Monya's skin was pasty and her hands were clammy. Cartier knew her friend wasn't inside that empty shell. She wished Janet would allow her friend to rest in peace, yet, she didn't know how she'd be able to she her in a grave.

Jason was the strong one, giving Cartier all the support she needed. He helped her climb the stately steps of the funeral parlor and even helped her dress that dreaded morning.

When it came time for family and friends to speak, Jason nudged Cartier. He knew she needed to say her piece. Cartier exhaled and stood up. She looked over at Bam and Lil Momma and gave them both a nod. Her legs wobbled as she approached the podium and cleared her throat. There was a sea of faces, some she knew, others she didn't.

She began, "I've known Shanine almost all my life . . . I can still remember the white and blue Pro-Ked sneakers she wore that were always untied when we were in the third grade." Cartier laughed slightly as tears streamed down her cheeks. "When we were little girls you couldn't see one of us without seeing the other four: Me, Monya, Bam, and Lil Momma. We were all once close as sisters and then something went wrong."

Cartier shook her head wildly and began to sob uncontrollably. Someone called out, "Take your time . . ."

Soon she regained her composure and continued. "I went wrong. Back then, I thought it all made sense . . . I thought that together we could conquer the world. Most of y'all know us as the Cartier Cartel." Cartier snorted her disgust. "That was my first mistake. Back then, I thought the only important thing in life were labels. I had us running in and out of department stores, stealing their merchandise and actually thinking that society owed us something. When that didn't quench my thirst, I exposed my best friends to selling drugs."

Cartier watched as a few people squirmed in their seats. They weren't ready to handle the truth.

"It was all my idea," she stated. "Every negative action the Cartel did was all mines. These were good girls . . . we were good girls and I don't know what turned me. And then, I turned them, and Shanine would be alive and Monya would be here too if it weren't for me," Cartier choked up and began to sob uncontrollably.

Jason ran to the podium and walked her down. She collapsed in his hands and for a while was inconsolable.

When the service was over, Bam and Lil Momma approached Cartier. They wanted Cartier to know that Shanine's death wasn't her burden to carry.

"This ain't your fault," Bam said. "We all made our own decisions. You can't take the blame all by yourself."

"We all wanted the same things you did," Lil Momma encouraged. "Shanine and Monya knew what they were getting themselves into. You didn't have anything to do with that."

"Excuse me, Cartier."

Cartier turned around as she heard a familiar voice and looked into eyes from the past.

"Ryan . . . what a surprise," Cartier stated.

Ryan cleared his throat, leaned down, and gave Cartier a quick peck on her cheek. The last time she'd seen him, he'd promised to do her bid with her. Time had taken any animosity she might have had.

"You're looking good," Ryan began. "I just came through to show my support."

"How nice . . . I'm surprised you remembered Shanine."

"Yeah, I remembered her. That was your home girl. I

remember everything," he stated. "That was some powerful shit you said up there."

"I was just speaking my truth," Cartier said and peered over her shoulder. Jason was clocking her intensely from across the room. Cartier gave him a warm smile and he relaxed. "You remember Lil Momma and Bam, right?"

"How y'all doing?" he asked.

They both shook their heads. Even if Cartier wasn't holding a grudge, they still were. They didn't care for how he handled her.

Ryan continued, "Do the police have any leads on what happened to them? I mean, I know that Monya is still alive, right? Is she talking?"

Cartier shook her head wildly. "They don't know nothing. We call down their every day, and I don't even think they are working on the case."

"Those hillbilly-ass police don't know how to do their job," Ryan said.

"Oh yeah, that's right. Don't you live down there now? I almost forgot."

"Nah, not no more," Ryan lied. "I got out of there. I mean, I still got property down there, but I don't rest my head there."

"That's good. I just wish . . ." Cartier couldn't finish her sentence.

Ryan wanted to continue where he left off. He needed to know Monya's status. "Can't the other girl help?"

Cartier's tears began to flow again. "No, she can't. She's brain dead and they don't expect her to ever wake up."

Cartier clutched her stomach and began to rock back and forth from pain. Jason ran over to her and decided to get her out of there. He purposely bumped into Ryan as he walked past him and purposely didn't pardon himself.

Ryan just laughed that his presence could still intimate Jason. He didn't give two fucks about Cartier. He'd gotten what he'd come for.

The next morning, the burial was just as sad. As Cartier and Jason walked toward their limousine, she began to reflect on her life.

"Jason, I want a new beginning," Cartier said.

He shook his head. "Me too, baby. Me too."

"Then let's start over. Let's move away from New York."

"We could put the house on the market and buy a house in Jersey or Philly," Jason responded.

"No . . . won't nothing be different in Jersey in Philly," Cartier replied. "We need a new lifestyle and leave the hood behind. How about we go far away, where nobody knows us? We could go to Venice Beach in Los Angeles and get a small apartment. The kids would love the weather."

"Are you serious?" Jason retorted.

"Jason, I'm more serious than I can express. I just need you to want to do this."

"Well, I'm not leaving here without my son," Jason replied.

"I already spoke to Janet about it and she said she's too old to take care of Monya's kid. She said Monya would love it if we raised Jason Junior. I told her I needed to speak to you first, but I had already made up my mind. I got to do this for Monya. We need to give her child a good, stable home. That's why she was out there hustling, to give her son a better life."

"The captain has turned on the 'fasten your seatbelt' signs. We're preparing for landing," the flight attendant stated. Cartier looked down at Christian and then glanced over at Jason and Jason Junior. In a matter of minutes they'd be arriving at LAX and beginning their new lives. Cartier was still torn up over Monya, who was still lying lifeless in a sterile hospital room. She knew her best friend wasn't ever going to wake up. She was as good as dead.

She hated to leave her mother and siblings behind, but Trina wasn't ready to leave the hood. She used Janet as an excuse and Cartier had to accept her decision. Trina was a grown woman. Cartier felt in her gut that if they didn't leave New York and soon, she'd get that dreadful call one day that something had happened to Jason. She couldn't take any chances.

When the plane finally landed, Jason scooped up his son, she grabbed Christian, and they exited the plane and walked hand in hand toward their future while leaving all the unhappy memories about the Cartier Cartel behind them.

Once they were settled into their rent-a-car, Cartier clicked back on her cell phone. She had thirteen messages. As she listened to each disturbing message tears streamed down her flushed cheeks. Anger began to rise up and form a lump in her throat. She swallowed hard and tried to contain her composure. Cartier couldn't believe what she'd just heard. The reality of the situation seemed almost improbable, yet it all made sense. Her hands trembled as she closed her cell phone so she clasped them together to stop them from shaking.

Jason glanced over and noticed that she was crying.

"Yo, what happened now?" he asked in a panicked voice. He almost didn't want to hear the news.

Cartier's voice was laced with malice and rage. "I just got several messages from Bam saying word out on the street is that Ryan's the one who rocked Monya and Shanine to sleep. She said that Big Mike told her that Monya and Shanine were going to meet up with his homeboy after they left Ryan. They never made it. On everything I love he gotta get it! He don't deserve to breathe the same air as me. Understand?"

Jason nodded. "Don't even worry about it, ma. I'ma push that nigga's wig back. I put that on everything I love!"

Download & Print

our Order Form Online at:

MelodramaPublishing.com/books.php

MelodramaPublishing.com

The Saga Continues...

Book 2 Coming in October 2010

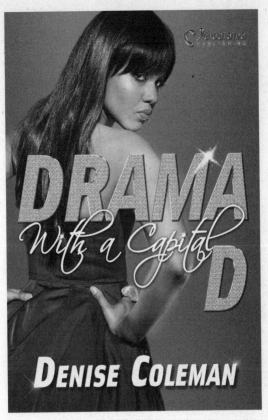

Drama with a Capital D by Denise Coleman
Available Now!

Lonnie, a strong, independent, career-minded sista isn't one for drama or unnecessary bull. In fact, she's not even sure if having a man in her life is worth the trouble it can cause. However, when she meets John, everything changes, and her comfortable life as a single career woman goes flying out the window. She's in love, and things couldn't be better. Then all hell breaks loose.

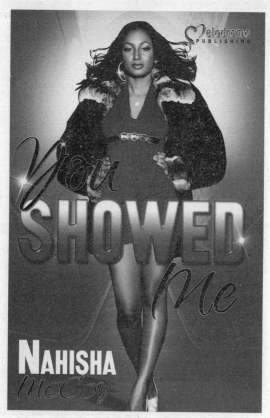

You Showed Me by Nahisha McCoy
Available Now!

Dating a hustler was never on Naheema's to-do list. But after
the charming yet deceptive Mike sweeps her off her feet, dating
a hustler is the least of her worries. Mike's charming sweetness
toward Naheema turns sour when the abuse, cheating, and his
street mentality kicks in. The life of a hustler's woman takes its
toll on Naheema physically, mentally, and emotionally, taking her
from a fairy tale to a horror flick.

Who's Notorious Now? by Kiki Swinson
November 2010!

Criminal defense attorney Yoshi Lomax finds herself on the other side of the bars in the third book of the riveting Notorious series. While Yoshi tries to prepare herself to face the music once she's extradited back to Miami, the ordeal she encounters en route is more than she could have anticipated. Knowing deep down in her heart that she isn't equipped to handle all of this strife, she has no other alternative but to play the game to save herself.

Get
HOOD

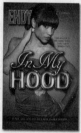

Visit us online

for excerpts, videos, discounts,

photos, and author information.

MelodramaPublishing.com

Also visit us on:

MySpace, Twitter, YouTube,

and Facebook

Find out
What All the
BLING
is About.

The
DiamonD
Syndicate

"The Diamond Syndicate is uncompromising
and drama-filled. Erica Hilton is unstoppable"
-National bestselling author Mark Anthony

**ERICA
HILTON**